To Melissa,

O—

The Fabliss Life

of

Bella Mellman

"There's a little bit of Bella in everyone."

11/15/15

Shirley Sacks

Love

Shirley

D0556175

BooksEndependent.com

This is a work of fiction. All of the characters, organizations, and events portrayed in this novel are either the products of the author's imagination or are used fictitiously.

The Fabliss Life of Bella Mellman

All rights reserved.
Published by BooksEndependent, LLC
www.BooksEndependent.com
Copyright © 2015 by Shirley Sacks
Drawings by Shirley Sacks
Photo of the Author by Bianca Simchowitz
Cover and Book Design by J.D. Woods Consulting
Editor - Shari Goodhartz

ISBN: 978-0-9887687-8-9

Table Contents

Dedication

To Manfred Simchowitz,
who has consistently supported me in all my endeavors.

Chapter 1 -
Living Well
"To live a life takes courage."

Bella was forever changing things around: moving furniture or rehanging art. She liked to think of her living room, which included a dining area and an artist's easel, as more of a studio. Her bedroom also had multiple incarnations. The bed was against one wall, then the other - even in the middle of the room. The walls were painted and papered many times.

Now the theme was birds. Bella loved birds. She thought birds were the closest things to God - inexplicable, soaring, living close but still far away, their nests hidden from human eyes. Bella had papered the walls with an old chinoiserie bird pattern found on eBay, and on the walls facing the queen-size bed, she hung unmatched, antique avian prints.

Across the window, cinnamon-coloured linen drapes hung three inches past the floor. Bella knew this was out of fashion, but she didn't care. She loved the way the curtains puddled onto the celadon wool carpet. It made her think of country estates with tall French doors opening onto pebbled courtyards, or elegant homes facing London's garden squares. She appreciated this type of discreet grandeur. In fact, when she thought of whom she would like to have been born - were she not born Bella Mellman, only daughter of middleclass Barney (though everyone called him Speedy) and Joyce Mellman, the children of immigrants from the shtetlach of Lithuania - she would be the daughter of an English Lord or a French Intellectual. The English upper classes had a natural

1

confidence that she admired, and the French had an inimitable, impossible-to-copy style. However, Bella was born in South Africa in the 1940s, and there was neither anything aristocratic nor intellectual about her background; although Speedy Mellman was said to have been a brilliant lawyer before alcoholism took over his mind, and cirrhosis destroyed his body.

Bella's queen-size bed was her refuge. A soft, cotton Indian quilt, one of many collected over time, covered the foot of the bed. Ralph Lauren–patterned sheets and pillowcases bought over the years on eBay dressed the bed, even though Bella was aware that sophisticates considered white sheets essential. "I don't like white linens, white towels, or white walls. I don't even like white clothes," she declared.

Besides almond milk, which she drank instead of cow's milk ever since she read about the trauma that was involved obtaining cow's milk, and other than sea salt and a couple of white bras, there was almost nothing white in Bella's home. Even the ceilings were a soft blush.

When her housekeeper, Julietta, changed the patterned bedding, which she did once a week, Bella's bedroom looked different. This pleased her to no end. Julietta took such care with making Bella's bed that Bella bought her housekeeper a couple of sets of Ralph Lauren bed linens. This generosity made Bella feel less guilty about the relatively good fortune into which she'd been born - despite her aristocratic yearnings. Julietta was from El Salvador. Her husband was from Guatemala. Julietta had a grown son she left in El Salvador who was not fathered by her present husband. From him, she had two more sons. One was a teacher and one was still at school.

Bella suffered from a disease aptly diagnosed as Jewish Guilt. It arose when she watched the garbage truck from her kitchen window, knowing for certain that no child started out thinking, "I want to be a garbage collector." She felt guilt when she watched economy-class passengers - especially older women - settling into their tiny seats, while she travelled business class on every long-haul trip. "If I feel this bad, I should change seats with that old woman." The altruistic thought flitted through her mind, and flew off, leaving Bella with a familiar combination of guilt and relief as she settled into the larger seat, which she decided was worth paying for so dearly.

She felt guilty having such luxuries as a barely utilized second bedroom. "I should foster a child, or offer the room to someone needy." But then she imagined having to actually live with another human being, let alone an angry, abused teenager. She made every effort to replace the guilt with gratitude that she had a comfortable guest room for the odd friend or relative who came to stay.

Her granddaughter, Chloe, slept at Bella's most Friday nights - not in the guest room, but beside Bella. She had done so since she was six months old. "I feel like a princess when I sleep here. When I grow up, I want a fabliss bedroom just like yours." Ever since Chloe could verbalize, she was captivated by the carvings of angels - one with a broken wing, one with a broken foot - atop the huge, antique framed mirror hanging on the wall, as well as the stories Bella spun about how they were damaged. Chloe also insisted the word was "fabliss," and not, as Bella corrected, fabulous.

Bella purchased the mirror in London when she moved there after her divorce from Guy. It moved back with her when she returned, like an injured homing pigeon, to South Africa after what was then called, "a nervous breakdown." The mirror had witnessed her battles with depression and alcoholism, and reflected her image as she conquered both - the first with modern medications, the second with the awakening of some kind of faith and the brilliant program of Alcoholics Anonymous. "If children were taught the steps of AA at school, the world would be a better place," she often proclaimed.

The angel mirror was one of the few things Bella brought to America, plus books she thought she could not live without (and never read), a set of silverware left to her by her grandmother-on-her-father's-side, and a hand-embroidered table-cloth - ecru-and-cream linen - made by her grandmother-on-her-mother's-side. The tablecloth disappeared she knew not when. When her daughter, Jessica, asked if she could borrow it for a wedding shower she was hosting, it was nowhere to be found.

Bella was sometimes astonished to see in the beautifully worn silver of that mirror - in the light reflected from the outrageously expensive chandelier she had anguished about before buying in a West Hollywood showroom - that she was no longer young. Thrice-weekly sessions with Sven down in the condo gym did something for the floppy flesh under her arms, but she felt more confident wearing clothes with longer sleeves. And no matter how many stomach crunches Sven encouraged, her belly would not flatten. Not that her stomach had ever been like one of those washboards, even when she was young. In fact, her rounded tummy was a feature that turned men on, or so they said.

Sven adored Bella. He had trained her for at least ten years, from the time Jessica insisted her mother do something to lift herself from a debilitating depression, which was caused when Bella stopped taking her antidepressants.

Sven was an odd mixture. He loved anything to do with power and fitness, whilst at the same time he was a romantic, and was always enthused about one creative project or another. Lately, he was turning a briefcase into a portable bar. When Bella first began training with Sven, he was fashioning a huge scrapbook for his latest love, Chanel, a dark beauty from a small town in Nebraska.

Chanel had, like so many pretty girls from all over America, come to LA to make her mark in the movies. She was attractive enough, but not smart enough to avoid LA's pitfalls: shady producers, directors with promises, and - above all - cocaine.

Sven brought the finished scrapbook to show Bella. It was touching, but Bella knew Chanel would not appreciate it. She wanted a movie role, or at least a handbag that matched her name.

Bella complained a lot in the gym. She grumbled whilst doing squats and lunges, but she did them, which Sven respected. He encouraged her, but sometimes he pushed too hard and she begged for mercy. "No more, please! I love you, but no more!"

Sven told Bella that he appreciated that she never judged him. This was not true, but she did it in such a pleasant manner. "Find a decent woman, not another stripper," she told him as, after Chanel, he fell for one after another of the type: tawny skinned, always with a cute figure, and frequently Asian. He didn't mind fake boobs, which was something Bella found fascinating about men. How could caressing or admiring silicone be a turn on?

Sven was part of a different world. He and his friends went to strip clubs. He knew a lot of rock stars. He was once the personal trainer to an entire band and went on tour with them as they travelled the world. When he did that, Sven left Bella in the care of one of his friends, who wasn't half as wonderful as Sven. Tania didn't talk or smile, and she seemed to get sadistic pleasure from making Bella do endless leg lifts. Sven was also happy when he got back. The actual life of a rock band was not as glamorous as he'd imagined.

"Hotels, travelling, and so many girls…When you have caviar every day, it gets boring."

"I am so past the rock-star part of my life," Bella said.

"Me, too," Sven agreed.

"No, that's not quite true. I've never had a rock-star part of my life to get over." And Bella was not one bit sorry about that, either.

In addition to forcing herself to exercise, Bella was vigilant when it came to her skin care. She never went to bed without washing her face. Since she was twenty-five years old, and thought she was getting old, she started using moisturizers. There was hardly a brand she hadn't tried; though of late, new creams

- supposedly more scientifically concocted - had become so ridiculously expensive, she was almost ready to go back to Pond's, which her mother used and swore by her entire life. And Joyce Mellman did have the most marvelous skin. Not a wrinkle even in her eighties, and only a fattish double chin. Working out helped Bella in the chin part, but she had lines above and below her lips that her mother did not. And Joyce had smoked, like Bella, until her forties.

Bella took attentive care of her insides, too. She swallowed a slew of vitamins and life-enhancing potions like riboflavin, which was very expensive, but supposedly worth every penny. She thought that some occasional Botox to remove frown lines, crow's-feet, and nasolabial folds, made her look - and there it was, that most awful adage - "good for her age."

People frequently complimented her with that damned "good for your age" description, which she hated so much but could not help using herself. And she did look good. She had a certain style, which, like her furnishings, she changed from time to time. Her hair had been short and platinum, red, highlighted blonde, and every length and colour in between. She was forever growing her hair, and when she had it cut, she immediately felt regret. Recently, she had taken to wearing intense red lipstick after years of pale pink, and her hair was a mélange of auburn and brown and, as usual, growing.

In summer, Bella often wore tunics made of fine cotton which she ordered online from an Indian/Pakistani website. During winter, she went for dark indigo jeans and long-sleeved T-shirts from Gap. She could not wear wool against her skin, not even cashmere. Anyway, California was too warm, and since the menopause, her body temperature had changed.

When she could wear an outfit that didn't require a bra she was delighted, but of late, having read in a book of style by Ines de Fressange - the one-time muse of Yves Saint Laurent and a Parisian fashion maven - that all women should wear a bra at all times, Bella decided that her days of being free of constraint were over. She went straight to the underwear department at Neiman Marcus.

Seeing Bella's new purchases, her good friend, Greta Mallory, said, "If you're spending on La Perla, don't tell me you haven't got a man in mind."

"I don't."

"You must have spent a fortune!" Greta exclaimed.

Greta was careful with money and often admired Bella's more cavalier attitude. Greta knew the price of milk, and the Greek yogurt she almost lived on. She read the small print, she saved, and she was precise and orderly. She didn't have to buy the latest anything and her cell phone was almost antique, as was her Mercedes. She took great care with most things, other than her relationships with men.

Bella had never seen Greta without her dark hair blown dead straight in a never-changing, timeless, mid-length bob with bangs that were never too short or too long. She never had grey roots. She had briefly worked as a manicurist, and her nails, short with burgundy polish, were never chipped. However, what made Bella really notice Greta's beautiful hands and perfect nails was that she always painted two nails, the ring-finger nails, of both hands, with a different colour - blue, gold, silver, and so on.

After working for very little remuneration in a variety of art galleries, Greta became a consultant, advising companies on their creative purchases. She earned a bit more, but not nearly what people thought. That was because she always managed to find great buys at sales.

Bella constantly told her friend, "You look like the editor of an Italian fashion magazine."

Greta's apartment, rent-controlled, was as simply elegant as she was. Her mother left her some fine art-deco pieces that were valuable, though she would never think of selling them: an oval table which she used as a desk; a divine dressing table; two stocky, worn-leather club chairs; plus silverware, vases, and ornaments. Other than one colourful contemporary painting, the apartment was a symphony of muted tones. A hushed note of exuberance was the art-deco bed, which Greta happily admitted had "a hint of Las Vegas," with its mirror-trimmed, fanned-out headboard.

"So, who is it?" Greta admired Bella's bra purchases: lacy mauve, dark green, and black with matching panties.

"It's me, for me, myself. So when I see myself in the mirror, I feel better about myself."

"I think you have a secret life," Greta added. "Bella Bond."

"I'm transparent. I don't have secrets from anyone other than my kids. And that's only because they would not be happy to know everything about their mother."

Greta had another idea. "Maybe you're having an affair with a married man?"

Bella darted. "That's your domain, darling!"

"Maybe he's a politician?"

"Republican, Democrat, or Independent?" Bella quipped.

"Wait, I've got it. You're doing research for a sex manual?"

"I'm not doing a sex manual." Bella guffawed, and then announced, "I want to write a book about getting older and being single."

Greta picked up on that and, for Bella's birthday, presented a beautiful Florentine notebook. On the inside of the marbled cover, Greta wrote, "All you need now is a pen."

And so, one night, not long after her sixty-ninth birthday, as the festivities of Christmas and the New Year faded into January, Bella made a start.

Chapter 2 -
A Woman of a Certain Age
"After sixty-nine, what is there? Seventy."

Bella slipped into the cool, soft sheets of her bed and arranged her pillows - two regular, one king-size, and a neck roll - precisely as she liked them. Then she opened the Florentine notebook and felt the smoothness of the cream, hand-cut paper. She picked up her bright-yellow Lamy fountain pen - if she didn't write with a fine nibbed fountain pen she herself could not read her own handwriting - and printed her name in purple ink on the inside cover.

Bella went back to her single name - Mellman - after her father died, instead of carrying on with either one of the two last names she was known by, both from ex-husbands: the first - and only one that counted - Guy Rufus, and the second brief mistake, Phil Varelly.

Now, she lived alone - and had done so for well over twenty-five years - in a two-bedroom condo at The Portland, a four-story apartment building with little authentic architectural merit, situated on a tree-lined street in the flats of Beverly Hills. Bella could hardly believe it had been so long, both being single and living in one abode. Bella wrote down some words she thought might help focus her on something to write: *Regrets. Mistakes.* She crossed out those words, and wrote one of her mantras. *"Only regret the things you haven't done."*

She then wrote in huge letters: *Perseverance. Taking chances. Adventures.* She added, *Love.*

Bella's family was close in both distance and spirit. Her daughter,

Jessica, and eight-year-old granddaughter, Chloe, lived in a tiny, though perfectly decorated, cottage in West Hollywood. Jessica's ex - tall, dark, and handsome, and useless for anything other than his pretty genes - had, thankfully, gone back to Boston where his shrill mother supported him in whatever he did (which was nothing that could possibly make a family a decent living). Jess was left to do reasonably well as an interior designer. Bella and Jess had their moments, as Bella learned the hard way to give no advice unless asked. Their relationship was now a fine one.

Bella's son, Ivan - five years younger than Jess - also lived nearby, at least when he was in town, which was not often since Ivan had become the best friend and mentor of Farrel Bootch.

Farrel was the imprudent scion of Bootch Communications and, like many scions, had reverted to type. He spent his days chasing models and playing at being a movie producer.

Farrel's father, Digby, first met Ivan at a barbershop, and was so impressed by his charm and considerable intellect that he offered Ivan a substantial retainer to guide his errant heir into becoming a responsible individual. "It was an offer I could not refuse," Ivan told his mother. Bella thought Ivan could do better than playing nanny to a grown man - who did nothing but travel the world in a private jet - while making sure that Farrel was where he should be at particular times: the Cannes Film Festival, scuba diving in still-surviving reefs, skiing, art festivals in various European cities, or even in Beijing and a couple of the more-welcoming Arab countries.

"I know what I'm doing, Mom," Ivan said. And Bella knew not to argue, for Ivan did know what he was doing and always had, ever since he was a four-year-old and refused to take part in the school concert, managing to do so not only without antagonizing his teacher, but making her adore him even more than she already did.

Creativity. That might be something to write about.

Though fame and fortune had not been the result, Bella made art all her life and she thought of herself as an artist. Her storeroom was filled with canvasses gathering dust. In her guest closet, portfolios filled with drawings hid behind old clothes she could not bear to get rid of, like the outfit she had worn to Jessica's wedding - an olive-green Issey Miyake dress and matching jacket that made her look like a pleated pear - and various old coats, unsuitable for the mild California winter.

When anyone asked if she was lonely without a man in her life, Bella had a stock answer: *"Being creative is like having company. It's always there, and when you don't feel like company, you can ignore it."*

However, of late she did not feel creative. She wasn't depressed. That comrade-in-arms was well taken care of with modern medicine. It was more a feeling of being of no use. As if her purpose in life was done.

Her old friend in South Africa, Marina Painter - whom Bella often called in the middle of the night, when it was daytime there - said, "You are suffering from existential angst. I have it all the time."

When Bella complained about how she was feeling, Dr. Fehrer, Bella's internist, suggested she take up a sport.

Bella thought this an excellent idea. So did her friend Greta. However, when Scott of "Pete's Ultimate Kayak" explained that one of the things they would have to learn was how to turn rightside up, after turning upside down, they eye-rolled each other and informed him that kayaking wasn't for them.

"What about lawn bowling?" Scott thought he was being funny.

A young man who happened to overhear the conversation said, "Don't pay attention to him. He's a jerk and everyone knows it. Let me tell you" - he quickly assessed Bella - "You're in great shape for your age."

She would have liked to tell that fool Scott that she did lunges with her Swedish-born trainer, and she regularly walked, without difficulty, at a 7.5 slant on the treadmill! Instead, she and Greta left in a huff, which soon changed to hysterical laughter as they imagined themselves stuck upside down in the cold ocean in a kayak.

 Bella wrote, *Marriage. Divorce. Single. Happiness!*

She knew that most people, at least most people her age, and in particular most married men, thought her life was incomplete because she didn't have a partner.

"How come a woman like you doesn't have a man?" It was meant to be a compliment, but she'd never worked out a reply that was sufficiently amusing without sounding bitter.

When she wondered why she wasn't married, Bella came to the conclusion that, having been married twice - even though the second one barely counted - she didn't like it, or else she would have remained married or married yet again. That was in line with one of her many firm opinions about such matters: "*What people say they want to do does not count. What they do is what they actually want to do.*"

Bella was aware that many women tolerated much worse than she ever did without resorting to divorce. So Guy Rufus was a womanizer; that was no big deal. That Phil Varelly's confession that he thought he was gay after three weeks of marriage was troublesome, but she knew more than one woman with a gay husband whose marriage worked well enough.

Bella asked her young neighbor from across the street, Nicole Behrmann, a delightfully optimistic creature who worked as a model-booking agent, "What do you think makes for a good marriage?"

Nicole thought and then replied, "Lots of nudity, sex, good music, not getting in a routine, and not letting your kids spoil your fun." Nicole was twenty-four and had never had a serious boy-friend. Bella wondered whether Nicole's generation might do better than hers when it came to marriage. Just about everyone Bella knew had been divorced at least once.

There were times when Bella was quite amazed by her longtime single status. She was a relaxed and fairly good cook, something she knew men appreciated. She was amusing, nice looking, and had a sense of fun. That question, "How come you're not married?" was not without merit.

It was not as if she was wary of relationships. She remembered times gone by when she hugged her pillow and sobbed into its unresponsive down, quite desperate for the affection of a caring lover. Thankfully, with diminished hormones, Bella could say unequivocally that a man was not the answer.

However - and this was, for her, a most annoying "however" - deeply embedded in the alleles fixed within her double helix, there was a vexing and totally superfluous set of genes that kept her romantic muscle operational.

That muscle flexed when Bella entered a room filled with people and she made a quick sweep to note the dearth of potential liaisons. It trembled ever so slightly when an attractive older man walked past her in the street. It contracted with displeasure when she saw old men with young women. It stretched when she detected a man her age who might have possibilities.

It had done so recently when she went to see some old master drawings at Sotheby's LA showroom. She would not have known about the drawings - or for that matter, that Sotheby's had a showroom in Los Angeles - had her ex-husband, the successful, handsome, womanizing Narcissist Guy, not suggested she go see the work.

So off she went, to please this man from whom she was divorced for decades, a man who broke her heart a thousand times with his infidelities, then remarried, had a child a little older than their grandchild, and got divorced again. After all that time, all that separation, and all that hurt, Guy was still, unaccountably, the man in her life. At least according to Edna Feather, Bella's delightfully named and exceptionally perceptive therapist.

Other than the two elegant, eager-to-please Sotheby's employees - who brought the old master drawings to Los Angeles with the hopes that some Hollywood producer or movie star might bite when the auction took place in London some months down the line - there was no one else there when Bella arrived. It didn't take her long to peruse the Raphael sketch and the few other small period drawings on show.

She pretended to appear interested in Raphael's small sketch of a man's face - "One of the most important drawings we've ever had, and so indicative of the period," enthused the lady from Sotheby's - when a man entered. Bella's romantic muscle involuntarily flexed, and in a nanosecond an impossibly idealized scenario was painted.

"What an irony! Guy sends me here and I find love. Imagine that. Falling in love at Sotheby's examining drawings by masters of the Renaissance, a period I am well able to discuss, having studied the period at University."

The man in question could not be called handsome, but he was tall and he wore no ring indicating he was married. And if he was at Sotheby's assessing drawings by Renaissance masters with prices that began in the millions, then Bella could see their plot line expanding in the story of how they met. He was well-known, from the manner in which he was fawned over.

Bella was introduced and they all stood chatting for a while, in that mindless way people talk about things when they have nothing to say. Bella noted the man's greenish teeth. Why did he not fix them? He must have the means. Was his camel-coloured sweater cashmere? It was grubby. Old cashmere with fuzz balls. His shoes? Bella always noted men's shoes. Yes, no, maybe? Could they be ignored? Despite how well Bella was dressed - she was going on from Sotheby's to a dance recital in which her granddaughter was performing - as well as her friendly and appropriately flirtatious attitude, the man showed no sparkle in his eye. And then, just as she was wondering whether she could ever kiss the pallid skin with the yellow teeth, the man pointedly addressed the Sotheby's employee: "We have that Boldini. Remember we bought it…"

Thus ended the romance that would never have happened, for she could no more sleep with the man with flaccid skin and stained teeth than afford the forty-seven million that was eventually paid for the Raphael sketch - a mere doodle in her opinion - that was the main draw of the show.

On the inside cover of the Florentine notebook - where Bella inscribed her name and address - she added swirls and flourishes. Before she could add more curlicues, and before she thought more about rich and unattractive men with dubious toiletry habits, Bella remembered she was going to write about being older and single.

For days she mulled upon how to proceed. She made a list of titles that sounded like Hallmark cards. And she wrote not-very-absurd chapter titles: *Fleshing Out Flabby Arms, Decorate Your Double Chin,* and *Varieties of Varicose Veins.* But then her "No You Can't" channel - Nike's flourishing competition - switched on. "Why do you think that would interest anyone?"

Bella didn't think aging was funny. She detested those endless cartoons about getting old that friends kept e-mailing, and she soon decided she no longer wanted to write about getting older - single or otherwise.

Greta - Bella's most faithful friend - liked Bella's idea. "I might be younger than you, but I'm single, and you should write about your life."

Bella didn't press the point that twelve years was not insignif-icant. She knew that nobody could fully appreciate an older age until they'd reached that age.

Instead, she announced to Greta, "I am going to write about living in a condo in Beverly Hills."

Greta said, "If you are thinking of writing about The Portland, you will get sued."

"Sued for what? It would be fiction, a novel."

"I can't imagine anything more boring than a book about The Portland, with so many of its residents almost ready for Forest Lawn."

"That's so ageist." Bella was beginning to notice how disparagingly people spoke about the aged. Now that she was in that category she determined to point out the offence.

Bella's young neighbor, Nicole, thought the book would be a best seller, though she never read books, best sellers or otherwise.

However, after dabbling with "Condo Life" for a few weeks, Bella abandoned the idea. She wasn't sufficiently enthusiastic herself.

Chapter 3 -
The Portland

"If you want to understand why people go to war, live in a condo."

There were eighty-five condos at The Portland, which had been Bella's Beverly Hills home for the past twenty-five years. She expected to make many friends - or at least acquaintances - during her stay, but this was not the case. Friends were difficult to make at The Portland, and the surrounding streets - with their charming old duplexes - had also presented few possibilities. Signs of human habitation were demonstrated by overflowing trash cans and parked cars, but Bella hardly ever saw actual people when she walked her dog, Charlie.

Los Angeles was an unfriendly place. There were reasons for this, which sociologists tried their best to fathom. It was too spread out. It had no center. The wide streets precluded a sense of community. People were transient. Writers had chronicled about how unusual Los Angeles was, with its loosely joined mini-cities, of which Beverly Hills was the best known. Fame, fortune, and sunny weather lured the talented, the good-looking, and the ambitious, which resulted in a rootless population. There were some old LA families, but they kept to themselves. Outsiders were unwelcome.

Beverly Hills taxes ensured the city was kept pristine. Weeds were not allowed. Litter was banned. Street trees were trimmed the moment they showed a burst of enthusiasm, which Bella found so egregious that she wrote a letter to The City in which she forcefully complained about the brutal manner of pruning. *Beautiful trees that should have many main and cross branches are made into tragic amputees. The moment trees leaf sufficiently to give some needed shade, their leaves are lopped off. This relentless dismemberment continues all summer. Leaves clean the air. We need more clean air, not less.*

"When branches are allowed to fall, the city is sued," she was informed politely when an official actually took the trouble to address her complaint. "Our city has been voted the best treed city in America," he said. "They have to be trimmed so that they will grow."

"That's like cutting your hair to make it grow. It's simply not true." Bella wondered why some things, so patently false, were accepted as truth.

Bella learned the hard way not to rely on friendships for amusement. Aside from the difficulty of making connections, her friends eventually moved. Even Greta, who loved Los Angeles and said she'd never leave, did so. She returned after three months, having learned that the man she ran to in Portland, Oregon, was not at all what he said he was - such as single. Fortunately, she never gave up her apartment. "I don't care if I marry a billionaire with houses all over of the world, I will never give it up."

Debbie Bently – who once lived on Bella's floor and with whom she had become very close, sharing their life stories as they walked their dogs together every morning and evening – married a man who lived in Florida.

Dotty Marriot, with whom Bella had fun learning to play bridge, went back to Dallas when her daughter married and had twins. When she left, Bella gave up bridge, which was no fun without Dot.

Lately, Bella had become friendly with newly divorced Shelly Davidson, who moved into the apartment next door. Shelly recently arrived from Stockton in Northern California, filled with hope that she would be able to find husband number three. Shelly was a California blonde and would be so till the day she died. "You're only as old as you feel" was her maxim, which might account for her short skirts and tight pants. Her generous divorce settlement might account for her love of designer labels. When Bella asked Shelly how she managed to walk in such high heels, she said, "I'm used to it. I've worn them since I was fifteen."

"So that's about forty years?"

"Not as much as that!" Shelly was one of those women who never divulged her real age. She was a bit like Bella's mother, who, when asked, always said with a coquettish smile, "I am twenty-nine."

Shelly had three grown daughters: the eldest from husband number one, a heart surgeon who left her for his nurse, and two from the second husband - also a doctor whom she had left, she told Bella, "Because he was boring, he drank too much, and I needed some romance in my life."

Had Shelly known Bella before she moved, Bella could have told her that Beverly Hills was not a city in which to find romance, especially for women over thirty. She would have also warned Shelly that most men are boring after two years, and "better the devil you know." But it was too late for that. However, Bella did ask, "You've been married twice. Why do you want to marry again?"

"I like being married," Shelly replied.

"Why?"

"I like reading the papers together on Sunday."

"There is more to marriage than reading the Sunday papers together! There's the rest of the week."

Shelly reiterated, "I like being married."

"Then you should have stayed married."

Shelly changed the subject, "I think I know why so many Jewish men marry Asian women - They're small. Everywhere."

Imperiously, Bella inquired, "And who told you that?"

"I like my men big - even bulky." Shelly was upset at the unfairness that so many Jewish men she knew, men her age, men she would like to go out with - even marry - went for Asian women.

"Do you like Asian men?" Shelly asked.

"I once saw a Japanese man in Hawaii who was so handsome I never forgot him. He didn't even look my way. There are some Japanese, I think they're from the North, who are gorgeous. I did have a brief romance with a Pakistani called Yunis, though that's not the kind of Asian we're talking about. Yunis lived in the same block of flats that I did, when I lived in London. He said he was a cricketer in his better days, but he was a liar. He was Muslim, and he drank like a fish. He was also married."

"Was he a good lover?" Shelly asked.

"A good lover - a good lover is someone you love, even if it's only for the moment."

"What if I don't find someone to love? Even as you say, 'for the moment?'" Shelly asked.

"Get a vibrator," Bella advised. "It's more reliable."

"It's not the same," Shelly replied, having never tried one.

"It's better."

"When was the last time you were in love?" Shelly asked.

With a wash of nostalgia, Bella remembered the mad passion she once shared with JP before she came to America. "My gangsta lover," she called him, a factual description that always elicited a laugh. "He was charming, as such men can be. He reminded me of a ruthless bounty hunter in an old cowboy movie: dark, wide-shouldered, and a wiry six-foot-four, with furrows down his cheeks and hooded, sexy eyes. The one you're supposed to hate, but actually find devilishly attractive. He was a sociopath."

The affair, rightfully, shocked Bella's friends and dismayed her family.

"I realized, long afterwards, that in a way JP helped me get over the failure of my idiotic marriage to Phil Varelly. I came here, partly, to get away from him."

"And since you've been here?" Shelly asked.

"You know, I've never had a love affair with an American. The last romance I had here was with a pompous Englishman aptly named Wulf Beauregard. He claimed to be a Shakespearean scholar and told me how he enjoyed living on a boat in the marina, though he never once took me to see it, nor gave me his telephone number. This was in the days before everyone had cell phones, and our romance ignited through e-mails. You can get very seductive through e-mails. You don't have to gaze in each other's eyes. Or rather, he didn't have to face me. Jessica says I have the worst taste in men, and she has a point. I thought Wulf would be the last great love of my life, but three months into the romance, he went off to Australia to visit his brother - he said - and I never saw him again. I had nobody to even ask about him. I was heartbroken. Months later, he sent me a handsome Christmas card from Melbourne. The card took the form of a poem, printed on antiqued parchment, proving to Wulf - at least - how brilliant he was. He included his address, and to the flourish of his signature added, *I'd love to hear from you.* I heard he'd married his wealthy Australian girlfriend, who'd supported him for years."

"What did you do?" Shelly asked.

"I tore the card up. He sent me an equally fanciful card the next year. I tore that up, too."

Bella thought there was something quite vulnerable about Shelly, despite her outward bravado - newly inflated breasts, a colour-and-cut from the one and only Chris McMillan Salon, and fashionable clothes that showed off her toned figure a tad more than Bella deemed necessary.

"I was like you when I first came to live here," Bella told Shelly. "I was a bit younger than you are now, and filled with anticipation. And a bit scared."

"You, scared?"

"Do you think I'm not human?" Bella laughed.

"You seem to be so confident, so self-assured - especially for someone who isn't married, or rich, or famous."

Bella didn't take offence, and instead gave Shelly some insight into getting around in Los Angeles, which she wished she'd been given when she first arrived. "West is to the beach. East is towards downtown. North is to the mountains. Remember that when you see street signs. Sometimes they only provide compass points."

Shelly was grateful. "You have no idea how much that helped me."

Bella knew. "When I first drove here, I got lost all the time. After one dinner in Beverly Hills, I found myself in the Valley and I had no idea where I was. I saw stores I thought I recognized, but it took me a while to realize that what we have this side of the Hollywood Hills is replicated in the Valley."

Bella introduced Shelly to her internist, her gynecologist, her optometrist, her chiropractor, and her therapist, Edna Feather. Shelly liked Edna and made a regular weekly appointment. Bella saw Edna only occasionally in times of desperation. Edna was far too expensive, and medical insurance didn't cover the mind.

Bella also warned Shelly, "There are more crazy people in Los Angeles than anywhere else. I don't mean beggars or the poor, but truly, certifiably insane human beings."

Shelly replied, "That's because Ronald Reagan closed all the asylums."

"That's what everyone says."

"Some of them live here at The Portland," Bella laughed.

Amongst those Bella deemed suited for the defunct asylums was Mr. Finn, who hurried down the corridor carrying the most enormous black-leather briefcase, and who wore a moustache that slicked up into sideburns. Mr. Finn never greeted Bella, but threatened to kick her dog, Charlie, should he approach.

Bella told Finn, "You kick my dog and I will kick you!"

Felix, one of the valets, told her that Mr. Finn was the illegitimate son of an old movie star who paid for his upkeep. "And a bit loco." Felix made the sign depicting insanity.

Paranoid Rhonda - whom Bella had to unfriend in the days before Facebook - felt under constant threat, despite security cameras, strict control of door locks, and twenty-four-hour valet service. Rhonda walked around the block with pepper spray and a whistle. She told Bella she'd seen a raccoon, the size of a German shepherd, up a tree that wanted to attack her, and could surely kill Charlie.

"It was probably a coyote," Bella replied. "But I don't think they climb trees."

"I know what a coyote looks like," Rhonda insisted.

In all her years at The Portland, Bella never saw a raccoon. She did see some possums, which though incredibly ugly, she knew were scared of people. Most animals were, and rightly so. She'd heard that coyotes came down from the hills to scavenge. Some were spotted in built-up areas. Jessica saw one near her house in West Hollywood. Everyone had a coyote story.

The Fays - he with the worst hairpiece, she with a permanent scowl - behaved as if they owned the building. They never parked their own cars - matching white BMWs with plates reading "Faymrs" and "Faymr" - no matter the congestion in the driveway. "It's what we pay for," Bella overheard Mrs. Fay telling the Building Manager, Mrs. Barkley.

Bella wanted say something every time she saw one of the Fay cars gumming up the driveway, but she desisted. There was a time, long ago, when she might have spoken up, but wisdom struck her once she stopped drinking and went to Alcoholics Anonymous, where she learned - some of the time - to mind her own business. "Practice restraint of tongue and pen" was a worthwhile motto.

At ten thirty one night, Bella's doorbell rang. It was Asa Ghobani. "I hope it's not too late." Bella thought Asa had something important to share. Bella and Asa exchanged pleasantries, and Asa was difficult not to notice. Tiny, skinny - other than inflated breasts - with thick flowing black hair, Asa dressed like a diminutive fashion model. Bella often complimented Asa on her outfits, which came from the designer floor at Neiman Marcus. "I'm a Neiman's girl," Asa said coyly, as if she was the daughter of Mr. Marcus. Asa added, just in case Bella might wonder, "I'm not snobby or any-thing. I just like their service."

"It does beat Kmart," Bella replied.

Bella thus did a double take at the vision of Asa in a floor-length, fuzzy, old chenille robe. She'd never seen Asa without full makeup, smooth long black hair, and dressed to go to lunch or dinner with her most seriously envious girlfriends.

"Please forgive the late hour, but do you hear noise coming from my condo?" Asa lived above Bella.

"Not from yours, but the people above you; their little girl cries a lot." Bella did not tell Asa that she'd discussed the matter with Mrs. Barkley and had called Child Protective Services.

Asa was not complaining about the crying. She was bothered by the Plotskys' late-night stomping. "I don't know what they do in the middle of the night. Bang, bang, like they're dancing, or jump-ing up and down."

Eventually, Asa began banging on her ceiling with a broom han-dle to shut up the Plotskys, who answered in kind. All that noise did reverberate down to Bella's condo, but she chose not to get further involved. The Plotskys and Asa ended up on the precipice of a court case, and each of their lawyers asked Bella for a state-ment. "They're both nuts," she told the respective legal representa-tives, who wanted testimony either for or against.

The Plotskys moved out, renting their apartment to a non-stomper. Bella never found out what happened with Child Services. She also avoided Asa, who came out of the Plotsky affair suf-ficiently vindicated to begin vigorous complaints about children using the pool without wearing diapers, the colourways of the impatiens planted in the front flower beds in summer, and how the valets didn't open the door fast enough when she obviously had packages. "I see them sitting at the front desk doing nothing. You should see how the valets jump to attention when I visit my friends at the Wilshire Corridor." Bella wanted to ask Asa why she didn't move to one of those buildings. And recently, when Bella bumped into her, resplendent in pink-and-grey Chanel, Bella found out that Asa had done exactly that.

Once their children had grown, a number of older couples chose The Portland after downsizing from their family home. Widows were created whilst living at The Portland, although the nature of the building was that hardly anyone knew anything about anyone living there, dead or alive.

Bella was horrified to discover she had no idea that Mrs. Bergen, one of the few residents Bella really liked, had been dead for over a year. Mrs. Bergen, who always instructed Bella, "Please call me Gertie," became a widow at The Portland. She had no children. After her ailing husband died, and even before, she made The Portland her baby, for which Bella was most grateful, seeing as she - Bella could simply not call her Gertie - nearly ran the Homeowners Committee single-handedly, organizing things efficiently and without fuss.

"You would think she owned the building," some residents huffed, but Bella always defended the birdlike creature. "We're lucky she bothers, when you and I don't."

Frequently an ambulance - always accompanied by a fire engine - arrived to cart off a resident who had succumbed to a fall, a stroke, a heart attack, or one of the many other ailments that beset the elderly. Bella thought it a terrible waste of money to have a fire truck, with lights flashing and engine running while the medics attended to the patient inside the building; but she was informed, when she called The City, that this was necessary in case the paramedics had to cut someone out of something.

After she discovered the passing of Mrs. Bergen, Bella suggested to the Board that a monthly newsletter would be neighborly to provide. "We'd be more aware, and know when to offer condolences or congratulations. I could do it myself."

"We will let you know," replied Maxfield Yudelman, the long-time Chairman of the Board, and that was the end of that. Bella was not sufficiently enthusiastic to pursue the matter.

Once, hoping to initiate a neighborly feeling amongst two single women who lived on her floor, Bella held a Sunday brunch.

Jen Edwards, in real estate, and Edith Binder, in wholesale fashion jewelry, made their appearance: Jen in a two-tone, black-and-purple tracksuit, popular with certain older women, and Edith in black pants and a black turtleneck, which showed off her severe haircut and one of the ethnic necklaces she always wore. They arrived at the same time. Jen brought a hostess gift, a candy dish with "candy" written on the outside, one of a dozen she'd bought wholesale four years prior. Edith carried a bottle of wine.

Bella gave the obligatory tour of her condo. Jen made no comment other than to remark, "I see you made your breakfast nook into an office area." Edith was more complimentary. "You are so creative. And so brave with colour."

Bella served her easy-to-make carrot soufflé and scrambled eggs mixed with chopped onions. Jen toyed with her soufflé: she was on a diet. Edith didn't eat eggs. Bella wished she could add vodka to the virgin Bloody Mary she served, but she didn't have any. Having stopped drinking, she sometimes forgot that others still did. So she opened the bottle of wine that Edith brought. "I don't normally drink red during the day," Edith claimed. Together with Jen, who said the same thing, they polished off the bottle. This finally eased the awkwardness between the three women, who were challenged to find something to talk about other than a mutual disdain for the Architectural Committee, which consisted of Fanny Moskowitz, Hazel Rudenbeck, and Mr. Leon.

Bella was relieved neither woman reciprocated her hospitality, although Jen was now much more friendly when she and Bella bumped into each other down the corridor. Edith on the other hand, was less so.

The Building Manager, Mrs. Barkley, did her best to keep a lid on irate homeowners and was so successful at it that she had kept the job for over twenty years. Bella had a lot of sympathy for Mrs. Barkley, even though she herself once had some words with the poor woman. The ice-smooth helmet of Mrs. Barkley's jet-black hair was something of a weapon, but she surely often wished she had something more substantial to ward off the vituperation of residents who blamed her for everything from loud televisions and noise at the pool to bad plumbing. The Portland, like all of Los Angeles, suffered from bad plumbing.

Mrs. Barkley's office was adjacent to the party room that, like the common areas of The Portland, had been newly updated to kitsch perfection by the Architectural Committee.

The monthly Board meeting was held in the party room. Bella could never get over the incongruity of Native-American pastoral scenes in fake antique-bronze frames hanging against the dusty-pink-striped, damask-patterned wallpaper. However, after seeing Fanny Moskowitz's condo when Bella went to look at an antique desk that Fanny wanted to sell, she understood.

When Bella first moved into The Portland she attended the monthly Board meetings, but soon gave this up and, like most residents, only showed up at the Annual General Meeting where new Board members were elected. Lobbying usually kept the old Board in power, other than when some newcomer moved in and wanted to change things, which he or she did not, once they were elected. Although one time, after the Englishman Dr. Rupert Barr moved in, he not only got elected, due to his Manchester accent, which Americans mistook for upper class, but got the Board to approve - and the homeowners to finance, by way of a special assessment - the refurbishing of a perfectly fine paved drive way. This not only resulted in general outrage, but also Dr. Barr's indignant resignation.

When Bella discovered that the staff was not provided with health insurance, she used the Annual General Meeting to make an impassioned plea for its provision. "We are privileged to live in Beverly Hills, ..." she began her speech. And from then onwards health insurance was part of the employment package, though it did not include husbands, wives, or children.

Most homeowners had less socially conscious issues. Mr. Hochenfuller - who always announced, "I have been in the business of property for over fifty years," before he said anything - frequently attacked the Board concerning financials. Although Bella could see he was drunk and did not even know what he was saying, Fanny Moskowitz always took offence and stated, "I have never been spoken to like this."

Asa Ghobani almost got physical with Mr. Leon of the Architectural Committee about the pending cost of new carpets for the entrance. Mrs. Leon - who joined the fray in defence of her diminutive, snapping husband - hit Asa with her rolled-up Order of Events. Some ladies pulled Mrs. Leon away from Asa, who shrieked, "You hit me! You hit me?" People shouted for everyone to calm down, which caused exactly the opposite. And so, if one little building managed to cause such fury, Bella knew that there could never be peace in the world.

Greta was complaining about how she bought a hugely expensive winter coat for nothing, as her trip to New York had been cancelled. Bella complained, too, about her lack of progress in her writing. "All I can do is think of titles. It's like people who think of names of restaurants, products, and stores they plan to open, and never do."

"Don't you think Graffiti would be a good name for a restaurant?

Street artists could paint the wall inside." Greta thought of the name long ago, even before graffiti artists became fashionable. "I'm surprised nobody has done it."

"Me, too," Bella agreed. "Seriously, I wish I'd never started this book idea. It's making me crazy."

"You were already crazy," Greta laughed. "Anyway, it hasn't been long since you began the book. You've only been sixty-nine for three months. And you know what?"

"What?" Bella wondered what brilliant idea Greta would have now.

"When it's spring, you always get a rush of energy."

Bella agreed on that point. She had long noticed that when spring sprung she began moving furniture, rearranging collections, and tidying those unused drawers where she put things she didn't quite want and had no place for in designated drawers. There was a good reason it was named "Spring Cleaning." The process of tidying up after settling in for the winter was genetically programmed. Bella loved when she discovered a deep-seated reason for the mysteries of life.

Soon after walking out of a film - one everyone else loved but she didn't - Bella decided to try her hand at writing a movie. And, almost like a god-given gift, she remembered one of the seven short stories she wrote when she first came to live in Los Angeles: "The Lions of A'marula," which was set in South Africa where she was born. At least she now had something from which to begin, and she thought the title was excellent.

"I am finally going to be like everyone else in Los Angeles and write a movie," she told Greta.

"It's called a screenplay or a script."

Bella replied, "I know that!"

It was not as if Bella had nothing to do. She still took under-privileged children on nature walks, trying to instill in them some appreciation for the little that was left of the wetlands near Los Angeles. More recently she'd taken up teaching illiterate adults how to read. The Getty and LACMA once used her services as a docent. She did a stint at The Museum of Tolerance where she guided high school tours. She could always go back there and do some good, but volunteering never fully satisfied Bella. She learned a lot, but she always felt a little bit too separate from the other volunteers, who were far more dedicated than she was.

Aside from unpaid altruism, Bella had gym with Sven three times a week and once-a-week French lessons.

Bella always wanted to learn to speak French, and when she read that learning a new language could help prevent Alzheimer's, she enrolled in a class. After three years of lessons, Bella had to agree with Greta who said knowingly, "There are two things you can't learn when you are older. Tennis and French."

The septet of South African short stories were not the only things Bella had written over the years. There were memoirs, which she planned to complete one day and give to her children to pass on to theirs so that her descendants might know about her life. Bella wished she knew more about her grandparents and their parents. All she knew was that on her mother's side they were Cockneys from London. "They were born under the sound of the Bow Bells," Joyce said, as if announcing their aristocratic lineage, but which truly meant they were born within earshot of St. Mary-le-Bow in East London's Cheapside. On her father's side, her ancestors came from Lithuania. Bella didn't know from what shtetl.

At a particularly difficult time in her life - after divorcing Guy - Bella wrote about the trials and tribulations of a newly divorced woman trying to find love again, in what she thought were amusing rhyming couplets. She sent a selection to a few literary agents. The only one who replied with more than a form rejection letter wrote that the poems were too scatological. Bella did not know the word and had to look it up.

Then, encouraged by Edna Feather, Bella sent her seven short stories off with hopes of finding an agent. The only personalised rejection letter she received stated that there was no market for short stories set in Africa from an unknown white author. The agent added, "Now, if you were Nadine Gordimer, it would be different." Nadine Gordimer was a Nobel Prize winner.

Edna told Bella she had accomplished something merely by completing and sending off the work. But it didn't feel like an accomplishment to her.

Chapter 4 -
The Green Eyed Monster
"Jealousy tried to come in disguise."

With regard to character defects, Bella knew there was a particular one hardly anyone admitted to possessing. People didn't mind admitting that they were procrastinators, that they were slothful or greedy, or filled with pride, and so on. The big character flaws that went unannounced, the ones to be most ashamed of, the ones nobody ever admitted to having, were jealousy or envy. The two words were interchangeable to some degree, though philosophers and the dictionary tried to distinguish them.

Envy's ignominy trumped malice, another motivation denied by all. Bella believed there was a certain deviously satisfying payoff in some malice - as in "Don't get mad, get even" - but for jealousy and envy, she saw no such reward.

When jealousy simmered, Bella tried counteracting it by admiration. This worked often, as in "Charlize Theron is gorgeous." How could anyone *not* envy her fellow South African's face, figure, and talent? Or Bella thought, "She is so talented and has the most marvelous taste," whilst drooling over the New York apartment of Diane von Furstenberg, a woman of similar age to Bella, though with superior achievements as well as a far more intelligent choice of husbands.

Then there were those women who had no idea of the part they played in invoking envy. Everyone had one or two of those.

For Bella, one was Annie Frederiks when they were both teenagers. One grade above Bella, Annie was the most beautiful girl at school. Bella watched her at assembly and hated her for her turned-up nose and incredibly pretty face, not to mention her bubbly personality and appealing laugh.

Later there was Veronica, with her Cheshire cat grin, married to an English aristocrat who was sent to South Africa to run a branch of his family's banking business. Guy and other men in their social set were besotted with Veronica.

After Bella's first divorce, Veronica was replaced by Felicity, who tried to entrance every man she met with a languid sexuality she knew precisely how - and when - to use.

Where did envy come from? Was it formed in the glial cells, in the axons? Did it lie in wait, ready to dispatch hurtful signals when certain triggers were stimulated? Evolution must have some use for envy. It seemed to be a universal emotion. Even dogs revealed envy's sting. Stroke one dog and a nearby pooch comes for a pat, too. Did dogs learn envy from humans?

Like a tsunami, envy surged when Bella heard that Guy's second ex-wife - the cold, unfeeling, and avaricious woman who Bella called only by her position, "Wife Number Two" - got engaged. The man in question was a Belgian-born billionaire whose inherited wealth derived from a specific component used in the manufacture of armaments, which made Bella recall a famous quote: "If you want to know what God thinks of money, look at the people He gives it to."

Bella's sheets were changed that day, and the red-checked set of the past week - her favorite with a coordinating quilt - was replaced by blue and white. She smooshed the pillows to her liking and switched on the television. Then she decided she'd rather read, but she was unable to concentrate.

Instead, Bella imagined getting married again. She didn't like the thought, so why was she envious? What was the cause? Logic didn't help. Did she covet his billion? Maybe… There was comfort in being cared for in a grand manner. But Bella didn't hanker for more than she could afford. Shopping at Neiman's could be fun, but she was happy with Gap and even Old Navy; and with the addition of a scarf, some interesting costume jewelry, and occasionally a hat, she felt just fine. Bella was frequently complimented on her unique style. She liked where she lived. She loved her Subaru, as the ads said. She didn't spend more than a minute desiring anything she couldn't easily afford.

Bella spoke to Charlie, who jumped on the bed for some affection, "I am happy living on my own with just you, my little darling boy. We don't want to wake up with some big, fat man in our bed, do we?" Charlie rolled on his back for a tummy tickle. "We don't have to listen to a man snoring. Why do all men snore? The temperature of my electric blanket is to *my* liking. Nobody tells me, 'Let's go now,' when I'm having a good time. And when I'm not, I can leave."

As if to lend weight to her chatter, Charlie began a light snore. Bella loved it, however, when Charlie snored. His sounds demonstrated how happy he was, and how much he appreciated being rescued and receiving care.

Bella found Charlie five years prior, running down Wall Street near the flower market, where Bella had gone to buy some orchids. Kong, her thirteen-year-old Pekingese had just died and she wanted another dog. Bella knew Charlie was godsent, and whilst not a Pekingese - which she declared were the only dogs she would ever have - he had many marvelous Pekingese characteristics: inscrutable, independent, self-assured, and fearless. In addition, Charlie was calm; he almost never barked, and if he ever made a mess in the house, he did so on a piece of newspaper specially put out for such accidents.

When Bella thought back - which she didn't do often, but which she did during this envy attack - she thought of Harry Whitehouse, a rich boyfriend she'd briefly had during the five years she lived in London forty years ago. Farrel Bootch, whom Bella's son Ivan had been employed to nanny, reminded her of Harry. They shared the same "I am special" insolence, with an intelligent demeanor that belied their lack of interest in anything meaningful.

Harry was left a fortune by his heiress wife, who committed suicide; leaving him with two young daughters, a large house in Belgravia, a smaller house in the South of France, and sufficient funds to take good care of them all.

Harry's life was spent going out to dinner and discos, parties, gambling, holidays at his French house, and cocaine, which at the time was considered not addictive.

"It's the most exhilarating drug," Harry informed Bella, who after using it twice and becoming - as Harry said she would - exhilarated, suffered a bad nosebleed and never touched the white powder again.

Acting as Harry's hostess at his house in Chester Square, one of the best addresses in all of London, Bella tried her best to fit in with Harry's moneyed friends - and failed.

Harry coldly informed her after a dinner party, "You were showing off."

"I was showing off I had opinions," she replied, feeling her eyes well with tears.

Harry was overly concerned at not offending his most illustrious guests, Sir Herbert and his horse-faced wife, Pru.

Pru was a distant cousin of the Queen, and Bella - having lived in London for a few years - realized that people like Harry who did not have upper-class roots were enormously impressed by the slimmest connections to royalty or the peerage.

"I was telling them about apartheid and why it will end. They asked."

"They were being polite. They didn't really expect you to go on. And on."

"How do you know?"

"I know."

The worst thing was that Bella still wanted Harry, even knowing he was so shallow, knowing he was so cruel. What caused attraction? The chemistry between people was unfathomable. Thankfully, by the time Harry moved on and found himself the widow of an impecunious Earl, Bella was long over him.

She'd dated quite a few men like Harry. They were momentary passions that died out like fire made using only newsprint. A few beaus had been more important, like the mad affair with JP, and Roland, her first romance after she and Guy parted. But Guy was the only man whom she still loved in a way nobody could truly understand, especially herself. She knew it was really love, for if he was unhappy, she felt for him. If he was sick, she cared and prayed for him to be well. She knew his bravado hid his weaknesses. She appreciated his strengths, too, which were many, and she was deeply grateful for his generosity towards her. She didn't know what she would have done had he not helped her financially. Maybe she would have gotten married again? Maybe she would have been more diligent in finding a market for her art? Maybe...

Bella didn't like "maybe." Maybe if she'd become famous as a painter, she would've been run over by a bus whilst on the way to the gallery? "Maybe" if she'd remarried, her husband would have gotten early onset Alzheimer's, and she would have had to take care of him?

Just that had happened to Devora when she married the charming and well-heeled Blackie Fielding. Everyone thought Devora fortunate to have bagged him. He was handsome, sweet, adored Devora's children, and liked by her friends. Even his children were pleased. A year into the marriage he came down with that dreaded disease, and to help herself cope Devora took so many pills she became a drug addict. Totally out of her mind, she sometimes telephoned Bella in the middle of the night. Bella always offered to take Devora to an AA meeting, but when Bella called to pick her up, Devora wouldn't answer her phone.

"Poor Devora," Bella said to the air. Charlie's ears perked up. "I don't think dogs get Alzheimer's."

Bella sometimes shared the Envies with her chiropractor Dr. Tea Francine. These mainly took the form of disparaging Wife Number Two.

"She is so pretentious. She told someone, 'Guy and I even eat hamburgers.'"

Dr. Francine laughed. "I suppose her alimentary canal is constructed from something exhalted."

"She believes driving east of La Cienega is a danger only to be faced when going to one of the downtown cultural centers for a gala dinner where she can wear one of her many designer outfits. What she spends on clothes, most families can live on for a year!"

However, though Bella and Dr. Francine did have a laugh at Wife Number Two's expense, Bella mostly brought the subject back to Guy.

Dr. Francine asked Bella, "What about your father?"

Bella often spoke about her mother, and how much she missed her now that she was gone, but not a word about her father. Dr. Francine said so much of what a woman is came from the father. In her case, Dr. Francine's father was a military man, and rather cruel, which she believed was one of the reasons she not only picked a kind man as a husband, but a career in which compassion was paramount.

Bella described Speedy Mellman: "He was an extraordinarily charismatic personality, a brilliant architect. He could use either of his hands to draw. Totally ambidextrous. People called him a genius, but always with the addendum, 'if he hadn't been a drunk.' He had ideas that were long before his time. When I was probably about six years old, he told me that one day, there would be no such thing as white people. Everyone would be Coloured and the melding of races would be a good thing. He was right. But because of his alcoholism, he died young. He was also unfaithful to my mom, and utterly unreliable. If he said he'd do something, he had no problem letting me down. His favorite quote was, 'The world is a tale told by an idiot, full of sound and fury, signifying nothing.'"

"Is Guy like your father?"

"Yes and no. My father was irresponsible. Guy isn't. Guy hardly drinks. My father was a charmer. Women loved him. Guy is charismatic, but he doesn't really like people. Funnily enough, my father liked Guy. In a way, Guy was the son my father wished he'd had."

"And Guy, did he like your father?"

"Yes, he did."

Dr. Francine was no wiser, but she wished Bella would find love. And like so many others, could not understand why she hadn't.

Bella continued contemplating her Envies - and how to get rid of them - as she waited to have her hair trimmed at La Fontaine, the salon in Beverly Hills that she'd been going to since she first moved to LA. Her Austrian hairdresser, Peter, attended to a flock of older society women who all seemed to know each other and never invited Bella anywhere, even when she was brand new in Los Angeles.

"They have husbands," Peter laughed. "They don't want you around."

Adrianna Wegener was one of the wives who elicited Bella's envy. She seemed to always be there when Bella went to La Fontaine, although Peter told her Adrianna lived in Santa Barbara, or rather Montecito.

"She met her husband here," Peter told Bella. "I cut his hair for years. Then one day, Adrianna came in. He fell for her on the spot."

Bella knew men didn't fall for her on the spot. Men had fallen in love with her, but that took time. Bella was like a tea bag. She had to be swooshed around to give up her flavor.

Adrianna had a blousy confidence, aided by milky skin, red hair, and a flat face like a Persian cat. She wore a Bulgari Serpenti gold watch that snaked around her pale wrist, large blobs of gold earrings that were real, and red clothes, which she knew suited her.

Blonde and petite Michaela Broome was another of Peter's well-heeled clients who brought out Bella's envy, especially so when she bumped into Michaela and her husband one Christmas season at Neiman Marcus.

Bella had told her granddaughter Chloe that she could pick five ornaments from the decorated Christmas tree that Neiman's always set up on their housewares floor. The year prior, when she was four, Bella allowed her to choose four. Next year, it would be six.

They were having the most fun choosing when Michaela appeared, riding down the escalator with an attractive man in tow.

"This is my husband, David," she said, hooking her arm into his.

David was wearing one of the internationally accepted rich-men's uniforms: slip-on Gucci moccasins, a blue gingham shirt with simple gold cuff links, and a pale blue cashmere sweater casually slung about his shoulders. He reeked of affluence: steel-grey hair, not too balding, and a tan.

Spoiling the marvelous moment Bella was having with Chloe, the envy-tipped dart struck. Of course Michaela had a rich man on her arm. Michaela was beautiful. And thin.

The next time Bella saw Michaela at the hairdresser, she noted that the circle of large, marquise-shaped diamonds that served as Michaela's wedding ring was missing. Unexpectedly, for Michaela had never had anything resembling an actual conversation with Bella, the beauty began a sorry tale.

"I was at The Health Spa in Arizona and I don't know what made me do it… I was suspicious, I suppose. I came back early and found David in my bed, our bed, with a hooker. She wasn't the first one. He was addicted. He'd spent so much money on them, once I began checking our finances. This whore received flowers every week, from my florist and on my account."

Bella asked, "What did you do?"

"I kicked him out."

"I hope it costs him," Bella declared. She'd learned that when husbands were caught cheating in America, their wives were expected to be vengeful.

"It's going to cost me!"

"How come?"

"I have to pay him alimony. For three years. Ten grand a month."

Bella read about women having to compensate men, but she'd never known one who actually had to pay out.

Dr. Francine pointed out, "You see, the outside doesn't show the inside story. You should know that by now." Then Dr. Francine took Bella's hands in hers. "Jealously is a very human feeling, but the emotion won't last. The brain can't seem to function at such an intense level for too long, neither for the good things, like being madly in love, nor the bad feelings, like jealousy."

Dr. Francine was correct. When Bella next heard about Wife Number Two, she'd had her boobs both lifted and enlarged, her lips puffed, and her face so vigorously smoothed that it seemed to have been polished with beeswax. Her Belgian fiancé had dumped her for a budding French movie star, and in revenge she actually married a young Brazilian tango dancer.

Bella was ashamed that she was pleased. The thought of Wife Number Two, who had no music in her soul - or rather no soul - attempting the tango made her giggle. When Shelly reported she heard that the tango dancer - whose name was an unromantic Lew Pinto - had been on the lookout for a Green Card via marriage since he arrived in Los Angeles, Bella's envy was stripped away like wax removes unwanted hair. Jealousy was replaced by a wave of gratitude that she, Bella Mellman, didn't have to deal with any man at this point of her life: tango-dancing ones, sponging ones, married or single ones - even one like Guy, who, whilst she still loved him, was horrible to live with.

Bella picked up her Florentine notebook. She decided to make a list of all the men she'd had sex with. She listed the lesser ones: one-night stands, brief flings, holiday romances, and ones whose names she couldn't remember, whom she labeled: *The one who took me to Marbella. One who liked oriental cats. One who cooked paella? One who knocked at the door all night? One I took to hospital with a kidney complaint. One with the large nose. One I met at Claire's office.*

Finally, she fell asleep. And when she woke the next morning, the Envies were still there, accompanied by a splitting headache which required two doses of Tylenol before lifting.

Chapter 5 -
The Romance Virus
"Romance is an appropriate name for a perfume."

Shortly after Bella got over the Envies, she came down with a Romance Virus. This took the form of longing for what she knew did not exist: a loving, adoring, man of substance, who would be content sharing Bella with the life she'd made for herself, and who wouldn't intrude when not needed.

It wasn't that hard to fathom what caused the Inflammation: Guy, at the age of seventy-three, had fallen in love.

Since he and Wife Number Two divorced, Guy had dredged up old lovers, tried out a couple of gorgeous women who purported to be something other than what they were, and avoided most of the appropriate divorcées his friends pestered him to meet. Bella realized there'd be someone - sooner or later - and there were moments she wondered whether it could even be her; though their passion, such as it was, could never be rekindled. They might love each other, but theirs was a love best sustained by distance.

Irina was a genetic mix of Turkish, Danish, Irish, French, Swiss, and Portuguese, or so she said. Bella's daughter, Jessica, thought Irina sounded Latina. "She's a year younger than I am! Is that crazy or what? Dad's so dumb. He thinks we're going to become friends."

That this age difference was ludicrous made little difference to Guy, who was lit by that particular glow one gets - at any age - with a fresh romance.

Bella had been divorced from Guy for almost thirty-five years; and still, when he found his last love - for this was surely to be his last - she was pained so badly that huge splinters of ice shot up through her body, finally falling, falling, like a river of acid down her old cheeks.

Old cheeks. That's what she had. Damn him. Guy had a young cheek to caress, and she couldn't even blame him, seeing as old cheeks were not appealing to her, either.

Bella was stung by more than that. Not only was Irina young, but Guy had found love. And as Shelly so aptly remarked, "A woman is lucky to be a man's last love."

Jessica called to inform Bella that her father had introduced Irina to her. "'Meet the love of my life,' he said. For god's sake, she's my age!" Jess was horrified. "I'll come over and tell you all about her."

"No, I'm going out." Bella did not want Jessica to see her tears. She knew the minute she saw Jess, she wouldn't be able to control them.

Bella called Greta, "I have smoked salmon."

"I'll pick up some bagels."

There was a time - long ago - when Bella lost her appetite when she was upset.

"Get a grip now, girl," Greta hugged Bella. "He's a fool. You know there's no fool like an old fool. He's grasping at love with someone he can't possibly have anything in common with. I wish you'd see it as it is: pathetic. I wish you didn't care."

"Perhaps it's a karmic thing that I do care?" Bella shrugged.

"There is no such thing."

"Maybe there is. It explains the inexplicable."

In Bella's late teens and early twenties, she dabbled amongst various esoteric ideas - Gnosticism, Theosophy, Zoroastrianism,

Science of Mind - in order to find something that might comfort her from the unbearable realization that life ended. None were particularly comforting, including reincarnation, for what was the point in coming back over and over again if you didn't remember you were here in the first place?

"Why don't you try and seduce Guy?" Greta made a bold suggestion.

"Don't be ridiculous!"

"It's not so ridiculous."

"It's not like that between us. Guy is like an old pair of slippers that are so worn out they no longer keep your feet warm," Bella reflected.

"Get rid of them!" Greta replied. "Let his young mongrel have him."

"Maybe I should never have gotten divorced? Dr. Feather told me that if Guy and I had been married today, a bit of therapy could have saved our marriage."

"That's because she's a therapist," Greta pointed out.

"When we got divorced, it was almost the thing to do. Nobody understood the consequences. I didn't. It was the early seventies, a time that was all about finding yourself, especially if you were a woman. If you were unhappy, you moved on, not for a moment thinking of the future or the children. They were expected to handle it."

Eventually, after endless examinations of Bella's feelings, Guy's state of mind, Irina's motivations, Wife Number Two, Bella's second marriage mistake, and a recounting of Bella's various failed romances, Greta said she had to leave.

"Glen is coming over."

"I thought this time you were really and truly never going to see him again?"

"He's going to help me with my taxes."

"That's a truly pathetic excuse."

Bella had little sympathy for Greta when it came to Glen Short.

It was not that she didn't understand the passion of an illicit romance: what she couldn't fathom was how Greta believed Glen's promises. His words were archetypical of the straying married man: "I love my wife, but I am not in love with her; I need to wait for the right time to tell her; I don't want to hurt my wife; Give me time." And those seductive, honeyed words: "I love you."

Bella undressed. She gazed at her aging body, not in the antique mirror in her bedroom, but in the harsh light of the mirrors that lined her soon-to-be-renovated bathroom. She finally decided to take the plunge and organize a remodel. Like a falling face, the out-of-date decor needed some injectables. Bella had been researching tiles and fixtures.

Bella was certainly still attractive, if she didn't stare too close. Her breasts were not bad, her legs were smooth, and her skin was soft. She'd always had soft skin. Her pubic hair had thinned to almost nothing, but that was fashionable these days when women waxed themselves so that their private parts appeared more like those of prepubescent girls. Bella grimaced at the thought of sex. She couldn't imagine throwing her old body over another old body.

Elderly intercourse gave Bella a feeling of - she couldn't quite think of the right word, but it was close to distaste, or even revulsion. Bella did a little wiggle in front of the mirror. Someone once suggested that when she felt blue, she should do the twist naked, watching herself in a full-length mirror; she couldn't keep a straight face.

Maybe it was the fact that her long-married friends, Owen and Maggie Lowenthal, were leaving on yet another extended trip to a faraway place - this time Russia - also caused the Romance Virus to flare. Bella could never quite fathom how Maggie managed to tolerate Owen all these years. He was insufferably bossy and his breath stank. He was rich though, or at least his late mother was. She had inherited the bulk of a South African mining fortune, which she passed on to Owen, her only son.

Bella was not a traveller. She would have liked to go to Russia, to India, or to China, but aside from not having the funds to travel first-class, which is how she wanted to travel, she did not like going away on her own. She wasn't the kind of person who could find someone to chat with, or enjoyed making instant best friends.

Bella hadn't noticed lovers for years, but that Saturday all she saw were people holding hands, kissing in the street, walking close together. Most were young, but there were a few oldies who obviously still cared by the way they leaned into each other for support.

She decided that a movie would surely take her mind off herself, so she drove towards the mall. She switched on the car radio. And as if the universe was mocking her, there was a talk on Jane Austen's *Pride and Prejudice* to commemorate the two hundredth anniversary of the novel's publication. Bella listened to the accolades given to this all-time-great romantic novel, where the intelligent, spunky heroine gets the handsome, rich man.

"I am intelligent," she thought. "And spunky. Why didn't I get a Darcy?" That was the trouble with romantic novels. "I got a womanizer. I got a gay man. I got a gangster and any number of - " Bella couldn't even think of a word to describe the litany of her mostly tawdry affairs. Why did the Romantic Virus remain in the body? There was no biological reason for a woman, long past childbearing age, to hanker after romance. Looking for love didn't make any sense from an evolutionary point of view. No sense at all. But then, she knew, life didn't make sense: the creation of the universe, evolution, extinction, love, hate, and death. She was forever thinking about those things. The great search hung about her neck like a string of heavy and unevenly shaped beads.

When she took Charlie out on her return, Nicole emerged to walk with them, and Bella asked her about the meaning of life.

"I think life is…"

At that exact moment, Charlie decided to do his business.

"That's what I think." Nicole laughed and so did Bella. It was the first time she laughed that whole envy-filled day, and she felt the better for it.

Greta glanced at the Florentine notebook she'd given Bella, which was sitting like an ornament beside her collection of antique Venetian paperweights. "How's the writing going?"

"It's not going," Bella sighed. "It's too hot to think," was her lame excuse. "It's supposed to be spring and it's ninety degrees today. And the rest of the week it's going to be the same."

"Imagine if doctors decided not to treat patients when the weather was not to their liking," Greta quipped as she picked up the notebook.

"There's nothing to see. I'm not a writer. I'm fooling myself."

Greta ruffled through the mostly empty pages. On one, Bella had drawn a woman's face. She had slightly smiling lips, curly hair, and no eyes.

Greta said, "Why don't you go back to drawing?"

Chapter 6 -
At the Ivy

*"Avoiding trends because they are trendy
is a form of snobbery."*

Bella usually took out-of-town guests to The Ivy, on the border of West Hollywood and Beverly Hills. She thought it the prettiest and most charming restaurant in all of Los Angeles.

This wasn't such an accolade, as she considered LA almost devoid of charm.

The decor of The Ivy was a mix of Mexican, French, and English country. The food was excellent and the portions large. There was always an array of beautiful people dining both on the terrace and inside. A meal at The Ivy didn't come cheap, and she was amazed that so many people were rich enough to keep the restaurant full for lunch and dinner every day, all year round. But then any trip to Neiman Marcus, Saks Fifth Avenue, Barneys, or Madeo - Bella's favorite expensive Italian restaurant - made her realize how many wealthy people lived in Los Angeles. Digby Bootch, Farrel's father, was always there when Bella occasionally went to Madeo. "They keep his table, in case he comes in," Ivan told her. "If he isn't there by six-thirty - he won't eat later than that - they give it up."

Seeing as her son worked for Digby's son, Bella once introduced herself to Digby when she went to The Ivy with her rich friends, the Blausses. He was polite, but distant. Ivan said, "It's because people are always trying to get money out of him."

Bella replied, "They certainly aren't getting a smile."

The Ivy was an experience which commenced when valets - as handsome as models or movie stars, wearing pink shirts and khaki chinos - parked customer's cars: Teslas, Mercedeses, BMWs, Porsches, and Bentleys, with the odd Audi throw in. Bella's new Subaru didn't make the cut, but the cute four-wheel drive had a certain élan, which she liked, even though Greta told her - after the salesman at the dealership informed her how Subaru served a niche market - "Lesbians drive Subarus."

"Maybe I'll attract a woman? God knows, I haven't attracted a man in years."

"That's a lie," Greta replied. Greta was irritated when Bella said men didn't like her. They did, but she was too fussy. Who did she think she was that she could so disdainfully discard every man - some really nice ones in Greta's opinion - who showed any interest?

Hoping to snap a shot of anyone vaguely well-known dining at The Ivy, paparazzi waited in front of the white picket fence that shielded the flower-bedecked patio dining area from the street. On the patio, where those who wanted to see and be seen preferred to dine, fashionably dressed women picked at salad. Men - whom Bella imagined were Hollywood producers but were more likely in property - dined with starlets or, on occasion, wives.

Bella usually chose to sit inside, away from the trendy bustle. But for lunch with Becky Blumenthal, her old friend from high school who was visiting from Florida with her husband, Brian, Bella booked a patio table. Becky, who loved all things she believed were exclusive - from handbags and face creams to restaurants and holiday spots - would enjoy the scene.

Bella persuaded Greta to join them. "I need support. I've known Becky forever, but she insists on feeling sorry for me so she can feel that life with her philandering husband has some meaning. You can back me up. Not that I can't defend myself, but I want to bash her head in sometimes. Having you there will prevent me from spending the rest of my life in jail."

True to annoying form, Becky ordered Cobb Salad. "No bacon. No tomato. No onion. Dressing on the side, please."

Greta ordered Cobb Salad, too, trying hard not to sound

mocking when she said, "With everything."

Bella ordered Fish-and-Chips.

Becky refused a piece of the steaming, diminutive loaf of bread served on a cute, matching-size wooden board. "I'm gluten intolerant."

"Everyone is now gluten intolerant, it's the fashion," Bella said as she broke off a piece of bread.

Becky then launched into an energetic description of the exclusive, luxury cruise she and Brian took during the summer.

"Our cruise was nothing like those cruise packages advertised in the Sunday papers. We met quality people. Very high-end. The women dressed up, and when I say 'up,' I mean jewels, long gowns, and men in black tie. Very exclusive."

Greta said, "I love travelling, but I've never been on a cruise. I'm waiting to get older."

Bella added, "Neither have I. I don't like boats."

"Ships," Becky corrected. "There was a fabulous woman we met from LA., Margo Rogers, divorced from Rudy Rogers. You've heard of him of course. She's very involved with the Museum, or maybe it's with the Philharmonic. I can't remember exactly… but she's very well-known. In fact, I want you to meet her. I know you'd get along. But she's in New York at the moment. She has a place there, too."

Bella was utterly annoyed when women told her how she would get along with other women they knew, as if she was short of women friends. She didn't add that she'd never heard of either Margo Rogers or her rich ex, but then she didn't move in those circles.

"I think she's also a bit lonely since her divorce," Becky added.

"Also?"

Becky didn't pick up on the irritated tone in Bella's voice and, as if she wasn't present, addressed Greta. "I think Bella is incredibly brave. She's faced so much alone."

"Brave? What have I done that's brave?" Bella scooped a huge blob of mayonnaise on a french fry and almost waved the fat-inducing morsel under Becky's nose.

"Difficult then…" Becky shrugged.

Bella refused to let that pass. "Not difficult, interesting."

Greta almost bashed Becky's head in herself, but Bella motioned - in that imperceptible way good friends communicate - to let her comment go.

Bella tried to explain, "I am not lonely Becky, I am alone. There is a difference."

Bella found that couples could not comprehend how single people managed to actually survive.

"I like living on my own," she continued. "Once you get used to it, it's almost impossible to make the compromises necessary to live with another human being."

Becky stared longingly at the small, homemade loaf of bread on the cutting board.

"I admire you, Bella. You've made the best of a hard life. I respect you for that." Becky gave in, cut a slice, and layered it with the slimmest sliver of butter.

"There is nothing hard about my life. I am not working in a factory sticking labels on ketchup bottles. I'm not hauling rocks from a mine. I've been married and divorced. I've loved and lost and lived to love again, and again, and again. I've resided on three different continents. I have a capable and attentive daughter, and a decent son. I have my divine granddaughter, Chloe, whom I adore and who adores me. I have a more-than-pleasant roof over my head. I have all my senses."

Greta nodded. "And then some."

Becky scraped some butter off her bread.

Bella wished she could tell Becky how Brian had privately shared - soon after he and Becky married - that he always had a crush on Bella and how once, when he'd come to Los Angeles on a business trip, he'd called and invited her to join him at a conference in Boston. Brian was just one of many married men who had propositioned her, and she learned over the years to deflect their attention with a gentleness they did not deserve. Husbands seemed to think all single women were fair game.

"You could find a man; you're still very attractive," Becky proposed. "I'm sure there are men who would want a woman like you."

Greta added, "There are! Quite a few."

"Not ones I want." Bella glared at both Greta and Becky. "I'm fussy, it's true, but I'm not interested in having sex just to make myself feel wanted. I'm fine without that supposedly indispensable activity. Men want sex, and they want to screw till the day they die. And in case you haven't noticed from the TV ads, they're prepared to ingest great quantities of medications to keep their unresponsive members erect, despite the side effects. Imagine risking your eyesight for a fuck!"

Bella grew up at a time when cursing was not ladylike, and she rarely did, but the word was so perfect. "I don't need sex in the same way as a man - to prove myself - and when I have the desire, there are battery-powered devices that do a better job than any man, aided by Viagra or not."

The horrified expression on Becky's face was so blatant that Bella made a mental note to send her a vibrator for her next birthday.

"Secondly," Bella was on a roll, "most women know how to make a home. Most men don't. We're able to make ourselves comfortable. We know which cleaning products to buy and how to use them. We know the difference between single- and double-sheet toilet paper, and boil and broil. Most men haven't got a clue. Your Brian would be lost without you."

Becky pushed her bread off to the side. "You are so right."

Becky's cell phone buzzed. Apologetically she whispered, "I have to answer, it's Brian."

When she'd finished the brief call, Becky announced, "Brian is back at the hotel."

"Congratulations, he managed to find his way back without you."

"He wants me to come back after lunch." Browsing the boutiques down the street, which Becky was eagerly anticipating, was now no longer possible.

"You know what Brian is like," Becky said as Bella and Greta drove her to The Beverly Hilton. "I don't want him to get in a bad mood."

"You have to compromise if you want to live with another person," Greta pointed out after they dropped off Becky. "You have to pretend you love someone, when half the time you want to kill him. That's one of the reasons I never got married. I'd never be able to hide my feelings."

Bella laughed. "When I first dated Guy, I told him I liked watching rugby because he was a fan. I think the sport is much too violent. But when you are first in love, you lie. You lie to yourself, too." Bella was making a subtle reference to Greta's affair with Glen Short.

From what Greta told Bella about Glen, she couldn't have found anyone less suitable. "He makes me feel adored, cherished. He's very sensual."

"Well of course, that's all you do - make love." Bella wanted to say, "All you do is fuck," but she tried not to use that word again. When Greta showed Bella a photograph of Glen and his wife on a website called Switcheroo, Bella could barely believe the depths to which Greta had fallen. There was Glen - tall, dark, and, according to Greta, very handsome - wearing his wife's pastel-pink shift dress and T-strap heels, and holding her gold clutch handbag. His wife posed beside him, wearing Glen's much-too-large suit.

"He's certainly chirped you up." Bella smiled fondly at Greta, whom she had to admit was glowing with a slight tan, more highlights, high heels, and a low-cut, black chiffon blouse that showed her breasts - naturally pert - to advantage.

Bella was practical. "You'll end up with a broken heart. But so what? You'll have lived, and loved, and lost."

"Why do you say I'll lose?"

"Experience."

"I told you I don't want him to leave her. Maybe when the children are grown up?"

Bella guffawed. "That's at least seven more years. Do you honestly think this hot-and-heavy affair will continue so fervently for years to come?"

Much as she hated it, Greta knew this was the truth.

Bella was not a romantic. Romantic novels and movies didn't appeal to her. She didn't like romantic music. She was cynical about love, not because she hadn't loved, but because she had.

Her cynicism began early. She was six years old when she worked out that her father and her friend Della's mother were up to something. And whilst she didn't know exactly what that something was, she knew their deception had to do with romance, and that their duplicity was illicit. Della's mother would call. She'd allow the phone to ring three times and then hang up. If Speedy was home, he'd call back, and vice versa. Della and Bella - the girls loved their similar names - would laugh at their respective parents. "They're stupid; they think we don't know."

Bella got into her bed that night, luxuriating in the cool softness of the freshly laundered, favorite red-checked Ralph Lauren sheets. She arranged her pillows, propped her head against the monogrammed neck roll for support, and began reading. The book was a doorstopper, a dense biography of Catherine the Great whose moniker, Bella was learning, was well deserved.

An oft-repeated refrain started up in Bella's mind: "My life is unimportant. What have I done that is in any way special? Am I really happy living alone, or am I lying to myself?" Then her thoughts, as they so often did, turned to Guy.

Guy was dirt poor when they married, but he was rich enough now - and guilty enough about his many indiscretions - to help her purchase her condo, a car, and a decent way of life. Between what Guy gave her and her own income, Bella could afford weekly manicures, an occasional visit to Peter for her hair, and training with Sven.

Sven was her one consistent luxury, but seeing as she hated working out, he didn't seem an extravagance like massages, facials, Botox, or a drastic face-lift. She was certain Becky had a lift - damn her, she did look good.

Bella imagined Becky and Brian in their hotel, bickering away, in the manner couples did.

Then, with a wave of affection for Becky, for the past they shared so long ago in South Africa, Bella did what she knew would make her feel better. She prayed to the Good in the Universe: "May Brian and Becky have a happy marriage."

Bella read a few more pages about Catherine the Great before her eyes began to close. She switched off the bedside lamp - a mid-century Chinese figurine topped by a pale, melon-coloured silk shade that gave the whole room a comforting glow - turned on her side, and pushed the monogrammed neck roll so that she wouldn't squash her face and cause wrinkles. She listened to the tinkle coming from a fountain that the new neighbors had installed on their patio - which she was sure someone would complain about - and soon fell asleep.

Bella had doubts about whether *The Lions of A'marula* was the best story for her to tell now. There was one other of the seven she'd written that might work: *Kietekie.*

She planned to run the idea past Shelly over their next dinner at

Il Figo. They both liked the food and ambience there and, best of all, the neighborhood restaurant was near enough for them to walk there. This lightened their guilt about dessert, which they always shared.

"So what's the story about?"

"It's about a six-year-old white girl who was allegedly raped by a black man - a horrible story really - and the worst thing is that most of what happened is true. His name was Phineas Mawela, and he was the grown-up son of my maid, Anna."

"I might need more than iced tea for this." Shelly rarely drank. She had no problem with alcohol; she simply didn't like the taste.

She took off her leather bomber jacket. "I can't stand the heat!" They were sitting on the patio, which was pleasantly warmed by ceiling heaters. She asked the waiter to turn the heater down, which he did.

"They can't control the heaters." Shelly adamantly refused to admit she was menopausal, and fanning herself with the wine menu, asked Bella to tell her more.

"Phineas lived with his girlfriend, Mary, who worked for the Van der Merwe family, which included little Kietekie, her parents, and Kietekie's three older brothers. If they lived here, they'd be labeled Trailer-Park Trash. In South Africa, we call them Poor Whites. Phineas was allowed to sleep with Mary in her little room in the servant quarters in the backyard, because he was a mechanic and helped Mr. Van der Merwe with his old car. On the day of the rape, Phineas had to be at work at four in the afternoon. He walked to the garage, where he had an evening shift. This happened during the school holiday. Kietekie's older brothers and some of their friends were in and out of the house, as was her father, who was out of work."

"I don't believe the heaters were turned down!"

"Are you listening?"

"Of course I am!"

"Kietekie's Aunt came by during the day to see if her sister was back from work. Phineas greeted her as he walked down the driveway to go to work."

"Where did he work?"

"You're not listening. I told you, he worked at a nearby garage. Anyway, the aunt said at the trial that she noticed Kietekie walking strangely, but she didn't tell anyone at the time, nor did she ask Kietekie if anything was wrong. When Mrs. Van der Merwe came home from work, Kietekie said nothing. Odd no?"

Bella didn't wait for Shelly to agree and continued, "Kietekie's parents went out for the evening. Mary was left in charge of the kids, who fell asleep on the living-room floor. When the parents came home after midnight, Mary went off to her room and left the mother to put the children to bed. It was then that Kietekie complained she was sore down there. Mrs. Van der Merwe took her to the hospital, where a female doctor found Kietekie had abrasions, although her hymen was intact."

"That doesn't make sense. Then she wasn't raped?"

Bella laughed. "The judge didn't know what a hymen was. The doctor who gave evidence had to explain!"

"You can't be serious. Maybe he was gay?"

"No, he wasn't. Just ignorant. The court proceedings were so confusing: conducted in three different languages! The Van der Merwes spoke Afrikaans. Phineas, though fairly fluent in English, was Xhosa and was questioned in his native tongue. The Advocate spoke English. All this had to be translated back and forth. I didn't understand much Afrikaans, and no Xhosa. I sat there for three days."

"What about your maid, Anna?"

"She didn't want to come. She said that being present would upset her too much. But she wanted me at the trial. I had to get permission to be in the gallery because no spectators were allowed during the trial due to the age of the child. Kietekie gave evidence. You should have seen her. She wore a pink frilly dress, like she was going to a party. Her hair was in ringlets, tied with pink ribbons.

Her white socks had lace frills. The Van der Merwes and the mother's sister glared at me as if I was the rapist. I ignored them, but the sight of them made me sick."

"The child said that Phineas put a pillow over her face so she couldn't see him, but she still knew it was him."

"And you thought Phineas could be someone else?

"I thought the father, or perhaps the brothers or their friends, had been sexual with Kietekie. It sounded, to me as if the child was clearly coached to blame Phineas. The black Clerk of the Court told me, after Phineas was found guilty and sentenced to eight years in jail, that the verdict was a miscarriage of justice."

"And so?"

Bella wondered whether the horrible story - or Shelly's hot flushes - were affecting her lack of attention.

"The sentence indicated that even the Judge found something amiss: a black man raping a six-year-old white girl in apartheid South Africa. He could have got the death penalty. The case went to appeal in Pretoria's Supreme Court. Three Judges heard the evidence presented by a state-appointed Advocate, who was not the same as the one in the original case. He was a charming young lawyer, and I filled him in on what I suspected."

Shelly called the waiter and asked that the heater be totally switched off, but other guests complained of the cold. The heater was thus reignited. Bella bit her tongue.

"So tell me, what happened in the end?" Shelly took a piece of paper from her purse, folded it, and made a fan.

"The judgment was upheld. Phineas wasn't present, but I was permitted to speak in his favor. I felt important facing those three High-Court Judges, and for a moment I considered becoming a lawyer. I was in my forties. People went back to school and began different careers. Then I discovered I'd have to be able to speak Afrikaans if I wanted to obtain a law degree. I hated the language and the apartheid it stood for."

"But I've heard you speaking to another South African."

"I can make myself understood - Afrikaans was compulsory at school - but I'm no way near fluent. I never got more than a *C*."

"What happened to Anna?"

"She retired as our maid, but before that I took her to visit Phineas at the jail near Pretoria on Sundays. We waited outside and I watched the sad trail of visitors coming and going. Phineas sent me a letter with a drawing of hands in prayer, thanking me for my efforts on his behalf. I felt so sad when I read his words. As if I'd failed him."

Later, Bella rummaged for the letter in her antique Chinese, papier-mâché letter box, and showed it to Shelly.

"What do you think?"

Shelly read the letter. The lined paper was fragile and the writing was childish, but the sentiment was touching.

"Oh, it's so sad!"

"So you think the saga of Phineas and Kietekie would make a good movie?"

Shelly folded the letter and gave it back to her friend.

"Don't get me wrong, the story is dramatic. But the black–white false accusation thing…we've seen it too many times already. Not exactly, but similar. Remember, we've had fights for racial equality, too."

Bella knew Shelly was right.

The next day, Shelly called. "I've been thinking, you could make *Kietekie* work. Don't give up because of anything I said. I'm not giving up, either. I'm going on another blind date tonight."

❧ · ☙

Chapter 7 -
Hats and Stockings

"Hair today, gone tomorrow."

The first thing Bella noticed about a woman was her hair: its health, length, and style, and whether it was tinted, highlighted, or natural. Redheads invariably had the best hair. When Bella admired a fellow client at her hairdresser the woman explained, "We have thicker shafts."

"I never knew that." Bella was amazed.

"Our hair shafts are thicker, but our skin is thinner."

"That's life." Bella laughed. "Always a downside to the upside."

More and more, Bella observed how women had thinning hair on top, just like men. That terrified her, for her grandmother-on-her-mother's-side ended up balding, and wore a curly silver wig, which she perched on her head without much regard for its placement.

Balding must be the result of evolution. And if it was evolution, why was balding not something to be admired? It showed an advance, like not having body hair. Women shaved their legs and under-arms, and waxed their pubic area. Men had begun to get rid of their body hair. No hair was acceptable, except on the head.

Bella never coped well with her hair. When she was young, no matter how many times she told her mother that she got headaches when it was pulled back, Joyce would nag, "I wish you wouldn't hide behind that hair. You have such a pretty face, and are much prettier with your hair off it."

Miss Willoughby, Bella's English teacher, teased her almost daily.

"Here comes the 'Wreck of the Hesperus.'" For some reason, Miss Willoughby found it amusing to liken Bella's hair to the sad poem by Henry Wadsworth Longfellow, in which a sea captain's pride in deciding to sail - despite a pending hurricane - results in both his and his daughter's tragic deaths.

Over the years, Bella could not imagine how much money she had spent in the quest for something that would improve her hair. Hundreds of products, available for every kind of hair condition, were evidence that she was not alone in her quest.

Bella was bothered that magazines showed models with hair that was simply not naturally possible without extensions. Movie stars wore extensions and wigs. How else were those updos created with braids and curls so full and thick - particularly in period pieces?

When Bella first arrived in Los Angeles around twenty-seven years ago, after cutting her hair and hating it, she decided to invest in some hair extensions. The Chinese technician promised, "You will not notice that you have them in your hair. You can swim with them and shower."

This was a lie. Tiny bits of glue attaching the fake hair to the real hair felt like broken matchsticks. Bella couldn't sleep. The matchsticks dug into her scalp like nails. Though told she could do anything, she was unable to run a comb through it after her morning shower.

"We can't give you back your money," the technician huffed at Bella, who called the moment the salon opened.

"I can't stand it, I have to have it all taken out. Now! Today. I don't care about the money, just get them out." Bella fought back tears.

Nowadays, Bella believed hair extensions were less bothersome. Shelly often had them put in before meeting a man she thought would be "the one," and claimed she barely noticed them. Shelly also claimed that men didn't notice them, either. "I can't believe men are so unobservant," Bella said.

"You could have some natural-looking extensions added to your hair, when you next have a date." Shelly knew Bella hadn't had a date in years.

When Bella was about thirty, she fortunately discovered the power of the hat, which not only hid her unruly (or unwashed) hair, but also gave her a distinguished, somewhat European air. Her mother told her, "If you want to make an impression, wear a hat." Of course, Joyce grew up in an era when women wore not only hats and gloves, but also stockings, which were kept in place by corsets or suspender belts. Panty hose did away with those torturous articles of clothing, but the stocking-and-suspender combination cunningly remained part of the lexicon of erotic apparel, and men claimed that panty hose were a turn off.

Joyce had a millinery collection from way back, when hats were worn "to go to town" during the day, as well as tiny cocktail hats - often with seductive nets over the eyes - which were worn to nightclubs. As a child, Bella adored trying on her mother's hats, all nestled safely in decorative hatboxes on one side of Joyce's bedroom. Joyce never got rid of her hats, not even after her second husband died and she moved into a retirement home. Those hatboxes had pride of place - stacked like a contemporary art piece - almost to the ceiling.

Bella was less fastidious about her hats, most of which she slung on a Victorian coat stand. These were not the confections Joyce collected, but were chosen for their ability to be plonked on the head at the last minute.

Bella was glad that everyday fashion had become less formal, but she also thought it became too relaxed, especially in Los Angeles, where people wore jeans to funerals, to the theatre, and even to the ballet. That was stepping over the line, as far as she was concerned.

"I think you should hide three things that begin with B when you get dressed," Bella told Nicole, whom Bella thought in need of some garment guidance. "No bras, no belly buttons, and no butts."

Nicole giggled. She was wearing denim jeans with purposefully ripped knees, topped by a soft, black T-shirt that slipped off one shoulder to show a lime-green bra strap.

"You may laugh, dear Nicole, but dressing like that is not the way to find a boyfriend."

"Who says I want to do that?" Nicole pulled up her top, hiding the bra strap, and thus baring her navel.

Bella ignored that query. She listened to Nicole enough to know differently.

"You think if you dress like that you'll attract a man?"

"Men like it."

"For a minute. But you, darling girl, you want a boyfriend. Maybe even a husband? At least someone who will commit to you alone. And in case you don't know, there's serious competition available at the click of a mouse. Compared to a living, breathing woman, that's inexpensive."

"You are so right." Nicole respected Bella, whom she found wise and experienced. She loved listening to Bella's anecdotes, especially stories about her past romances. Nicole imagined Bella's life was exciting and adventurous.

"You young ladies may dress like porn stars in all their varieties, from innocent baby dolls to black-leather dominatrices. But when men go to the Internet they find Missy Maureen who likes doing all kinds of things you don't, or Sweet Lulu with lips as thick as bananas and bodily orifices that are forever waiting to be filled."

"Ew!" Nicole grimaced.

"And, my darling Nicole, these cyber women don't want commitment. Nor do they nag to be understood or heard. They don't have period pains. No hormonal ups and downs. And they are available for less than the price of a dinner at a mediocre restaurant."

At Bella's nail bar, a truly beautiful woman from Texas - typically blonde, tall, and probably around thirty-five, with a huge diamond on her ring finger and a pale-blue Hermès bag blinking on the floor beside her - said, "I'll tell you, as I will probably never see you again. I am getting divorced because my husband is addicted to Internet porn. He'd rather jack off in front of the computer than have normal sex."

Internet sex was here to stay, Bella knew. You couldn't put that genie back into the bottle. Photoshop might correct the surface imperfections of famous models in *Vogue*, but the application was used to retouch rashes and ingrown hairs on a plucked or shaved pubis, or anything unseemly or discoloured in a computer-rendered labia or butt. The pubis was often shown now, as hairless as a newborn, or trimmed like a military moustache. Lips - kissed by nothing remotely like affection - remained full, glossy, and just-so parted. Arched backs pushed out fake breasts that made no pretense at reality.

Bella pondered that. "Some men obviously don't care that the breasts they caress are silicone, or whatever new-fangled material those things are made of. Some men might even prefer them artificial. As for males in search of more exotic fare, whatever they fancy could be found online."

Greta told Bella that one of her friends had a son who was a Furry.

"What's that?"

"They take on an animal persona. And have sex with other Furries."

"What kind of animals?"

"All kinds. He's a tiger."

"Don't be ridiculous."

"No, seriously, it's a whole subculture."

Greta and Bella fell about giggling, and had one of those memorable, unstoppable, pants-wetting laughs. Later Bella searched the Internet for Furries. She saw Furry conventions, Furry costumes, statistics for sexual and nonsexual Furries, and Furry fandom - not all of it was devoted to sex, but still. Furries!

"What on earth has happened to the world?" Bella asked.

Greta said, "Everything changes, but it all stays the same."

"Only more accessible? Furries - how would they have found each other had it not been for the net?"

In all of Bella's fertile years, she was unaware of being hormonal. Jessica never mentioned the condition, though she often went on about how hungry she got before her period; which was fine, as Jessica was thin as a rail no matter what she ate.

In contrast, Nicole was forever hormonal, or about to be hormonal, or just finished being hormonal. One evening, whilst they walked Charlie around the block, Nicole was short, almost rude. "Give me a break will you! I'm hormonal."

Bella had enough.

"My periods came and went. I had some bad cramps, for which I took painkillers, but I was never aware of erratic mood swings. Perhaps I had them and didn't notice? There's no going back to find out. I had some miserable times, which I suppose could be termed hormonal. But they were situational, like thinking I was in love, waiting for the phone to ring, wondering when or if - that kind of misery. And you know what, Nicole, none of my friends ever talked about being hormonal, or having crazy moods when they had their periods. I think all this stuff about being hormonal is an excuse for treating people badly."

"You won't give me a pass will you?" Nicole said.

Nicole lived in a studio apartment, the smallest one of four in a

French Chateaux–style building opposite The Portland. Her apartment faced the street, and when she saw Bella outside, she often joined her to walk Charlie.

Other than Nicole's hormones and mood swings, Bella listened to Nicole's main two woes. The first consisted of not being appreciated at the modeling agency where she worked. Nicole hoped one day to become a director, instead of a trainee who was required to do everything and anything, including being sent off to buy endless cups of coffee and do other demeaning chores. But Nicole's more pressing problem was her failure to find true love.

"I don't understand men," Nicole complained when another potential romance failed to progress.

Bella put her straight. "Men don't understand us, and why the hell should they? We are different on the outside, so why shouldn't we be different on the inside?"

Nicole easily swung from being an ardent feminist who wanted to have sex like a man, to being a woman whose sole ambition was to find her soul mate, buy a home, and have a baby. "I fight my biological urges on a daily basis. I want a baby, I want to be pregnant," could segue into, "I can do anything a man can, and better."

Bella broke into the song from *Annie Get Your Gun*. She had seen the movie when she was young. Her grandparents took her with them to a matinee every Saturday afternoon. George, their driver, drove them in the black Packard. Neither of her paternal grandparents ever learned to drive. They were immigrants from Lithuania, who came to South Africa to make life for themselves and their potential children, and their children's children, and so on. And they succeeded because, despite their own lack of a formal education, they insisted their children get one.

Bella offered her own first child, Jessica, books about boy's things. She bought her fire trucks and helicopters, but Jess wasn't much interested. She never got into dolls either, but like almost all girls - and some boys too - she adored pink. And she loved her collection of little horses.

Ivan, born five years after Jessica, liked purple and showed no interest in dolls - male or female - or horses. "What was the lure of horses?" Bella wondered. "Why did horses intrigue little girls and not boys?" That was surely worth some kind of study. The little legs astride the wide back, the subtle control of a powerful animal? There were no boys in her granddaughter's riding class, and there never had been for over three years now, since Chloe began riding. In the competitions (that she was now good enough to enter), no boys took part. All the grown men who frequented the stables were gay.

Thus far in her life, Bella had seen one man knit, whilst she was on a train to Scotland. He was an English Eccentric, a particular type who wore a worn, navy-blue velvet jacket and scuffed patent-leather shoes, and didn't care much about personal hygiene. There was also that brilliant man Kaffe Fassett who knitted and embroidered and published marvelous books showing off his work. Personally, Bella had never seen a man embroider, though Ivan, when aged twelve, got her to show him how to do needlepoint when he wanted to make a cover for a set of tarot cards. Bella encouraged this hobby in Ivan, but his interest lasted about a week, and shortly after he also lost interest in the tarot.

Of course there was the fashion industry; but the men working there were mostly gay, and they didn't do the actual sewing. Farrel Bootch once told Bella that he was thinking of going into fashion, which made Bella wonder about him, but Ivan assured her that Farrel was not only not gay, but was something of a stud around women. Bella found this hard to believe, until she noticed the length of Farrel's fingers, which she'd once heard were analogous to other body parts. Length did not have the significance men believed, nor did girth for that matter. Or how long you "did it." Smart people knew the mind was the most powerful sex organ.

Bella wanted to be a fashion designer for a good part of her childhood. She drew detailed outfits - hats, gloves, matching handbags, and costume jewelry - and wrote, in flowing cursive, where and how each outfit should be worn. She wished her mother kept the drawings. They'd be an absolute treasure, but Joyce was not the sort of mother who did that. Joyce was utterly unsentimental, which Bella thought played a large part in her own lack of sentimentality. Detachment was in her genes.

At the age of eighteen, Bella took a course in sewing and patternmaking. She produced one simple A-line skirt and learned how to craft tailored buttonholes, and that was the end of that - though she had devoured magazines like *Vogue* and *Harper's Bazaar.*

Being aware of what was "in" in Paris, London, or Rome made Bella feel as if she was *au fait* with what was going on - which is something she always wanted to be despite living in the southern tip of Africa where even the seasons were opposite to those of the First World.

Magazines arrived on the African shores a few months after their publication, but the delay was quick enough for Bella to receive the satisfaction of knowing, for example, on what basis Robert Clergerie was *the* emerging Parisian shoe designer.

When she moved to Los Angeles, she scooped up the fashion and home-decorating magazines. Compared to what they cost in Africa, they were inexpensive and, best of all, current.

Now, as she approached the big birthday, the pages of those once-treasured magazines mocked, "You can't wear this anymore!"

From Bella's career as an advertising copywriter, she knew that she no longer belonged to the demographic to which such publications were aimed, even when they occasionally tried to include "older women," with issues devoted to "How to Look Good in Every Decade."

Bella decided to stop reading the glossy fashion magazines, and she succeeded for about a year, though when faced with the latest *Vogue* or *W* lying in a pile while at the hairdresser, or at the manicurist, or at her daughter's house, or even at Dr. Feather's office, she was thrilled. But she still scoffed at the triviality of headlines like, "Fur Is Fun Again." As if fur went away to a sanatorium to get over a bout of melancholy.

Then one day, she got an e-mail offering such a good deal on subscriptions, she simply could not resist. And so, every month they arrived to taunt her: *Vogue, Harper's Bazaar, Town & Country, Vanity Fair, Elle,* and *Architectural Digest.* She didn't read them with the enthusiasm she once felt, but she thought that having purchased the publications, she was obliged to page through them; which she did, with Greta, in one huge magazine binge on Sunday, together with the Sunday papers. And during every Magazine Marathon, Bella complained how reading the hyper-stylish magazine pages made her feel utterly, undeniably unremarkable.

"I can't wear any of these clothes," Bella complained as she flipped through a fashion spread titled, "Spring Forward with Lots of Colour." "Who actually pays four thousand dollars for a pair of beige pants? They aren't even special: beige twill."

"Everything is relative," Greta pointed out. "I bet Julietta would think you're crazy to spend what you do on your clothes, not to mention what you spend on face creams."

"True." With a mixture of shame and guilt, Bella made sure to never leave receipts lying around for Julietta to see. Not that Julietta would ever notice. Ask her about Bella and she'd say she had a generous employer. Bella gave a double check at Christmas, plus a good gift: silverware, dinnerware, sheet sets, and so on. When Julietta's grown son got into trouble in El Salvador, Bella paid for a lawyer to sort out the matter. Julietta presented Bella with a large white orchid as thanks, which touched Bella so much she bought Julietta some T-shirts from Lands' End.

"Just think how much more useful a laptop would be to an underprivileged student than this pair of Jimmy Choo, crystal-encrusted strappy sandals that, if they were lucky, would be worn a couple of times," noted Bella.

Greta looked at the picture. "If I had the money I'd buy them."

"What about this? Seventy-five hundred dollars for an evening purse. It's not even that special." Greta made no comment.

She didn't ask Bella why she bought the magazines when they so annoyed her. Greta loved paging through them, and was grateful to not spend the money to purchase them herself.

Bella went back to reading. She decided to keep silent about the spread featuring the Vanderpoodles, their three tousle-headed daughters, and their two English Springer Spaniels, all photographed at both their eighty-thousand-acre Montana spread and their fifteen-bedroom holiday cottage in Belize - where Sybilla Vanderpoodle preferred to entertain out-of-town guests. Inadvertently, the words came out: "And some people have no shoes."

Greta couldn't help herself. "Stop! Don't feel so damned guilty that you appreciate photographs of high fashion, and all the pretty models who we know are touched up with Photoshop so they don't even have pores, let alone wrinkles and pimples. We're women, we like this stuff. These magazines are made for us. If we didn't buy them, they wouldn't print them."

Bella conceded. "You have a point. I actually do like the information about skin care. And I realize that the pictures of happy families cavorting in their fabulous homes are not quite true. Remember that spread on the Hafts?"

"How could I forget?"

Biddy Haft, mother of the Hafts in the spread, had gone to college with Greta. They had remained such good friends that Biddy divulged that her son was in and out of drug rehabs, and her daughter-in-law's bespoke children's clothes company was - and had always been - a money loser, no matter what was said in *Town & Country*.

Bella shrugged, trying to raise herself out of the shallows. "I also read *The Christian Science Monitor* every week, and *Time* and - "

Greta interrupted. "Stop judging yourself so harshly. You're a woman. Women like fashion. Even nuns like shoes. And you do your bit - all that volunteering. I could never stand doing that. And you're no longer eating red meat, and you've given up milk for that awful almond stuff, so the poor animals don't suffer."

"I still eat fish, and I'm sure they feel pain, too."

"Well, I hope you never go that far, because I do like the smoked salmon you get from Costco. And remember, you did save Charlie from the pound."

Charlie's ears pricked up at the mention of his name. He almost seemed to nod.

Aside from *Kietekie* and *The Lions of A'marula*, there were still five more of her short stories for Bella to consider turning into a screenplay.

The Dermatologist's Wife had potential. The story line involved a woman who went to jail rather than pay a fine for employing a maid who did not have the required papers to work in Johannesburg. The apartheid government wanted to prevent blacks from the rural areas flooding the cities to find work, and employers were fined if they hired an illegal. The situation was a bit like that of the alien immigrants in The United States, except the illegal blacks were born in South Africa. However, Bella decided that writing about racism from a white person's point of view had no appeal.

Greta suggested, "Why don't you take a screenwriting class?

Bella made inquiries. She'd missed the start of the new term. She would have to wait. She felt relieved. She did not like classes.

Chapter 8 -
Depression

*"Some people are born happy
no matter what comes their way."*

Nicole had remained in bed the entire weekend. "I can't eat. I can't sleep. I can't get out of bed."

Jason, whom Nicole thought was "the one," had broken up with her. In addition, she was struggling with a new manager she was certain was angling to get her fired. What had begun a few weeks prior as feeling blue had progressed. "I feel dead inside. I don't want to kill myself, but I can't see the point of anything," said Nicole.

Bella told her normally cheerful young neighbor, "Everyone loses boyfriends and everyone has problems at work, but not everyone sinks into the pit you're in. Believe me, I know what I'm talking about. You need to be on an antidepressant, now, as soon as possible."

"A pill won't cure how I feel," Nicole said flatly. She was beyond tears. "I have to pull myself together." Bella noticed Nicole hadn't even washed and blow-dried her hair, which she did every day. Bella was surprised to see how curly Nicole's hair actually was.

"You can't 'pull yourself together' when you're down like this. You need something more than a belt. I hate that term, 'pull yourself together.' Only people who have never suffered from a depression suggest that as a cure. You need modern medicine."

"What if I become addicted?"

"You can't get addicted to antidepressants, no matter what anyone tells you. I don't know why antidepressants have such a bad rap. They're less toxic to the body than aspirin. It's not like a drink, or a drug you ingest, and suddenly you feel great. They take six weeks to kick in. But they do kick in. And it's not as if you feel the kick. One day you wake up and feel normal. And if one kind doesn't work, there's another that will. And you will feel better. I promise you that."

Nicole didn't believe Bella, but she went to her doctor and he prescribed an antidepressant. Every day, Bella asked if she'd taken the medication. "Don't give up. Six weeks, I promise."

And whilst Nicole waited to feel better, quite sure she never would, Bella shared about her own bouts of depression.

"The first episode I remember was after Ivan was born. Postpartum depression wasn't well-known then, at least not in South Africa. Dear, sensitive Guy chose that time to go on an extended business trip. And he wasn't alone all the time, I later found out."

"That must have been awful." Nicole still had the naiveté of youth.

"That's men for you. They are genetically programmed to be unfaithful."

"That makes me feel even more depressed." Nicole managed a tiny laugh.

Bella continued her tales of depression. "Dr. Lavin prescribed an antidepressant. I took the pills for two or three days and felt no better, so I stopped. He never mentioned that antidepressants took time to work. He probably didn't even know."

"Did you get better?" Nicole asked.

"Eventually the depression went away, and I forgot about how bad I once felt. Then, we divorced, and the dreaded black cloud returned. I don't know what possessed me, but on top of dealing with being newly single, I decided to give up smoking. I shoved all thoughts of failure aside and decided that I was now a gay divorcée, ready to have fun. It was Christmas time. Party time in South Africa. It's summer there, the opposite of here. I was filled with hope for a happier future, and was drinking too much, too. As I was about to leave my flat for yet another dinner party, it hit. I felt as if I was being crushed, like I couldn't breathe, but of course I could. Fortunately, by this time Prozac had come onto the market. Dr. Lavin informed me I was suffering from Acute Anxiety, probably a result of getting divorced, which was morphing into Clinical Depression.

"'Clinical Depression is a chemical imbalance,' Dr. Lavin said, differentiating the malady from hysteria, or run-of-the mill sadness, or feelings of melancholy or grief. At least my anguish had a name, which made me feel as if I was not merely a weak person. It was something tangible, a medical term.

"My friends whispered that I had a nervous breakdown. My utter despair was not something well understood in those days. I couldn't bear to listen to music. I couldn't watch television. I didn't want to observe people living their lives, even on a screen. I went about my life, doing what I had to do as if I was dragging a hundred-pound weight behind me. From the outside it might have looked like I was functioning; but inside, I was a mess. Guy already had a girlfriend and I don't think that helped, though I wouldn't admit it to anyone. Not even to myself.

"I started reading a novel. It was called *The Dice Man*, as I recall. The protagonist decided to make life choices according to the number that came up when he rolled his dice. Above six, make the call - below six, do not. Above six, have a drink - below six, don't. I began to feel myself in the protagonist's brain and, like him, becoming crazed. I was afraid that I wasn't sane enough to take care of my children."

Bella was never ashamed to talk about her suffering. Now, after multiple bouts of depression, she took daily medication. And she told anyone whom she thought might need the information about it. Her openness resulted in quite a few people being bolder in obtaining help.

Nicole's medication kicked in six weeks to the day. Bella didn't need Nicole to tell her. Her hair was shiny, and blown dead straight.

But Bella did warn her young friend, "The dark cloud might hover from time to time, for when you suffer from depression it tends to force its way back, something like the way an octopus knows how to squeeze into the tiniest crevice. And if the blackness returns you take meds again, never ever reduce or stop taking the pills because you think you're okay. I learned the hard way that is not a good idea."

Nicole listened to Bella, and four months later - under her doctor's supervision - she stopped taking the antidepressant. She didn't have a new boyfriend and her job was still difficult, but she wasn't depressed and she was just fine. She also signed up for a course in creative writing, which she said was "awesome."

Bella asked, "So what are you writing?"

"We had to write about a character, someone we knew. I wrote about you."

Bella wasn't sure if she wanted to know what Nicole wrote about her, but curiosity got the better of her so Nicole gave the piece to her to read:

Bella has lived the sort of life many people can only hope to recall in their yonder years. There is some argument as to some suspicious decision making, but in her defense this has only led to more experience to relay to her grandchild. After all, if one has no experience, what the hell are you supposed to talk about?

She has never lost her sense of curiosity, which has kept her mind alert and her commentary quick. This isn't the sort of woman you find at the bingo tournament or a country club. This is the comrade you go to with your embarrassing accounts from last night, where you're sure to find a slow, knowing nod and a wink.

"The teacher said my writing was well observed. He suggested I might base the short story we have to write for our final project on you."

After many failed efforts trying to create a script layout using Word, Bella paid for, and downloaded, a copy of Final Draft which was supposed to make script formatting simple.

That night she went to bed around four in the morning, having discovered the software wasn't quite as simple as advertised - at least for a fledgling screenwriter - and she had absolutely no idea how to begin her script, whatever subject she decided on.

This resulted in a purchase of numerous secondhand How To Do It books from Amazon.

Chapter 9 - Someone

*"By the time we learn life's lessons,
there isn't time to practice."*

"I don't really want to get married again," Shelly told Bella.

"That's progress," Bella said.

Then Shelly added, "But I do want to meet someone."

Bella always thought that "someone" was a strange term: It denoted a lack of specificity, as if anyone would do.

In her quest to find a third husband, or that "someone," Shelly took the contemporary route. She joined Match.com and JDate, hoping that, being Jewish, she'd find more sensible choices. Shelly had - though she didn't tell Bella until much later - paid three thousand dollars to join a personalized matchmaking service.

"If you told me before you wasted your money," Bella informed Shelly, "I would have told you that's a con. There was a woman here, Dotty Marriot, who became a good friend of mine. She was from Dallas and moved here thinking she'd have more fun. So, this very exclusive, personalized matchmaker promised a certain amount of highly compatible contacts. Eventually they came up with just one, and that one wasn't even a genuine member of the service. He was merely a friend helping out." Bella added, "I also told Dotty, though she didn't believe me, that if you want to find a man, Los Angeles is not the place. You'd be better off in Alaska."

"But I really do want someone, I'm not like you. I'm not happy on my own."

"You also weren't happy when you were with someone," Bella pointed out.

"That's true," Shelly conceded.

"Look how lucky you are," Bella said. "You own your own condo, with hardly any mortgage. Your parents will leave you enough so you don't have to worry when you're really old. You have three grown children."

Shelly added, "Two of them give me nothing but trouble."

"Yes, and what kind of man wants to deal with that? You'll also have to deal with his kids, whom you will find as spoiled and indulged as he will find yours. Then, you have to listen - as though it was all interesting - to him and his old friends tell stories over and over again about their misspent youth - which is funny only to them. You will not like his family, nor him yours. And his children will be furious that you might get some of his money, which I can assure you, you won't."

Shelly said, as she said so often it became a refrain, "I like the feeling of being married."

"Have you ever thought that there's a predicable trajectory to marriage? It's not simply straightforward for people who have been divorced, as in your case, twice."

"What do you mean?"

"You date, marry, move into a first apartment, get pregnant, buy your first house, have another child, move again. The kids go to school, they go to college, they get married. You become grand-parents. There's a blueprint for a successful marriage and women like you simply have not followed the plan."

"You sound like there is no hope."

"Hope. It's not about hope. More like a reality check. Take growing old; you do it together. Both of you slowly acclimatize to the ravages of age as they occur, in tiny increments. The breasts and testicles gently fall, the skin stretches, hair thins and greys. The steps become unsteady, the hands less sure. But it's a whole other thing to be suddenly faced with some man's old body, or have him face yours. And that's even if you're in good shape for your age. God I hate that term, 'for your age.' I hate it, and I can't help using the words myself."

"Oh Bella, you are just too cynical."

"I am." Bella grinned. She took this as a compliment.

Bella believed her cynicism began at the age of six, when she first understood that her father was having an affair with her best friend's mother. Joyce responded in kind, and Bella watched her parents battle and bicker until they finally divorced after her father ran off with his new secretary. Bella had come to the conclusion, long before she got married, that couples did nothing but bicker about anything and everything: when or how something occurred, who was there, who wasn't, and who said what or did what. The language of marriage was bickering.

"Most women still want to get married," Shelly insisted.

"That's because they are delusional. In my day, I think one of the reasons men married was so that they could have regular sex. There was no pill. A woman risked a lot if she had sex. Now women 'put out' for a cup of coffee." Bella shook her head. "'Put out!' What a horrible term. As if women doled out their genitals like canapés on a tray."

"What about kids? Women want children, at least when they're younger." Shelly was forlorn. Hard as she might try, she could simply not ignore the start of menopause, which had already been confirmed by her doctor.

Bella tried to be gentle. "You've had your children and you can't have any more. But men, they are able to carry on distributing their genes till they're ninety. But as the body ages, so does sperm and there are risks. Of course in the past, men didn't live as long, so it didn't matter." Bella added, "Old eggs can also be risky, but women at least have a clearly defined cut-off for birthing babies."

Shelly chirped, "Some older women do marry. It does happen."

"Occasionally, but in case you haven't noticed, men your age want younger women. And if they have the funds, and sometimes even if they haven't, they get them. I don't blame men. Young flesh is prettier. Even in the dark, younger skin feels better. Being with a father figure works for a while for her, too. She has a couple of kids, but once they're off to school and she has more time to herself, the age difference begins to matter. Other than the kids, they have nothing to talk about. They remember different music, different movies, different cultural happenings. He wants to relax and take it easy. Having had her kids, she now wants to prove herself. Being a mother isn't enough for her anymore. They're on two different life trajectories. So they divorce. She gets a settlement and begins to complain, a bit like you, that there are no decent men. If he has sufficient money after that, he picks another - even younger - woman. This one might have a young child or two, which he thinks, mistakenly, he can tolerate. On the other hand, he might find one of those left behind: a woman who wanted a career and suddenly finds herself thinking about what she missed. If he's lucky, she'll have missed the boat as far as kids are concerned, which will be a relief for his other children. This one stays with him until he gets old and sick. She becomes a loving, ever-available nurse as she waits out his death. He appreciates her care so much that he adds her to his will. The children are sometimes relieved there's someone else to take care of Dad; alternatively, they label her a gold digger."

"It's not always like that," Shelly said.

"No, not always," Bella admitted. "Perhaps you will find your someone. I'll pray that you do. I do pray, you know. I like praying for other people. Oh, I'm not a saint. I pray for myself, too, when I'm in trouble."

"You pray?"

"Yes, believe it or not. I don't like organized religion, but I pray to the Vast Unknown, the "Something" that's Beyond my Understanding - the Force, the Great Mother, the All Knowing Father, God. And if I can't find that kind of god, I marvel at nature. Like how trees release their leaves only when the fall wind blows. I wonder how birds fly, and where they live. We never see bird's nests. Where do crows in LA nest? There are around ten thousand different bird species, and two million tropical insects! I just read that, in case you think I have those kinds of statistics at my finger tips."

Bella gazed at her hands. "I can make my hand move, but the blood flows through my body on its own. And isn't it amazing that I can make odd movements with my tongue, and understandable speech comes out?"

"I think it's all scientific," Shelly said.

"Science may tell us how things work, but what's utterly mysterious is that anything exists at all."

"Well, then please pray for me to find someone." Shelly was very serious.

"I will, I told you I will. But you just might get that someone and live to regret it." Bella laughed.

The first How-To scriptwriting book arrived. The subject was about character development. One of the exercises was to write about someone who was problematic in your life: a warming-up exercise. Bella decided to write about Guy. She began: *How does Guy remember our time together?* That got her thinking of memories, and how two people recall the same event so differently. And after a few paragraphs, she knew she didn't want to write about Guy. She thought about him far too much anyhow. She didn't need his further intrusion.

Chapter 10 -
Gym and Mosque

"Exploring unusual places - and stomach crunches
- do a body good.."

The new homeowner was already on one of the two treadmills when Bella got down to the gym in the basement of The Portland. She immediately assessed him as her age. *Hmm.* Norman was not at all her type. He had some odd bumps on his face. She hated facial bumps. She hated bumps anywhere. She hated those that were appearing on her own body: roundlets of raised pigments that were not freckles, the skin doctor had pronounced, but "sun damage."

Norman once had good hair. What was left was tied in a ponytail. Bella imagined, correctly, that he would drive a black Porsche. And maybe own a Harley? Again she wasn't wrong.

He also wore tube socks. Washing had turned them off-white. He did not turn the tops down. The gold chain around his neck was "not quality." (Bella knew a woman who was known by the odd nickname Grottie, who was forever pronouncing anyone who didn't meet her standards, as such.)

Bella did not like men with chains, quality or otherwise, unless they were musicians or artists. Norman was also not a scientist - scientists could be forgiven for just about anything they wore, even off-white tube socks. He was a retired attorney.

"You obviously don't come from LA." Bella gave a welcoming smile when he introduced himself as Norman Hoffman and began to chat.

"You can tell?"

"Yes, people from Los Angeles don't chat." Bella's experience was that Los Angelenos avoided casual conversation. Neighbors walked past her and Charlie as if they were invisible, and Bella became so accustomed to the absence of a friendly smile or even a glance of acknowledgment - let alone a comment about the weather - that when someone did start a conversation, it was suspicious. Bella realized that even she had become like that, having lived in Los Angeles for more than twenty-five years.

Norman just moved to LA from Boston. His older son still lived there, but his younger son lived in The Valley, that nether region Grottie would surely label "not quality."

Norman's wife had recently died. "Cancer?" Bella asked, already knowing the answer.

Norman had the television in front of the treadmills switched on Fox News.

"I am liberal," Bella said, to forestall him saying something he might regret.

"So am I," Norman said, but after some small political discussion on health care and the minimum wage, Bella knew they were unlikely to agree on anything.

Norman walked fast, but on a flat gradient. Bella walked at a good slant, and slower. They were both sweating, as the day was unseasonably warm. Bella couldn't help being pleased that Norman looked more frazzled than she did.

Bella considered changing the subject to factory farming or global warming, but she didn't. The heat made any contentious subject too taxing to argue.

When Norman's trainer, Meghan, arrived, he introduced her to Bella. When his son's wife arrived to take a session with Meghan after him, he introduced her, too. When Sven arrived, Bella introduced him. The encounter was very chatty. Too chatty.

Two days later, after Bella almost finished her hated twenty minutes on the treadmill, Norman arrived. Hillary Clinton was being interviewed on TV.

"That bitch, she should be - "

Bella interrupted him from her perch on the treadmill, stating calmly, "Don't call her a bitch. A bitch is a female dog."

Norman attempted to backtrack. "You're right. It was not the right word to use. Especially since I own a female dog myself."

"You have a dog?"

"She's almost thirteen. Flossie, she's a Beagle. She was my wife's dog."

Bella gave him a pass for being a dog owner. Anyone who loved a dog had a good side.

She didn't see Norman again for a couple of weeks. Maybe he went back to Boston, where he had told her he still maintained a small apartment so that he could spend time with his son.

Bella wondered why she bothered thinking about Norman. Could it be because he was a man her age? He was not unattractive, when you took away the gold chain, the white sneakers, the tube socks, and the odd skin bumps. He should shave his head, rather than keep that ratty, grey ponytail. Perhaps, now that he's in LA, he would buy some better socks, and anything other than those old white sneakers. He was almost as tall as she liked. He wasn't in such bad shape. She was certain he had been a good husband and had never strayed, though Bella knew she couldn't ever be truly sure about that.

He was a good man. Why did she presume he was a good man? She imagined him kind and loving towards his dying wife. She thought about that and how she'd never had a loving, kind man. She went for the rotters, the liars, the cheats, and the charmers. Ah well, she had interesting stories to tell about them, not that she told them much anymore. They were her past, and Bella was not the kind of person who lived back there.

Instead, Bella always had the ability to find something new in which to immerse herself. At one time, she dove into Russian history. After the horror of 9/11, she read the Koran to find out more about Islam.

Bella made Greta accompany her to a local mosque. "I want to see for myself what's going on in there."

"Why?" Greta wondered.

The two of them took off one Friday morning - the Muslim Day of Prayer - modestly dressed in ankle-length skirts and long-sleeved tops, with large scarves to cover their hair and necks. They drove into the parking lot and told the suspicious guard that they were thinking of becoming Muslim. He beckoned a woman in a black chador who introduced herself as Fadia. She happily led them inside, indicated where to leave their shoes, and pointed them towards the upstairs women's section. This was empty, save for a couple of chairs set against the wall, a shelf with prayer books, and a wizened woman praying to herself in a corner. Bella selected a Koran, and grabbed one of the chairs. The Koran was in Arabic.

A beautiful young Indian woman in a pink sari arrived with a toddler. She smiled. "You are obviously not Muslim."

"How do you know?"

She gestured at the Koran, sitting on the floor. That was a big no-no, Bella discovered, as she further read about the religion, which she found as anachronistic as any other conceived in the distant past by men who pretended they knew all of life's answers, and strived to control those willing to admit they did not.

The only way to see what was going on downstairs - where the men were - was by peeping through a window that ran the length of the room; and so, Bella peeped.

"Stop doing that," Greta admonished, as she peeped herself, despite disapproving glances from the few women who straggled in, sat on the floor, and began to pray quietly.

The Imam's sermon was incendiary. He demanded the congregants do all they could to promote Islam, and stop the spread of Christianity. When Bella and Greta drove home and got down to analyzing the sermon, they decided the words were no more incendiary than a Christian preacher pressing the faithful to spread the message of their Savior.

After the sermon, there were a lot of prayers involving kneeling and prostrating on the floor, which was thankfully covered by plush, fitted carpet. Bella and Greta did their best not to giggle, as they copied the other women. But once Bella got into the rhythm of silent prayer, she had a moment when what she called "the chills" suffused throughout her body. It was a feeling she'd often experienced in the presence of Faith.

After the service ended, Fadia approached Bella and asked if she liked the service.

"What do you have to do to become Muslim?" Bella inquired.

Fadia didn't miss a beat. "You must bathe after your period."

"I don't have a period any longer."

Fadia excused herself to retrieve some instructional materials, which Bella read when she got back home. One particularly naive pamphlet proposed how all of Islam was scientifically proved to be true.

"We should do this again," Bella said when she dropped Greta at her home.

"I'd rather go skydiving than go back to that stuffy place and go up and down on my poor knees."

However, the following week Greta mentioned to one of her clients where she'd been, and he was thoroughly impressed.

"That's one of the reasons we trust you to purchase our art. Aside from your good taste - everyone comments favorably on the art you've chosen - you are a woman of substance."

Greta never told any of that to Bella.

One of Bella's How-To books suggested crafting a story outline using three-by-five-inch cards before commencing to write the actual script. And so she went to Staples, where she bought a pack of cards, in six different colours, some pencils, and an eraser.

In South Africa, they called erasers "rubbers." Before she knew the American meaning of the word, Bella made the mistake of saying, "I need a rubber." And it caused a good laugh. She also bought a pack of yellow legal pads. For her more serious writing, the Florentine notebook would be abandoned.

Chapter 11 -
Blauss

*"Sometimes you have to act as if
you're having fun."*

Olivia and Martin Blauss were seriously rich. Olivia was partly Swiss and partly Austrian, and at least ten years older than Bella. Martin was older still. Both Blausses were well preserved - Olivia by judicious surgery and exquisitely refined good taste, and Martin, by his money and Olivia's attentive care. Martin was almost like Olivia's doll, albeit a bad-tempered one who demanded utter obedience. Olivia made sure Martin had his hair cut at Cristophe. His clothes were East Coast luxe. He was a handsome adjunct to Olivia's classic Nordic beauty.

Bella was first introduced to Olivia and Martin at a party at The Beverly Hills Hotel. Bella was new to Los Angeles and for some reason the Blausses befriended her. She was invited to dinner by them on a regular basis, at least when they were in town.

The Blausses had a home in New York, but they travelled frequently and were almost never around. That is, until Martin - after a bout of intense depression - succumbed to old age and its handmaiden so frequently in attendance, dementia. The Blausses lived a rarified life, eschewing ostentation, though oozing luxury. Everything was understated, from the Chinese-imported pottery and the paintings by well-known artists - Kenneth Noland, Frank Stella, Ellsworth Kelly, and Sam Francis amongst them - judiciously scattered around their small but perfect Bel Air "cottage" to Olivia's closet, with its Armani suits and jackets, Hermès bags, and whatever else she wore. Everything was shades of taupe, white, and black. Any red, or for that matter anything outside Olivia's muted colour spectrum, would have resembled a wound.

The house, like its mistress, was a study in restraint, each room an example of flawless selectivity. The only room they actually used was the library, where Martin sat glued to Bloomberg TV even after his short-term memory went, and where Olivia kept up-to-date with worldly affairs by reading the latest political best sellers.

Over the years, Bella's friends often asked her, "Why don't the Blausses introduce you to someone?" As if the Blausses being rich meant they had to know a suitable single man for Bella.

Bella never once asked the Blausses to introduce her to anyone. In fact, she never asked anyone to introduce her to "someone." Even if she wanted to meet a special man, which she might have desired years ago, she couldn't bear sounding desperate, which - in her mind - is how women always sounded when they asked for this kind of introduction. Twenty years ago - when Bella first met the Blausses - Olivia asked Bella for permission to give some man her number.

"So, what do you look like?" he asked when he called. New to Los Angeles, and thinking perhaps this was the LA way, Bella launched into a brief description.

"How much do you weigh?" he interrupted.

"One hundred and twenty-five pounds."

"So you're plump?"

Despite Bella's desire to be accommodating, that was insulting. She stated, "I can see we will not get on with each other."

Bella wondered what Mr. R.U. Plump would think of her current weight, more than twenty-five pounds heavier. He'd probably label her obese, which is how she felt when she ventured - usually with her daughter Jessica - into trendy boutiques where sizes went from zero to ten. Size zero! Size nothing, naught, nada. It sounded absurd, like you weren't even there. Size Absolute Zero didn't exist when she was younger. At department stores, Bella found herself in a no-man's-land between "Large," a size still obtainable on the main floor, and "Extra-Large" in the Old-and-Fat Department. The domain of sizes larger than "Large" was discreetly situated, and drearily presented in a nether part of the store, hidden well away from enticing presentations of less voluminous current fashion, despite that the average size of American women was fourteen.

The next time the Blausses introduced Bella to a man went even worse. Wally Lazar was fairly pleasant when he met them for dinner at the Blausses' current favorite Italian restaurant, where the Blausses were treated as if they descended from Mount Olympus. This was the direct result of large and frequent tips. Martin had no illusions; he paid handsomely for what he wanted from life.

Wally invited Bella to dinner at his home the following week. His prowess in the kitchen was a subject of conversation at the restaurant, and Bella presumed - incorrectly so it turned out - that the Blausses would also be present. Wally's house was a nondescript Spanish style, and had walls and walls of books, which she thought was a good sign when she arrived. Then she read some of the titles - books of pornography emphasizing bondage. She made no comment, though she knew he expected her to do so.

Wary, she sat at the table set for two. A couple of glasses of wine helped her relax, but Bella's instinct was to keep her wits about her. As the evening progressed, Wally became more and more disdainful and argumentative, no matter what subject came up.

Bella was courteously rational. She was even flirtatious, hoping to charm him into civility, but Wally clearly wanted war. Finally, when Bella disagreed with him about something trivial - she could not remember later exactly what the topic was - he became so belligerent that Bella feared for her safety.

"I am leaving," she announced as she opened the front door and ran towards her car, which was parked in the street.

"Get out of here," he shouted. "Get the hell out!"

When Bella called Olivia to tell her about her awful evening, Olivia laughed. "I've heard he's a bit strange."

"A bit!" Bella replied.

"He's the only single man we know," Olivia said lamely.

This was a fact. The Blausses had no single male friends of suitable age. However, the Blausses did know a slew of well turned-out divorcées and widows, and sometimes when they invited Bella for dinner, the Blausses included one of their other women friends.

Bella had little in common with the rest of the single women the Blausses knew. They were all country club members (or seemed like they were). They dressed well, but cautiously. Lots of navy. Perfectly polished, midlength nails. A solid gold bracelet. A stainless steel and gold Cartier watch. Noreen Norell, a surgically altered and very pretty dealer in antiquities, long divorced from a well-known plastic surgeon, was the Blausses' single friend Bella liked most. She once invited Noreen to her birthday party, which was during the summer when guests could flow onto the large patio.

Noreen arrived late, and was so incongruously animated that Bella wondered if she'd taken some drugs. The next time she and Noreen were entertained by the Blausses at Martin's new favorite restaurant, Noreen told them that she'd met a group of gay designers who knew how to have serious fun. She bubbled, "You can't imagine what we get up to." Bella imagined Noreen's pleasures being pumped by the fuel of drugs and alcohol. When she bumped into Noreen a year or so later, the effervescent antiques dealer was a mess. Her fine blonde hair was dirty and under a baseball cap. She wore an old tracksuit and her skin was grey.

"I'm not well," Noreen admitted.

"I can see that," Bella could not say otherwise. She heard that Noreen's once flourishing business had closed down. "You know, I could take you to a meeting."

Noreen knew what kind of meeting Bella was talking about. "Thanks, but I'm not ready to do that."

Bella gave her a card. "If you ever want help, just call.

Bella went back to *The Lions of A'marula*. She colour-coded her cards: yellow for characters, blue for plot points, white for dialogue, and pink for timelines.

Then, as one of the How-To books suggested, she laid them out. For this she used the dining room table, a Heywood Wakefield design she bought when she first arrived in Los Angeles, a time when mid-century, modern tables were not in demand. Bella liked the table. It was made of maple wood and had two leaves and rounded ends. At a pinch, she could seat ten. However, even with two extra leaves, the table was not big enough for all her cards; they overlapped and shifted. Some fell onto the floor. Bella was reminded of working on a jigsaw puzzle - a favorite pastime she shared with her father, Speedy, when she was a young girl - but in this case, every piece was the same shape and there wasn't enough working space. Strong coffee did nothing to sharpen her powers of organization. A massive headache set in.

Bella long suffered from headaches, even as a child, just as her grandmother-on-her-mother's-side did. She took two Tylenol and decided to go to an early show. Sitting in the comforting dark watching a movie, grazing on popcorn - no butter, but copious amounts of salt preferably flavored with cheddar - and drinking diet cola to quench the thirst acquired by the salty popcorn, was a panacea for Bella's minor worries. Bella knew that carbonated drinks - whether sugared or not - gave her an acid stomach, but when she felt this way, she didn't care.

Chapter 12 -
At the Drugstore
"People who say they are happy getting old are lying."

Bella eventually got the hang of how unusually America marked the year as the months veered past July, though she thought - in the year's final months - there was a specificity that frequently matched neither the weather nor the mood.

Labor Day signified the official end of summer. Even if summer weather continued - with intermittent heat waves as it usually did - into November, summer was considered done. If the temperature reached the eighties, women still donned boots and switched to black, and the department stores were filled with cold-weather gear that made her sweat just seeing them. The weather may say otherwise, but after Labor Day, sandals and sundresses were out of place. The seasons had spoken: "It is fall."

Halloween followed, which Chloe anticipated months in advance, always bubbling over what she would wear. This year was Punk. "I'm eight," Chloe said proudly. "Almost double digits." The days of cheap, Chinese-made princess costumes were over.

Bella did not grow up with Halloween. She thought the day - derived from the ancient Celts - quite awful; people dressed like ghouls and monsters, wearing hideous rubber masks, and super-sugary candy was doled out to marauding children who acted as if they'd never tasted sweets. On one of her more recent trips to South Africa to visit family, in late October, Bella was horrified to see Halloween costumes displayed in stores.

Dotty Marriot, her neighbor from The Portland, invited Bella to her first Halloween party - a rather sad event where nobody knew anyone, even without their disguises.

Dotty was wearing something vaguely Italian because she'd bought a Venetian mask in New Orleans. Bella found a skeleton jumpsuit at a huge drugstore in West Hollywood. The romper was extremely comfortable and she didn't even have to wear a bra. All she did was step in, and tie the back neck. No zips or buttons.

Bella also wore her skeleton costume to the first and only Gay Pride Parade she attended in West Hollywood. She and Dotty went together and Bella hated every minute of it. Firstly, she hated crowds, and secondly, she lost Dotty in the crowds she hated. Thinking herself wise to stay in the last place she and Dotty were together, Bella ended up drinking far too much with a man who claimed he was straight, but liked dressing as a woman - and an old woman at that, with a plaid wool suit, an old-fashioned handbag with a handle like the Queen of England, gloves, mid-heel shoes, and a wig.

Bella had many tangible memories of that Pride-ful evening. She had the sense to take a camera and she still had a really gorgeous photograph of herself posing with three real policemen, plus there were others taken with the cross-dresser and a well-curated variety of crazily dressed people.

This year, Bella lent the skeleton jumpsuit to Nicole, who claimed as expected, "It's so comfortable," and then added the usual, "I had an awesome time."

The slight melancholy that Bella currently felt was not the depression that sometimes afflicted her, and for which she took medication. This was regular, normal, being-human sadness, which Bella attributed to the inevitable passing of time. Not just her own time, but the year, as months hurtled - or dribbled - away into the holiday season.

This feeling began in an aisle at the big drugstore opposite The Beverly Center, where Bella purchased her skeleton suit.

Bella usually frequented a smaller pharmacy near The Portland, but on the day before Thanksgiving - which was another holiday she hadn't grown up with and didn't particularly like - she passed by the big drugstore and decided to go shopping there.

Bella would be without her family this Thanksgiving since Jessica decided to join some friends in Palm Springs. "Do you mind Mom?" she asked, knowing full well Bella would say she didn't.

Ivan, who was usually in town for Thanksgiving, was not. Bella couldn't remember if he and Farrel were going with Digby - of course in Digby's private jet - to Morocco or Ibiza. Wherever the destination, her son would be somewhere fabulous, and Bella was fine with that. She was truly happy when her children were happy, which neither of them could totally comprehend.

Greta invited Bella to accompany her to visit some friends, who said they wanted to meet her. Shelly invited her to the home of her rich friends, the Moores. Even Nicole said Bella should come with her to a Thanksgiving dinner. But Bella declined all invites.

Greta said, "It's not nice to be on your own on a holiday."

"I like my own company," Belle replied, and she did.

Bella used baby oil to soften her skin. She poured a capful of the product into her baths, which she had done since she was a child.

Whilst searching for this effective tenderizer at the drugstore, she spied some shelves stocked with diapers, and zoomed in to what she thought was the baby section. However, on closer inspection, she realized that these diapers were intended for adults.

Bella was aware that adults became incontinent. She'd seen diapers in drugstores before, but her smaller pharmacy had nothing like the selection here. This adult diapers section took over an entire side of one long aisle.

Diapers, nothing but diapers, from the bottom shelf to the top.

Huge bags of diapers for night and day, for fat bodies and thin, for men and women, scented or not, and a multitude of brands, all touting their various absorbent capabilities.

Having for some years worked as an advertising copywriter, Bella understood why the diapers - like the larger-size women's clothes - were displayed in a back section of the store. They were products that did not need to be promoted, and thus displays were unnecessary; plus, seeing all those huge packets of diapers would horrify younger shoppers. They certainly shocked her, who had no idea - until she chanced upon them - that this need was so great.

It was no surprise that adult diapers were something people didn't discuss. Martin Blauss wore diapers. Bella saw them at the bottom of Olivia's cupboard, peeping out from amongst the Manolo Blahnik shoes.

Joyce, Bella's late mother, ended up wearing diapers.

Grace, a large black woman and Joyce's caregiver during the last years of her life, changed Joyce like she would a baby. Joyce never got over how kind Grace was, doing such a chore, and left Grace a nice chunk in her will. "You couldn't pay me to do what Grace does for me," Joyce said, insinuating her humiliation - rather than stating outright - about how the indignities of old age shamed her. "And she does it with such grace, like her name."

Bella was pleased Grace was there to care for her mother, particularly as Joyce lived so far away.

Bella noticed the inescapable path her own body was on, as her tissues slid ever rapidly towards decrepitude. Brown spots became more and more noticeable on her face. New ones showed up, like overnight mushrooms did in damp grass. At Bella's regular pharmacy, she noted the blossoming of facial creams that promised to help with uneven skin tones. Uneven skin tones! That was a euphemism for age spots. Being more specific, these creams promised to correct brown spots, as if they were some mistake that could be erased, like smudges on a drawing.

From Sephora's online store - Bella loved shopping online - she bought a dark-spot corrector that she studiously applied to two really bad dark spots: one on her cheek and one on her forehead. They faded a tiny bit, but so did the skin next to the spots. These dark spots were joined by an ever-increasing cluster on the underside of her cheek and on her temples, where the sun's damaging rays had hit year after year.

The accompanying correcting serum and face cream that she purchased was also supposed to help, but she found, despite daily application, the spots persisted. In addition, she recently discovered discoloured lesions on her legs that she previously saw only on old people. Was she already old? Was being just shy of seventy old? Bella knew "old" was actually relative. Jessica complained she was old when she turned forty. Little Chloe thought she was to be old at ten, when she got into double digits.

Shelly suggested Bella get rid of her varicose veins. "I have, and will do more if I get more. It doesn't even hurt. You have to wear a tight stocking for a few weeks. That's the worst part."

"Burst leg veins and dark spots are the alphabet of old age." Bella intoned.

"That's a good description, but you don't have to accept it."

"I can't be bothered. Anyway, I can't see them; they're at the back of my knees. What I can't see doesn't bother me. And on the rare occasions I wear a skirt, I wear dark tights."

Bella didn't tell Shelly, but she went to see Dr. Roberts.

Dr. Roberts had, like almost all dermatologists and ear-nose-and-throat doctors, moved into the realm of injectables. Once upon a time their clientele had been teenagers with acne; now they treated older people with wrinkles and brown spots.

"You would look great with a peel," Dr. Roberts said. "You won't look waxy," he promised, but Bella did not want to take the chance. A peel was a controlled application of toxic chemicals, which burned the skin so badly that new skin was encouraged to surface. There were different strengths of peel, but stronger ones gave the skin a finish like a giant, very light and smooth, scar. Bella had eagle eyes and noticed such things. She could tell when a woman had a peel. Augmented lips and breasts and newly smoothed wrinkles - she noticed them all. She used Botox herself and was pleased with the result. Her forehead didn't budge, but quite a few people told her how rested she appeared.

Her old friend Christine, whose husband was a highly regarded plastic surgeon in Miami, told her that all the TV anchors were surgically enhanced. "They've had cheekbones and chins altered, and - of course - their eyes. There is not a face on TV or in the movies, that is only God's creation."

 Shelly informed Bella, "I am going to have my neck done."

As if Bella couldn't tell, she added, "I had my eyes done and my forehead lifted a few years ago. My neck's gone all turkey."

Bella decided not to dissuade Shelly, for the skin of her neck no longer matched that on her face at all.

"At the same time I'm going to have a few hair plugs."

"Why? Your hair's great!"

"That's because I wear pieces. Take a look." Shelly turned her head down and showed Bella how her hair was, indeed, thinning.

Bella's late grandmother, her mother's mother, Granny Rachel, had gone bald at the top of her head. She wore a wig for special occasions, and didn't seem to notice that the silver-grey, curled hairpiece had a tendency to slip over her forehead. Bella hoped that she did not have the balding gene. Her mother had a fine head of hair when she died, as did her father. Ivan began to go bald in his thirties, and she much preferred a bald man to one with a hair-piece. But what were balding women like Shelly to do? There were more and more of them.

"I am sure one day everyone will be bald," Bella said. "We don't need hair on our heads any longer. At least, not for protection or to keep our heads warm. Maybe we'll evolve into hairless humans, at least once our hormones stop surging?"

"I like bald men," Shelly said. "You know that friend of yours, the party man. He's bald as an egg and so handsome.

"He's gay."

"I know," Shelly sighed. "The best-looking men are."

Bella met egghead Grant Butler and his circle of friends soon after she arrived in the United States in the late eighties. They were her first friends.

She tried her best to find them amusing, but the truth was she never felt totally at ease with the group. For one thing, they were overtly sexual with each other, which made Bella realize how much the presence of women restrained straight men. She was not a woman who was easily comfortable with gay friends, like Greta, who had a slew of them.

With Grant and his friends - some of whom had contracted the new, horrifying AIDS - Bella visited jazz clubs. She tried her best to be gay - or rather happy - with them. And she was for a time a frequent guest when Grant entertained in his high-rise on Wilshire Boulevard, though she always left Grant's events both starving and drunk. The food appeared to be exquisite but the portions were minute, which was mostly a relief as Grant tried out recipes using the oddest ingredients, like banana sauce on fish.

Grant was an event planner extraordinaire. His real name was Herman Smuklestein, and though he told everyone he was born during the British Raj in India - and his father knew Mahatma Gandhi - he was, in fact, from Liverpool.

Grant made a quick ascent from catering Beverly Hills Bar Mitzvahs to lavish parties and weddings for the ever richer and more famous, and he lovingly recounted the details of his latest event in a fake posh accent that he believed fooled Bella - it did not - but did impress his American clients.

His description of centerpieces and table decor made them sound like multiple orgasms, and his satisfied clients showered him with gifts - like the gold Rolex he received after the Venetian-style wedding he planned for Hollywood's latest heartthrob.

Though Bella had long since lost contact with Grant, she sometimes read of his continuing, and ever-glittering exploits in glossy magazines. She also heard that Grant wouldn't even consider doing a wedding for under a million dollars.

Bella knew that Grant's A-list clients usually ended up getting divorced, which she was sure cost a great deal more than their extravagant weddings.

"How's the writing going?" Bella wished Shelly wasn't so interested in her progress.

"It's been so long since I lived in Africa. I don't have its pulse any longer," Bella sighed.

"What about writing something new, something set here?"

"Any suggestions?"

"What about a story based on Grant and his clients?" Bella had told Shelly about Grant Butler, and the fascination she found for his luxe world and his clients. "We could go to all the smart stores for inspiration."

Bella didn't need much of an excuse, and thus off they went to peruse the three glorious monuments to opulence set close together on the same side of Wilshire Boulevard in Beverly Hills: Neiman Marcus, Saks Fifth Avenue, and Barneys.

At Barneys, they gaped as a Middle Eastern mother in a black chador and her daughter - heavily made up, in tight jeans with an

Hermès silk scarf wrapped around her head - bought every single Annick Goutal scent. In contrast, Bella and Shelly anguished over which expensive perfume, if any, to choose.

In the shoe department at Saks, they tried not to giggle as they spied on a petite Chinese girl - who seemed no more than fifteen, accompanied by an older man who was clearly not her father - hobble around on a variety platform boots that almost doubled her height.

Shelly managed to persuade Bella to try on some high heels, too. "I can't stand in these, let alone walk."

"You're not trying," said Shelly, who wanted Bella to dress sexier. If she did, she'd attract a man, despite Bella's protestations she didn't want one.

They oohed and aahed on the designer floors at Neiman's and pretended they were shopping for something to wear for a family wedding. Afterwards, they went up to the men's department and had cappuccinos at the bar. There they flirted with a young barman - handsome as any movie star - and a charming, Argentinian octogenarian who said he was, unfortunately, waiting for his wife to join him.

Shelly was crazy enough to buy a pocket-handkerchief for her latest almost-boyfriend. The salesman was so delightful that Bella almost bought one for herself, as a neckerchief, but the silk square didn't fit around her neck.

Later, after wandering around the cosmetic counters, Bella bought a brick-red Christian Dior lipstick with a matching lip pencil. When Bella saw Norman the next day in The Portland lobby he commented, "Like the red!"

Bella was becoming more comfortable with the Final Draft software. The program was not as difficult as she first thought.

She decided *The Lions of A'marula* would begin with a Voice-Over. Simple as it eventually sounded, this little bit took a couple of days and nights of rewriting to make it work.

A'marula was the name of a game farm adjacent to South Africa's Kruger National Park. It was once owned by Millionaire George Agadees and was named for the Marula trees that grew on the property. George bought A'marula with some of the huge profits he earned from harvesting abalone off the East Coast of South Africa.

That was as far as Bella got. What the hell came next? Then - as one of the books suggested - on a yellow legal pad, she began to work out the basics of the plot, including timelines and characters. The three-by-five cards were just too confusing. Shifting them felt like playing a mad game of Bridge. Too many choices. And so, on the pad she started her outline, using a pencil in case she needed to erase.

The story will take place shortly before Nelson Mandela was freed, as South Africa moved from an apartheid state to racial equality. It will end after South Africa voted Mandela into power.

Her story could have taken place at any time, but Bella picked the moment when South Africa changed and began to reach for the stars, and moviegoers could do worse than learn a bit about an era they hardly knew anything about. Nicole didn't even know what apartheid meant.

Bella told her to do some research on the Internet, and the day after, when Nicole came out to join the walk with Charlie she couldn't wait to tell Bella, "I can't believe how similar apartheid was to America. Sort of like segregation in the South."

"Exactly. When the Nationalist Party came into power, they made apartheid the law of the land. The idea was that blacks would have rights, but only in their own tribal states. The Nationalists called them Bantustans, and they were supposed to be independently ruled. For example, Bophuthatswana was designated the state for the Tswana tribe. But instead of being one contiguous area, Bophuthatswana was a patchwork strung across an area of white South Africa. That way all the best farmland was left out."

"Would it be like Beverly Hills is part of Canada, or something like that?" Nicole's mind worked in strange and wonderful ways.

"Something like that."

"People were moved around like pieces on a chess board. Some poor Tswana woman who was born in Johannesburg and had never been to Bophuthatswana suddenly found herself having to live there, unable to work in the city in which she was born."

Nicole carried on with her analogy. "So I'd have to live and work in Canada, even though I hate the cold weather?"

"Exactly. And if you thought you had some possibility of remaining where you were born, you'd have to stand in a line at the Post Office for hours and then be told to come back the next day. And after that, you'd have to go stand in another line at the DMV with the hopes of getting different documents."

Nicole understood. "And then wait in line at the airport and as I get near to the front, the flight is called full."

"The system made for a lot of bribery. I can't tell you how many times I made the trip to the Labor Office, a bottle of scotch clearly visible, to get a passbook stamped so that someone could work for me."

Guy had a man he called his Fixer. Hendrick Broeder made a fortune helping English-speaking businessmen get everything from passes for their workers to telephones. The Afrikaans businessmen easily got anything they wanted. They were in power. South Africa was like two different countries for the whites. The English speakers were generally more liberal, and the right-wing Afrikaaners were encouraged and led by the racist Dutch Reformed Church.

"Supposed biblical evidence was quoted from The Book of Joshua, which said blacks were made to be hewers of wood and drawers of water, but then the bible says a lot of things that today would be unconscionable. And Jesus Christ would be horrified by what some did or even thought in his name."

Bella didn't want Nicole to think she was merely a passive bystander to these iniquities. "Many whites were against apartheid. We all voted for the Progressive Party, which had one single Member of Parliament, Helen Suzman. She held the torch against all those racist men. My late father knew her. She was his generation.

"When I was at college, we marched and protested when they banned black students from attending our University. When I got older, I joined the The Black Sash, which was a women's group that helped black people negotiate the tangle of laws that endeavored to keep blacks in their place. We stood on busy streets in absolute silence, wearing a black sash across our chests. Many people shouted insults, '*Kaffir boetie*,' which meant black brother. Once I had an egg thrown at me."

"Awesome!"

"Not awesome, but intimidating and even dangerous; also exciting to be part of a movement that demanded change. From today's perspective, I wish I'd done more."

When Nicole asked about The Soweto Riots, Bella was amazed. Nicole knew almost nothing about history, hers or any other. But she'd read up on the riots where school children, mandated to learn in the hated language of Afrikaans, protested and were killed. The Soweto Riots marked a defining moment. And commemorated in the New South Africa on June 16.

"So similar to America before civil rights," Nicole observed. "You know, my aunt went to a big march in Washington. She was the rebel of the family. She still is. She lives with a black man in New Orleans. They run a bar."

Bella was surprised. Nicole had only ever spoken about how boring her family was. Her father was a dentist, her mother was his receptionist, and her older sister was studying dentistry.

"I was living in London at the time of the riots. When I came back, things were beginning to unravel. The President, P. W. Botha, declared a State of Emergency. A friend of mine said he reminded him of walking dildo. He had a strangely shaped bald head and a horrible, flaccid, pear-shaped body. And he did all he could to stop the inevitable. One weekend, when the kids were with Guy, I gave shelter to three black men who were on the run. One man - he's the only one whose name I remember, Abel - arrived holding Mao's *Little Red Book*, only it was black. Abel told me he had a cache of weapons buried in Bophuthatswana, where his mother lived. They all drank a lot. Abel passed out on the living-room floor. The two others slept in Ivan's room."

Having awoken Nicole's interest in Africa, Bella lent her a book, *Africa: A Biography of the Continent* by John Reader, which was not just about South Africa, but the whole continent. Bella was horrified to discover that Nicole didn't realize Egypt was in Africa, nor was she aware - as most people weren't - that the African landmass was bigger than the United States, Europe, China, India, Russia, and Japan combined, and that the continent contained over fifty different nations.

Bella asked Nicole a few times whether she'd read the book.

"Not yet, but I will."

After a couple of weeks, Bella bought a used copy on Amazon as a replacement, for she never wanted to be without a copy on hand. She didn't mind, for one of her maxims was that if you lent anything, you should never expect it to be returned.

Bella thought that Cape Town would make a wonderful backdrop to the beginning scenes of *The Lions of A'marula*. The Mother City, as it was affectionately called by some, was one of the most beautiful cities in the world and oddly a bit like LA, with Table Mountain right in the middle of the city, forcing the suburbs to spread out so that there was no center.

A lot of Bella's friends had moved to Cape Town after Johannesburg became dangerous, with endless robberies, hijackings, and murders. Just about everyone knew someone who had been murdered. Knew as in "really knew," not as in "my son's girlfriend's mother's sister" was murdered.

Bella's school friend Naomi Barrow's husband had been shot dead whilst waiting to pick up his grandson from a soccer game. And for what? A cell phone. Another friend was stabbed in his house in the tony suburb of Houghton, near where Nelson Mandela lived. Jessica's old art teacher had been held up in her studio, and when the robbers realized she had nothing of value, they shot her in the stomach. She lived, but left the country soon after, as so many people who had the means to do so did - not only white people, but black people, too.

The high hopes of The Rainbow Nation - as named by Archbishop Desmond Tutu to describe post-apartheid South Africa - was bogged down by crime and corruption. However *The Lions of A'marula* would take place before that. And the crimes in Bella's story were of a more privately sinister kind.

Though the main action takes place at A'marula, a game farm owned by George Agadees near Kruger Park, the story commences in Cape Town, where George, his wife Margaret, and their fourteen-year-old twins, Winston and Elizabeth, live in a magnificent Cape Dutch - style mansion, set against the foothills of Table Mountain.

At fourteen years, Winston Agadees is startlingly handsome. He has glossy, dark brown hair and olive skin. More than startling are his eyes. One is blue and one brown, the result of an unusual defect known as Horner's syndrome.

Horner's was something Bella only found out about a few weeks before she started her script. She'd gone to watch Chloe riding, which was one of her true pleasures in life. Not that Bella understood one thing about horses. As a young adult she had a couple of lessons with Guy. She wanted to find a sport they could both enjoy. The result was that Guy learned to ride well, and she learned that being high off the ground on an animal that could canter - Bella never even got to learning to gallop - was terrifying.

Whilst Bella was making conversation with a young mother watching her child in the ring with Chloe, Bella noticed this woman had one brown eye and one blue. Bella tried not to stare. But she couldn't help herself and eventually stated, as if the woman didn't know, "You have different coloured eyes."

The woman explained Horner's Syndrome: "Fortunately I have only the eye colour difference. Some people sweat on only one side." Bella did some research on the Internet and gave the syndrome to Winston, adding a slight droop to one eye, which she read was not uncommon.

Winston's twin, Elizabeth, is her father's favorite. Winston is jealous.

Whilst the twins are swimming in the pool, set on a lower terrace out of sight of the main house, Elizabeth knocks her head against the diving board and falls unconscious into the pool.

Winston makes no effort to save her. Nobody suspects he was with her at the time of the tragedy.

As the now-cherished, remaining twin, Winston has everything he could want. He attends a prestigious South African boarding school, and after matriculating is sent to Europe for a gap year to gain life experience.

He returns from Europe with a new friend, Charles Somerville. Charles is the second son of an Earl and, like many second sons, is lost with what to do with his life.

English-speaking South Africans were impressed by the British aristocracy. They furnished their homes like English country houses, sent their kids to schools fashioned on British Public

Schools. They did their very best to affect what they thought was a good English accent. George wanted Winston to fit in with the upper-class, English-speaking South Africans, even though he - being of Greek origin - might not. Bella remembered her time living in London with her young children, trying to fit in. That was when she began to drink more. But her increased consumption of alcoholic beverages didn't help. She wasn't English enough, and never would be. This fact took her a breakdown to realize, which is why she returned to South Africa.

Winston drinks too much, and he misses work. He is not turning out as his father wishes and never will.

The final straw for George: whilst on one of many visits to A'marula, Winston shoots a huge, black-maned lion affectionately known as Big Baas, quite aware of how much his father abhors hunting for sport.

Bella wanted to have the South African bushveld in her story. This wild world was the part of South Africa she loved best. There was magic to the bush, and she couldn't fathom that some people were unappreciative. She'd taken Ivan and Jess into the bushveld many times. They loved it, too.

George threatens to disinherit Winston, so Winston pours sugar in the gas tank of George's small plane, which he flies from A'marula to Cape Town.

Again, nobody suspects Winston when George and Margaret are killed in the crash. Winston becomes sole heir to the Agadees' family fortune.

Bella felt as if she had accomplished a lot that day.

Chapter 13 -
Not a Match
"Never marry just to prove you can."

The Holiday Season was approaching when Keisha, the receptionist at The Portland, suggested that Bella go out with Mr. Dragozetti, a slender and very pale Italian bachelor - or maybe he was a widower who, like the tube sock-wearing Norman, lived on the penthouse floor. Mr. Dragozetti had a thin, old-fashioned moustache, and wore those insubstantial, slip-on, Italian-style shoes with weavings in the front that some men thought fashionable, but Bella found otherwise.

Keisha said, "He told me he wants someone sophisticated to take to some very fancy holiday parties. I thought of you."

Bella felt a bit insulted. Did Keisha truly believe Mr. Dragozetti was up to Bella's standards?

Bella imagined how Keisha saw her: a single, older woman desperately searching for a mate. This misperception happened, and not infrequently. Barry Slomowitz, the wizened husband of Bella's friend Renee, told her, "You could get lucky," as he recommended a hotel bar known for playing good jazz. This was said at a mutual friend's fiftieth wedding anniversary. (Did people really live together for so long?) Barry was of a generation that couldn't conceive of a woman being content without a husband, and her presence without a partner at the table for ten was disquieting to him.

As for Keisha's recommendation, Bella had never, not even once, given anyone at The Portland a reason to think she was not satisfied living on her own. She never inquired whether anyone knew that "someone" for her. She never sounded forlorn for being single. There were times she felt alone, but that wasn't the same as loneliness. Anyhow, being alone was her choice. Mr. Dragozetti, too, might have made the same choice, seeing as he never once glanced her way.

"You are too vital to give up on love," Shelly told Bella for the hundredth time.

"I haven't given up on love. I'm just not going out of my way to look for it. I don't want to go online to find a man," Bella calmly explained as Shelly, once again, tried to persuade her to at least look on Match.com.

"You can't win the lottery if you don't buy a ticket," Shelly trotted out the aphorism.

"There isn't a place for a man in my life. Where would he fit in? Not in my bed, not in my closet. Not with my family."

"He might have a house of his own, big enough for you and all your things," Shelly replied. "Have you considered that?"

"I've done some searches. Men around my age say they want walks on the beach holding hands with a soul mate. But I don't see beaches filled with old men and women holding hands. I don't like walking and I don't like the sand. They want to find their soul mate. In their late sixties and seventies! That kind of starry-eyed foolishness in a septuagenarian is enough to make me vomit."

"You're only as old as you feel," Shelly chipped in with her favorite cliché.

"I don't feel young enough to want to jump into bed with some old man. And they all want sex. They say so. 'I want an adventurous partner' - or - 'Romance is important to me.' That's a euphemism for sex."

"You make a loving relationship sound so horrible."

"You call sex with some old man you barely know love? And if I had sex with a man my age or older, it would have to be in the dark."

"We are not that old." Though almost fourteen years younger than Bella, Shelly felt as if they were the same age. She sighed, "Men our age do seem to want younger women. Many of them even say they don't mind having more kids."

"All those older children supplanted by cute new babies. The problems that arise from those circumstances keep therapists in business." Bella's laugh was hollow. "Men have grandchildren and children all at the same time."

Bella was never comfortable with the online dating scene. She understood the need for such a service, but thought it humiliating to advertise herself in the search for a mate. Younger people had fewer qualms about marketing themselves. They wanted a mate and did what was necessary to find one.

Years previously, long before Match.com had become another ho-hum part of modern life, Bella tried one of the first online sites. At that point, it had no photographs or e-mails. On her profile, she wrote that her favorite author was Eugène Marais - a challenge, as she was sure nobody else had ever heard of him - and immediately received a call. "Is that Eugène Marais the entomologist?" a man asked. It was four in the morning.

Marais was a South African author. He was handsome as the devil, an opium addict who wrote the one Afrikaans poem that Bella loved. The verses told a story about a young black girl called Mabalel who wandered down a path by the river and was grabbed by a crocodile. Anyone who'd heard of Eugène Marais must be interesting, regardless of his discourteous sense of time.

The man deduced from her accent that she was from South Africa. "Do you know Leonard Levin?"

Bella almost fell off her chair. Bella had adored Lenny when she was fifteen. She heard that after his marriage he moved to the United States, but Bella lost contact with him and anyone else they both might have known.

"We worked together, in computers," the man informed Bella, and so she decided she'd be safe enough to meet him for coffee.

The second Bella entered the West Hollywood coffee shop she noticed the Eugène Marais aficionado. He stuck out like a sore thumb, wearing faded baggy shorts, an old Hawaiian shirt, and a freshly shaven face; though a few long hairs on the side stuck out, demonstrating lackadaisical grooming. She almost turned and walked out and, after she sat down and the man began talking compulsively, she wished she had. Afterwards, she realized that the computer-savvy man looked up Eugène Marais on the net.

At least ten years passed before Bella, gingerly and without enthusiasm, ventured onto a dating site again.

A Japanese man contacted her. He was an architect and his photograph showed a handsome, well-boned face. Bella thought the Japanese impressive: their aesthetic, their food, and their sense of design are even more refined than the French, which was saying something.

Bella arranged to meet Mr. Japan at his contemporary house before they went out for lunch. Greta said she knew the house in Westwood. The architecture was stark contemporary, and stuck out on a street of traditional cottages. Bella thought this was a positive sign.

When she arrived, a bit late as she said she might be, Mr. Japan had already eaten. He said he was so hungry he could not wait. A bad sign. He insisted on serving her take-out sushi and a bit of left-over apple pie which, being polite, she ate whilst he talked compulsively. What was it, Bella wondered, about her and compulsive talkers? She tried to give him a pass. He was, after all, a widower. He had no idea what to do with a date. After lunch, they went to the Getty Museum. He wanted to see an exhibition of photographs.

Had Bella been on her own, she would have whizzed through the show. But there she was, with a man, trying to make some sort of connection, so the whole thing took forever. When they finally left, both of them were exhausted from their mutually failed efforts to bond.

"One swallow doesn't make a summer." Shelly loved her aphorisms.

"I am not what men want," Bella replied.

"What do you think they want?" Shelly asked, "And don't go saying 'sex' again. That can't be true. They want true love, like we all do."

"Dr. Fehrer told me that when he works in the old-age home, all the men want prescriptions for Viagra."

The thought of rampant men in the old-age home was, to say the least, disquieting. Moreover, because there were many more older women than men in such places, men were in demand.

Shelly kept on nagging. "Try Match. Go on, be brave. I'll help you."

And so, being in a playful mood one evening, Bella followed Shelly's instruction and joined - for one month. This necessitated posting a photograph. There was also a section in which one had to write at least two hundred words about what she wanted. That was a struggle and she was determined - unlike Shelly in her profile - to be honest.

I want a man who is fabulous, confident, amusing, kind, intelligent, and rich enough; a man dedicated to a stimulating and fulfilling career (e.g., scientist, author, artist, politician or something out of the ordinary, like a think tanker). I do not want passionate sex for starters, that has to come later. I am not going for long romantic walks on the beach. I hate walking. I am old-fashioned enough to expect a man to pay my way. No economy flights unless local.

I also have a lot of baggage. I have, after all, lived a life. What you might get: a creative, amusing, attractive and challenging woman. At least for a cup of coffee.

"Well, nobody is going to reply to that."

After one week Bella had one response. *I am not interested. But I celebrate your candid profile. No bullshit there. I hope you find your man.*

She replied: *I hope that was a compliment. I wish you good luck in*

113

finding someone, too.

He messaged back. *I was being complimentary.*

Had Bella found him even a little bit attractive, she might have written more. But she didn't and, furthermore, he lived in Tulare, which Bella discovered was in California's Central Valley. Bella received two further "winks." One from a man who lived in a retirement village in Arizona. Another from a man whose ideal date was "champagne with a bit of OJ, either on a mountaintop or beach, enjoying loving words and caressing on a blanket, gazing at the full moon, and listening to music." He also wanted a woman to help him complete his memoir titled, "Thirty Jobs in Thirty Years." She did not return either wink.

However, Bella's non-adventures on Match.com worked like a charm - the Romance Virus abated, and she was left with energy to pursue more creative ventures. She began a series of drawings based on her interpretation of Fractals and Fibonacci Patterns and the Theory of Evolution, in which the tiniest mutations accumulate into big differences. She also went to the wool shop, where she always spent a fortune. "What's the point of spending all that time knitting with cheap wool?"

Knitting one of her exquisite and unusual multicoloured scarves whilst she half-watched the news, Bella saw a piece about the Cannes Film Festival. She imagined how she would feel to be a star, dressing up and parading down a red carpet, smiling, and answering silly questions.

To the question, "Who are you wearing?" she imagined herself answering, "Oh, this princess satin sheath stretched over three sets of Spanx that are squishing my liver into my stomach and my boobs into my neck? I call her Priscilla."

On the other hand, when Jessica got married, a professional did Bella's hair and makeup and she felt like a movie star. Still, looking as marvelous as she did at the wedding, Bella was uncomfortable walking with Jessica and Guy down the aisle. She did not like being the center of attention.

Publically showing her own art was awkward for Bella. This was one of the reasons her artistic career was not as successful as it could have been. The acclaim that Bella so sorely needed felt more like a scratchy wool sweater, and she was aware of the dichotomy.

No, she would not like walking on the Red Carpet!

Later on that evening, Jessica called to chat. She had lunch with Guy, a rare occasion since her father had taken up with his European Mongrel, which was what Bella decided to call Irina.

"Dad was swooning over Irina."

"She makes him feel young."

"She makes him look ridiculous."

"He's still an extremely handsome man. Women are attracted to him."

"Not for his looks," Jess replied.

"He can be charming, when he wants to be."

Bella felt the stirrings of that damned Romantic Virus, and so she logged onto Match.com. Merely logging on worked like an antibiotic.

"NICE'nEASY" wrote: *I would like to meet a woman with a sense of humor who can put up with an old man that is set in his ways. I'm very loving and a great cook. Travel is my life. I enjoy meeting open-minded people who enjoy exploring new places and trying new things. Anyone who is easygoing, sociable, and loves to laugh will get along great with me.*

There was not one thing wrong with this. He could cook. He liked travelling. He was open-minded. Did that mean he liked threesomes? The Romance Virus went into lockdown.

"UPMAN" wrote something similar: *I am a genuine, down-to-earth guy with a welcoming sense of humor. I have very eclectic taste in music and movies, and am always interested in trying something new. I love to laugh and joke around.*

Both men wrote that they wanted try something new. They maintained they were genuine and wanted the same, and they claimed to have a good sense of humor. At the age of eighty, they still wanted to find romance. Bella thought this was either incredibly sad - or incredibly sustaining - to live with such hope. All she knew was that the probability of finding true love at her age was as remote as finding a diamond in the grass.

Like an irritating itch that gave her pleasure to scratch, Bella returned to *The Lions of A'marula*.

Three acts. Plot points. Midpoints. Inciting incidents. Climax. Every How-To book seemed to note the brilliance of two famous films: *Chinatown* and *Casablanca*. "Maybe you can tell a professional the story, and they can write the script for you," Greta suggested.

"But the whole point is that I want to write."

"Then write." Greta was not at all sympathetic. Bella attributed this indifference to her dashed hopes when she found out the "perfect man" she met at the optician was - like Glen Short, Greta's long-time married lover - unavailable.

"He's separated," Greta said, weakly.

Bella read up on how successful screenwriters went about their work.

There were Ten Tips from Billy Wilder. One was, "Know where you're going."

Bella knew where she was going, but she didn't know how to get there. Mr. Wilder also said, "If you have a problem with the third act, the problem is in the first act." He didn't advise Voice-Overs. She wished she could make her whole movie a Voice-Over. One writer advised, "Ignore all rules and create your own."

Bella looked at the time. The tiny, red, enamel-cased clock on her desk read 11:25 p.m. Bella liked the night. The Portland was on a quiet street, but there was something different about the silence of the night. Bella made herself some coffee, knowing she wouldn't be able to sleep. She tried to work on character arcs.

She called Greta, who was always awake late at night. "I hope you're not occupied."

"I'm alone, if that's what you mean," Greta replied.

Bella explained Winston's character arc. Greta laughed, "Maybe you should make a painting of an arc."

Bella ignored that. "I hate this arc thing. Life doesn't have arcs. People muddle along, and situations evolve without tidy resolution."

"I know you will work it out Bella, you always have all the answers." Greta didn't feel like being sympathetic.

Receiving no comfort from Greta, Bella called her old friend Marina Painter in Cape Town. Nobody was better named than Marina, who became a well-known painter of South African landscapes, many of which were of historical scenes - like the Battle of Blood River, in which Boers numbering four hundred seventy slaughtered more than three thousand Zulu warriors. Big corporations that liked the idea of South African history, at least when whites won, snapped up her paintings of the famous defeated Zulu Chieftains Shaka and Dingane.

Marina told Bella that she had bumped into Tucker Jessop.

After her divorce from Guy, Bella had a brief but intense affair with Tucker. He was one of those reprobate Englishmen sent to Africa by their aristocratic families, like Charles Somerville in *The Lions of A'marula*. After Tuck dumped her, he became engaged to a well-connected American divorcée. The marriage failed, and the last she heard was that he'd lost the family fortune, which included substantial land ownership in Dorset. He now lived in Cape Town.

"You would not believe how dissipated he looks," Marina told her.

Bella was ashamed, but admitted she was pleased.

After that conversation, she gave some thought to making Winston a redhead and English, like Tuck. Or maybe blond like Leonardo DiCaprio, who was her favorite actor, although lately he was being overtaken by Matthew McConaughey. Maybe she should model Winston on Farrel Bootch and make him somewhat more effeminate? After all, she imagined Digby Bootch, Farrel's father, when she brought George Agadees to life. Perhaps Winston's twin, Elizabeth, should be evil? One of Bella's How-To books encouraged the power of making choices.

At two in the morning, Bella's best idea should have been choosing to go to bed, which she finally did, just as the day began.

Chapter 14 -
Maurice, Ugh!
"Life is absurd."

"Should we go to The Tennis Club for lunch?" Jessica called her mother, as she usually did, every morning. "I'm feeling miserable and missing Gran."

Bella's mother, Joyce, died a year previously, and Jess and Joyce were close. Bella missed her mother terribly, too. She didn't imagine how much she'd miss her until she was gone.

Bella heard this from other women who lost their mothers, but only after Joyce's death did she understand how deeply common was her sorrow. It didn't matter that mothers were as annoying, critical, irritating, intrusive, or as imperfect as daughters believed they were. However flawed, when mothers were gone, they seemed to be universally missed. Bella shared this with Keisha, the receptionist at The Portland, whose mother died more or less at the same time as Joyce. Their shared grief was a comforting bond.

The Tennis Club wasn't busy that Monday, and Bella arrived before Jessica. The day was crisp and sunny. Bella chose to sit outside, where luxuriant potted petunias and a glittering, turquoise swimming pool reminded her how fortunate she was to live in California.

She picked up the main section of *The New York Times*, abandoned on a nearby table. Bella liked *The New York Times*. She had the *Los Angeles Times* delivered daily, but read *The New York Times* online: the Opinion pages, Fashion and Style, and the Science section.

By the time Jess arrived, Bella was done with the paper and decided once again, after reading about greed, inequality, and ineptitude, that the Revolution was nigh and that Capitalism was failing.

Bella and Jessica had finished their Cobb Salad (Bella's without bacon or chicken), when an older - and from a distance, handsome - man showed up. For a moment, Bella thought it was Guy, even though this was impossible as he was in Europe. The man ignored both Jessica and Bella as he strolled nonchalantly past them into the dining room.

"You'd think we're invisible," Bella observed.

"Maybe he's shortsighted, or is it long-sighted?" Jess suggested.

When the man walked back outside, as if to inspect the swimming pool, Bella stared at him. "I am going to make him acknowledge us," she told Jess. "Just to see if I can."

Bella always said, "If you stare at someone they know it," and despite the man's forced nonchalance - as if he did not notice the only two people sitting outside having lunch that day - he eventually walked over and introduced himself as Maurice Sevrillo.

He was luxuriously and immaculately dressed: a perfectly laundered, soft-pink twill shirt, a brown crocodile belt with a subtle brass buckle, and navy suede Tod's loafers. A recent tan and a head of well-cut grey hair completed the picture.

"Where's the tan from?" Bella inquired.

"Palm Springs."

Maurice was a stockbroker or some kind of trader, and he possessed the kind of charm and easy manner of a man who had the wherewithal to follow the sun. He said he was from Connecticut, where his wife and two children lived.

This was Maurice's second wife. His first marriage lasted two years and produced a son, now sixteen. He married for the second time at the age of sixty, and his second brood was six and four.

"My daughter's eight," Jessica told Maurice.

"Are you married?"

"Divorced."

"I am separated," Maurice smiled.

They talked about the coming election, the state of the nation, the state of the world, the mess that was health care, and the mess that was the Middle East, Africa, and Europe. Bella had opinions. Maurice had other opinions. Bella could hold her own in most discussions. Her interests were eclectic and fairly extensive: science, psychology, politics, art, fashion, and anthropology. She liked to keep up with things.

Maurice was smooth, but sufficiently handsome for Bella to discard the fact that his smoothness veered towards slippery. She wondered whether he found her intelligent conversation to be captivating.

Then, staring directly at Bella, Maurice asked, "Can I have your number?"

More taken aback than anything, Bella mumbled, "What for?"

Jessica jumped in, "Why do you want her number?"

Now, directly looking to Jessica, Maurice replied, "You're a single woman, aren't you? Why shouldn't I want your number?"

Oh, how to save face! Bella was relieved she did not blush, and silently thanked her God that she had not eagerly fished into her purse for her silver card case.

Bella couldn't remember the conversation after that, and once she managed to somewhat compose herself stated, "Jessica is too young for you." She added, "And I am too old."

Bella hoped she sounded both witty and wise. The last thing she wanted was for Maurice to suspect her humiliation.

Jessica stated the obvious, "You are a womanizer."

"I like women," Maurice smiled with assurance.

"How do you keep fit?" Bella changed the conversation.

"I don't. My shoulder is giving me trouble. I can't play tennis at the moment."

He was just the kind of man who'd play tennis, Bella thought.

"I might need surgery. My shoulder doesn't work." Then glancing down at his crotch, he added, "But this still does."

Bella became brutal. "Most women don't care if your equipment doesn't work. They don't want sex, they want money." She was suddenly quite certain - without asking - that his second wife, with her two toddlers, was at least twenty-five years younger than he was.

"You mean security," Maurice corrected.

Bella lobbed, "Call it what you want."

"And don't give us that BS," Jessica pinched. "You are not separated."

Bella wanted to reach across the table and plant a kiss on Jessica's cheek.

"We don't get on anymore," Maurice said, failing to sound genuine.

On this subject - older men with younger women - Bella's judgments were well-formed.

"You want to relax, she wants to have fun?"

"That's true."

"She wants to find something to do with her life. You want her to cater to you?"

"True."

"You can't understand why she can't just appreciate not having to work for a living, and enjoy going out to dinner, or watching you play golf or tennis or whatever? She's sick of your old friends? She thinks your first set of children are so spoiled. She's always telling you how much you spoil them."

"How do you know?"

"I know," Bella smiled.

"You are very smart," Maurice said, "I should talk to you, instead of my psychiatrist."

"It won't cost you as much," Jessica laughed.

"And there's my wife's therapist and my children's therapist."

With that, Bella had enough of Maurice.

"I have to go, Jess, I have an appointment." She added, looking at Maurice, "Not with a psychiatrist."

They all rose to leave.

Jessica ran to the club's front office, wrote out Bella's number on a small piece of paper, and handed it to Maurice. "You need a woman friend, someone your own age, to talk to."

Bella thought that so sweet of Jessica, seeing as Bella had often said she didn't miss having a partner, but did on occasion miss being able to talk to a man closer to her own age. A friend. Not a lover, not a husband, not a partner. A friend.

In the car, Bella said, "I felt so awkward, and all I can say is that I'm so happy I didn't give him my card."

"He was staring directly at you when he asked for your number. He wasn't interested in me. He might call you... I think he liked talking to you."

"No, he won't. Men like that don't want to know the truth. They want to think that women, however young and unsuitable, still want that part of them that they claim works."

With vigor and delight, they commenced to pull Maurice apart. His fine appearance became pure sleaze; his clothes, affectation; and his conversation, inane.

Jessica said, "I can't imagine going out with such an old man."

Bella mused, "If he had a yacht in the South of France and invited you to go to dinner in Paris on his private plane, might you consider it?"

"No. He's just too old for me. I don't care what he has."

"He's too crass for me," Bella said firmly. And she tried to not give Maurice Sevrillo another thought.

Bella imagined Maurice as a much older version of Winston

Agadees. Charming when he wanted to be, confident, assured, handsome, and not for a moment concerned about anyone but himself. She pictured him as a young man. Of course women would have fallen for him as Lena did for Winston.

This brought her to Brown Vongani and his beautiful eighteen-year-old daughter Lena, who were important characters in *The Lions of A'marula.*

> *Lena is a member of the indigenous Tsonga tribe who live and work at A'marula.*
>
> *She is the only and beloved daughter of Brown, the Tsonga Headman, who is employed as "Boss Boy."*
>
> *Though relations between blacks and whites are more than frowned upon, Lena can't help being flattered when Winston flagrantly flirts with her.*

Bella tried to flesh out Lena.

> *She has the smoothest brown skin. Her teeth shine like pearls against her plush purple lips. She is lean and muscular like a model. When she walks, it is with confidence.*
>
> *Brown is strong, decent, and noble.*

Bella didn't want Brown to be the stereotypical noble tribesman. Maybe he could be short and fat? Or skinny with a limp?

Bella now felt as if all her characters were contrived: Winston too bad, Brown too good, and Lena too seductive.

Chapter 15 -
Everyone Has a Sociopath
"Seeming sane is not the same as being sane."

Bella was not that surprised when Shelly fell for Alex Diabello. Countless disappointing encounters through Match.com, money wasted on supposedly more selective dating services, and an unremitting desire to find true love all conspired to make Shelly ready for a man like Alex. She met him inside an elevator whilst on her way to see her accountant. "We glanced at each other; it was instant attraction. And then he kissed me."

"Just like that?" Bella asked.

"Just like that."

And just like that the affair began, on one ordinary spring afternoon. Only Alex Diabello did not inform Shelly he was married - there wasn't much time - as after Shelly finished her appointment and Alex did whatever he came to do, Alex followed Shelly back to The Portland. There they shared, Shelly said with her face glowing and her eyes sparkling, "The most wonderful connection."

"Have you thought that his last name sounds a bit like the devil?" Bella asked.

"I've never been loved like this. He makes me feel like a woman."

"You are a woman," Bella quipped.

"You know what I mean. He's the first man I've felt 'that thing' with. You know how I've tried; I've had lots of dates. But there wasn't one man with whom I felt 'that thing.'"

"In your case 'that thing' is called insanity. I have had 'that thing' a few times in my life, but nothing was like the madness I had with

JP. He was not only married, but a bona fide sociopath."

The affair between Bella and JP lasted one-and-a-half years. "Six months to get him, six months to have him, and six months to get rid of him. In fact, the only way I really got rid of him was to leave South Africa. I wasn't the first woman JP managed to make crazy."

"Alex says I'm the first woman he's had an affair with, after twenty years of marriage."

"Oh yes," Bella's voice dripped sarcasm.

"I believe him."

"I suppose he swears on the graves of his kids or his mother?"

"As a matter of fact, he does swear he's never felt this way."

"For sure he's a sociopath."

"You've never met him."

"I don't have to meet Alex, but I guarantee he drinks too much, or takes drugs. I bet he loves status symbols - Rolex watches, Mercedes cars, things like that."

Shelly replied, "So? Lots of people drive Mercedes, and wear a Rolex."

Bella continued, "He doesn't worry about things that you think he should worry about - court cases, creditors, the future, or being found out. JP didn't react to pain when he was hurt. I saw him get beat up outside a hotel bar, and he completely ignored the gash across his eye. When it was cold and he was not warmly dressed, he paid no attention, as if his skin didn't react normally to temperature. Of course the main thing about sociopaths is that they don't have empathy. They can mouth words of love, but their actions don't match. They are con artists. I think they believe their own lies whilst they are telling them."

Though Shelly didn't comment, Bella knew she'd struck a chord.

Every few weeks Shelly told Bella another wonderful story about Alex's plans for their future. "We are going to live in Spain...We're going to buy a wine estate in Napa...Alex is starting a company to sell antique, hand-woven carpets from Afghanistan...Someone he knows has millions and wants to invest in a movie."

"And what about his wife?" Bella asked.

"I don't want to break up his marriage. I've told him that."

"But you are doing the one thing that could." Bella continued, "You'd better hope he doesn't leave his wife. My JP had a mad wife; only someone mad would marry him. I think she was also a sociopath. After she left JP, directly as a result of our affair, she married again. I later heard she left South Africa as she was about to be arrested for fraud. She was a stockbroker."

The delusions of a woman addicted to love came out loud and clear, as Shelly proclaimed, "Alex is not a bad person. He loves his wife, but he's not in love with her."

"That's what all married men say, sociopathic or not, as they embark on an affair."

Shelly was thrilled when, after about six months of intense ups and downs, Alex bought a house where they would live, in Beverly Hills splendor, once he filed for divorce.

The sale went all the way up to the day before escrow closed, just before Christmas. "It'll be your Christmas present," Alex told Shelly. "I'm putting it in your name. You'll always have it to fall back on, no matter what happens to me."

Shelly spent hours going through the Design Center and choosing furnishings. She was happily overwhelmed deciding whether to go Modern or Spanish, or perhaps French or maybe Italian, or a mix of everything. Bella was required to give her opinion on colour schemes, fabric swatches, tiles and floor coverings. She hoped Shelly would be more adventurous than she was in her apartment, which was - to say the least - predictable: all beige other than a white piano, which Shelly couldn't play but liked the shiny surface as an extravagant platform to display numerous photographs in silver frames. There were pictures of Shelly at gala events; Shelly on a yacht; Shelly in Hawaii, New York, and Acapulco; and one with her ex-husband and President Clinton, as well as many photographs of her children.

"I knew nothing would come of anything Alex promised," Bella told Shelly as escrow came and went without the deal closing. "Surely by now you knew too?" Bella stated more than asked.

"How could you be so sure?" Tears rolled down Shelly's cheeks. She was used to crying as Alex let her down, over and over again.

Bella couldn't blame her friend. "People like Alex are charming and intriguing, I give you that, but at heart they are nothing but common con men. And never truly successful in the end. Oh, they might have a bit of success, but whatever they may achieve always eventually fails. One minute they are throwing money around, and the next there is no money for a pack of cigarettes. JP smoked unfiltered Camels. Two packs a day at least. I didn't smoke and managed to ignore the smell. That's how besotted with JP I was, even when I discovered he was a sociopath."

"How did you know?" Shelly asked.

"A magazine article in *Fairlady* - it's a well-known South African publication. There was JP in black and white. A classic example. The writer quoted from a book called *The Mask of Sanity* by Hervey Cleckley. And once I read that book, I knew. The description of the sociopath was illuminating. Cleckley is still, today, an acknowledged expert on sociopathy, or psychopathy, or antisocial personality disorder. Whatever they want to call the condition."

"I'd like to read that book," Shelly said.

"The book is out of print. Maybe you can find a secondhand copy? There isn't that much to read on the sociopath. They don't present themselves for treatment. When you have one in your life, you know what havoc they cause. The sociopath doesn't suffer, but the people with whom sociopaths interact, they are the ones who go for therapy. They don't feel guilt. Their pathology is the opposite of the neurotic who worries about everything. Sociopaths simply do not truly fret, at least not sincerely, though they can pretend feelings, like they can pretend to love. Let me ask you: Did Alex fret knowing full well he was not going to buy that house?"

The question was rhetorical, for Shelly had tearfully reported that Alex was extremely calm when the deal fell through, as he knew from the very start he didn't have the funds to buy a house.

"Alex tells you he loves you, but disappoints you all the time. He uses honeyed words, and those words trap you. I'm sure they trap his wife, and all the women who came before you."

After the collapse of the sale, Alex told Shelly that his wife was beginning to suspect. She found a message from Shelly on his cell phone. He admitted to being careless, and had even more excuses for letting Shelly down. "She'll take everything I have, if I'm not more careful." Or, "You have to let me play this the right way. For us. For our future."

Shelly finally told Bella how Alex had conned her. "He sounded thoughtful as he 'allowed' me to charge the bill from the hotel in Santa Barbara to my American Express card. "You earn the mileage," he said, "I'll give you the cash when we get back to LA."

"You got out cheap," Bella told her, when Shelly declared her New Year's Resolution to finally get rid of Alex. By that time, Shelly had lost twenty pounds, more than a few thousand dollars, and the confidence of her own good judgment.

"I've heard your resolutions before," Bella said.

"I've got my appetite back. It's over."

"Thank the Lord!"

"I'm not sorry I had the affair with him. I learned a lot," Shelly said.

"What did you learn?"

She didn't reply; instead Shelly asked Bella, "What did you learn after JP?"

"The most important thing I learned was to detect the type almost instantly, even as I'm being charmed, for that kind of man attracts me. I've also learned to have some sympathy for sociopaths, as they're born that way and there is no cure. It's a bit like diabetes, only there's no insulin to keep sociopathy in check."

"I can tell you another thing you learned," Shelly said. "You learned how to help a friend who was in the clutches of one."

That night Bella lay in her bed and thought back on her romance with JP. None of her friends understood how she, Bella Mellman, had fallen in love with a low-life gangster who, when they asked him what he did, said quite proudly and truthfully, "I am a thief."

Bella didn't understand until many years later that she fell into JP's arms soon after she stopped seeing Jack Flattery. Jack was also married. He said he was in love with Bella; however when his wife became pregnant with their second daughter, Bella ended their affair.

Bella did not regret Jack, and she did not regret JP.

Bella once read that you should only regret things you have not done, not things you did. Bella agreed.

The clock read 1:20 a.m. when Bella mistakenly erased all she'd written so far on Final Draft.

She actually screamed out loud. One of the residents called the Front Desk, and the Night Valet rang to find out if everything was in order. Bella told him why she screamed. He sympathized.

Bella spent the next few hours driving herself insane trying to fix the problem herself. There was nobody at Apple to ask: they were closed until the morning.

Poor Charlie! He became so desperate to go outside, he made a poo in the guest room. When Bella finally took him out, a large rat rushed in front of her and across the street. She screamed again, but other than a light going on in a house across the road, nobody came to see what happened. Then she stepped on a snail. The crunch was sickening, and Bella felt more grief than befitted the demise of the poor mollusk. Her mind, at this dark hour, took to contemplating how she would die. Cancer? Heart failure? Accident? There was no way she wanted to go. "I wish I could live forever," she said to the sweep of black sky where only the brightest of stars could be seen. "I want to see my grandchildren marry and have children, and then know their children. I want to be here forever."

These gloomy thoughts shifted towards more general catastrophes that were constantly being forecasted in the news, and which Bella, being a big reader of such matters, was well aware: earthquakes, droughts, incurable illnesses due to antibiotic overuse, ozone depletion, global warming. And seeing as she especially enjoyed reading about the cosmos, she knew the world was going to end sooner or later, certainly when the sun exhausted its nuclear fuel and bubbled out into a red giant. By that time, plants and animals will have long died out, the oceans will have evaporated and only the hardiest of microbes may be left. That is, provided they aren't engulfed and obliterated by the ballooning red giant that once was our sun. Bella could never get her mind around the vast enigma of the cosmos, no matter how many books she read, or how often she watched TV programs - like those featuring the enthusiastic Neil deGrasse Tyson - that tried their best to simplify the mystery.

Chapter 16 -
The Luncheon
*"The only people who enjoy catered affairs
are those who organize them.*

The benefit luncheon for The Circle, a group home for drug addicts, was the one charity event Bella attended every year. Bella never totally enjoyed the event. Afterwards, as she drove home, relieved it was over, she wondered why she didn't merely donate some money and skip the event. But she knew many of the people involved with The Circle, and she found it pleasant to see some of them, at least once every 360-some days.

Bella knew people who attended endless similar affairs, and whether they were upmarket or down, they all followed similar scenarios. The centerpiece flowers might be more inventive or costly; the tablecloths, food, and wine of better quality; the jewels or dresses the guests wore more haute, but a charity-do was a charity-do.

Bella knew what was required of her and she behaved accordingly. She browsed the silent auction, noting jewelry nobody in their right mind would either wear or want, baskets filled with creams and lotions made by unknown beauty houses, tickets to sports events, sports memorabilia, restaurant and hotel vouchers, and so on and on.

Bella had once won a Botox treatment donated by a dermatologist whose wife was on the hosting committee. She put the certificate away, in a very safe place, planning to use the poisonous injectable when her present Botox wore off. However, when the day came, she couldn't remember where she'd hidden it.

Wherever she was seated, Bella pretended to be delighted by the fellow guests at her table, whilst wishing that she were seated at that table over there, or there, with much more interesting-looking folk.

She was not bad at small talk, first to whoever was on her left, then her right. They were usually people she did not know, did not know well, or did not want to know better. She affected a laugh when the Master of Ceremonies made jokes. She wore a benign smile as philanthropists supporting the venture were lauded and acclaimed for everything but their ability to donate money.

She wondered whether she was alone in these cynical feelings. Perhaps other people liked people? Maybe they liked to dress up? That was the part she most enjoyed - seeing as her life was so casual, the occasional dress up was fun.

Bella may have been scornful of such events, but she was aware they were part of a worthwhile system. The charity made money, as did the hotel staff; the cooks; the waiters; the people who did the flowers; the food's producers, farmers, and wholesale suppliers; and the silverware makers. These events were a vital part of the endless chain of supply and demand that kept society functioning.

At this year's Circle event, Bella was placed at a table with followers of Trey Becker. She had never heard of Trey Becker, but she discovered that - aside from donating time and money to The Circle, for which he was one of the year's nominees for the Circle of Excellence - his claim to fame was teaching single people how to have successful relationships and find true love.

Bella was aghast, thinking, "The people in charge of seating believe I should go to a Trey Becker seminar!" Bella kicked herself for not requesting to be at the same table as Shelly. She'd hoped for a more interesting placing when the event planners were left to their own devices.

There were nine Trey Becker devotees. Bella was clearly an outsider.

"He's wonderful," claimed Graziella, the voluminously teased red-haired woman on Bella's left.

Graziella introduced Bella to her silent fiancé. "We didn't meet at Trey's seminar, but we're engaged. We go to Trey's talks together now. We love listening to him. It's not just for helping you meet someone, but Trey explains how to have a loving relationship once you have someone special. He's a relationship guru." Graziella giggled at what she thought was a bit of a joke.

"When are you getting married?" Bella inquired.

"Next year, in April."

Bella deduced the nuptials were fourteen months away. "Have you been married before?" Bella inquired.

"I have," Graziella replied. "Not Tony."

Bella wanted to tell Graziella that seeing as Tony had remained single up to this point, all the Trey Becker seminars in the world would not help her bag him; though looking at Tony, Bella could not imagine why anyone would want to do so. He was uncouth, his hair was plastered with grease across his bald patch, and he had stained teeth. He wore a brown sports coat and beige pants. Bella hated men in brown anything, other than shoes.

Bella turned to chat with the woman on her right. About forty, and utterly bland, she was there with her widowed father. They both went to Trey Becker. "He's changed my life," the daughter claimed. "Now, I want my dad to find someone."

"So, who have you found?" Bella asked the dull woman.

"I know what I'm looking for now," was the feckless reply.

Bella chose not to ask the father anything other than where he came from.

"How much do the seminars cost?" Bella was certain Trey Becker's clearly indispensible wisdom wasn't cheap.

"It depends," the daughter explained. "I have private sessions with Trey. You can have private, semiprivate, or go to group sessions. There are many different-sized groups. Or you can go to a big event. It's not very expensive to go to one of those. You should really try it," she said, staring at Bella's ringless left hand.

"I don't want a relationship," Bella replied. "I have had enough of them."

"That's what you say." The daughter was earnest. "You are like me, you chose the wrong people."

"Yes I did," Bella laughed.

Thankfully, the Master of Ceremonies asked for quiet and a video began, showing all the good things The Circle did.

Bella ate her starter salad. She picked at the ubiquitous, stuffed chicken breast.

She tried to see where Shelly was seated, but failed to find her in the huge ballroom. Then, before the announcement of the "Brown Nosing of the Year's" three recipients of The Circle of Excellence Awards, Bella excused herself to freshen up. Instead, she made her way to the garage, where she entered her car as if the Subaru Impreza was a chariot, and zoomed away into the late afternoon to meet her chosen Prince, anxiously waiting at home.

Charlie was as happy as ever to greet Bella. And as she walked around the block with him, she resolved to never again attend a Circle - or any charity - event. If anyone asked her to buy a ticket, she would refuse, and donate the same ticket price to PETA.

The patient man from Apple helped Bella to restore, not the file that was lost, but the one previous. The data loss wasn't as disastrous as she thought. After thanking him profusely, she returned to fleshing out another important character: Beatrice Agadees, George Agadees's spinster sister. Bella hated the word spinster, and its demeaning connotations. "Spinster" should be removed from the dictionary altogether.

Beatrice lives outside Nelspruit, which is the closest town to A'marula. She owns a small store selling a mix of homemade produce, like jams, as well as local art and African artifacts.

Since the death of George and Margaret, Winston is Beatrice's only living relative and she absolutely adores him.

Though Beatrice has never been married, she has a long-time lover: an architect named Delbert, who constantly asks her to marry him, despite her consistent refusals.

Bella imagined Beatrice to be a bit like herself. But she couldn't get a grip on Delbert, Beatrice's persistent lover. When she thought of Delbert, an image of Archie Miller - her late stepfather - kept cropping up.

Bella never understood why her mother married Archie, other than she was afraid to be alone after she and Bella's father divorced. There was something repulsive about Archie, though he never tried anything untoward. That was left to the most disgusting husband of one of her mother's friends. Bella never told her mother. She wished now that she had. She did tell her therapists, all of them, over the years and she understood that this event affected her more than she ever admitted. Bella was grateful it was now acceptable for women to talk about molestation. She was astonished to discover how prevalent such sexual abuse was. Greta shared that she had been molested by a neighbor, and like Bella, had not told anyone at the time. "In fact, you are the first person I've ever told." Greta, who said she never cried, dabbed her eyes with a lace-trimmed white handkerchief embroidered with her initials. "It's such a relief to tell someone. I thought I'd take it to my grave."

Shelly told Bella that a friend's father had tried. "I told my mother and she didn't say anything, but I wasn't allowed to ever go there again."

Chapter 17 -
The Old Boyfriend
"Do not collect old boyfriends.

When Roland Underwood - an Englishman with whom Bella had a love affair directly after her divorce from Guy - called Bella out of the blue to inform her that he was coming to Los Angeles on business, she suggested that instead of him staying at a hotel, he stay with her. For a moment Bella thought she might even climb into bed with him, just for old time's sake. Sex didn't really count with an ex.

Bella picked Roland up from the airport, which he said was unnecessary; but they had been close and he'd shown her that getting over Guy was possible, if only for a while.

The first thing she noticed about Roland as he emerged from Arrivals was lingering evidence around his cheeks and nose of a hard drinker, which he was when they had their affair. And which he still was, as Bella observed him heavily imbibing during the two days he spent in Los Angeles.

Almost the first thing he told Bella was, "I had prostate cancer." Just in case she didn't quite comprehend, he added, "I am not allowed to take Viagra." And so, Bella knew that she and Roland were not going to have sex, even for old time's sake. This was a little disappointing to Bella, as she hadn't had sex for ages, and with Roland intimacy would have felt familiar and safe.

At The Portland, Roland eschewed the combo shower and tub in the guest bath, and asked Bella, "Do you mind if I have a soak in your bathroom?"

Bella had no problem with that and drew him a bubble bath. As she watched the bubbles form she felt happy doing something for a man.

"Come sit with me, talk to me," Roland called, once he settled into the hot-and-milky, bubble water that covered most of his aging body.

Bella and Roland chatted easily. They had a natural rapport. When Roland finally got out of the bathtub Bella noticed - beneath his bulging stomach - a pair of hanging testicles.

"I've got fat?" Roland hoped Bella might deny the obvious.

"No, you look good."

"So do you. You never change."

Both of them knew they were lying.

After they returned from dinner at Bella's favorite Italian restaurant, she asked, "Do you want to sleep in my bed?"

Roland demurred, "I need to have a good night's sleep."

In the morning, Bella peeked to see if Roland was awake. He said nothing, but opened the covers for her to creep in beside him.

Bella lay there, comforted by the warmth of his body. His bulk smothered her, and she could hardly breathe, but she remained quiet, not moving. Then she began to cry softly, for what was, what might have been, and what would never be again. Her tears were without morbidity; Roland did and said nothing to stop her. Had he been a weeper, he would have cried himself, for the memory of their affair left only gentle marks on them after its slow-burning end. After a few minutes, Bella truly could not breathe under the weight and heat of Roland's body, and was forced to extricate herself.

"I must get up," Roland said. "I have a meeting at ten."

"I must get up, too," Bella said.

That night they went to dinner with Bella's grown-up children, who did not remember Roland as well as he remembered them. There was a stilted oddness about the evening, which was made uncomfortable by the high-decibel noise in the restaurant. Restaurants had dispensed with noise-muffling surfaces like carpets and curtains so conversation sounded more animated than it actually was. Noise equaled having fun, which in LA was - Bella supposed - understandable, as most people had nothing to say to each other, seeing as they usually barely knew each other.

The restaurant was mid-priced and Bella expected Roland to pay. After all, he'd spent two free nights with her. She'd driven him to two business meetings and picked him up, too. Since inheriting his father's mining machinery business, Roland was now rich. Instead, he split the bill with Ivan, which horrified Bella, who did not remember Roland being cheap.

Afterwards, he said, "I should have picked up the bill myself."

Bella replied, "Yes, you should have."

Not long after he returned home, Roland sent her an e-mail thanking her for her hospitality. He wrote, "You were the love of my life."

This pleased Bella no end. There was something gratifying about knowing that you were the love of some man's life, even though he didn't pay for dinner.

The How-To books said, "Write a backstory of each character." So Bella did the part she was enjoying the most: research.

She used Google to search boarding schools in South Africa, and decided Winston would have gone to Michaelhouse in the KwaZulu-Natal Midlands. The school was founded in 1896, and the founder, James Cameron Todd, wrote, "A man's tone, moral and spiritual, as well as intellectual, is largely determined for life, by his school."

Bella thought how proud she was of her own son, Ivan, who attended four different schools due to her transcontinental adventures. He'd faced schoolyard bullies in both England and South Africa - for different reasons - and his experiences resulted in a maturity and sense of the absurd that was utterly endearing. Ivan's backstory, like Jessica's, might have been quite different had either of them - as were both Bella and her father - been afflicted by alcoholism, which was now believed to possess a distinctly genetic component.

Chapter 18 - Praying

"God, if I can't be good, help me be better. "

Although she was Jewish, Bella's granddaughter, Chloe, went to an Episcopalian school.

"When they talk about Jesus in prayers, just substitute the word God," Jessica told her. Even in kindergarten, Chloe understood this perfectly.

Bella always had her family and a few friends over for Passover and she celebrated the Jewish New Year with a feast. She knew the Hebrew prayers for the wine and bread, and she also knew the words for "Silent Night." Bella's favorite prayer was The Serenity Prayer, which she became familiar with once she stopped drinking and went to Alcoholics Anonymous.

Bella found Judaism depressing. The prayers, understandably, sounded like they intoned sorrows all the way from the pyramids at Giza to the gates of Auschwitz.

She much preferred the romance she found in fanciful or majestic church edifices to the no-frills design in synagogues, where embellishment and soft lighting was thought - mistakenly, in her opinion - to detract from thoughts of God.

The downtown Catholic Cathedral was Bella's favorite modern building in Los Angeles, and she made it one of her stops when she showed out-of-town guests around her adopted city. Bella was quite the guide.

"Welcome to my Los Angeles tour!

"First, I will drive you around some streets in Beverly Hills, where you will see Tuscan Villas, French Chateaus, Spanish Haciendas, Tudor Mansions, and Iranian Extravaganzas. In these immaculate streets, you will see no people - other than Mexican gardeners who will be clipping hedges, torturing shrubs into a desired configuration, or attacking fallen leaves with electric blowers, which are like giant hair dryers. If you do see the occasional dog, a housekeeper will be walking the creature. You will see many Range Rovers, and other luxury vehicles, parked in the driveways."

Bella never planned a specific route around the residential streets of Beverly Hills, but whatever route she chose, there were houses displaying the whole stylistic gamut: from tasteful to vulgar.

"I will then drive you towards downtown. We will pass through Koreatown and the Mexican Marketplace, to the so-called Cultural Center, where the powers that be decided to build large theatres and museums as far away as possible from the people who use them."

As Bella drove towards downtown along Beverly Boulevard, her guests were duly amazed to note Korean, and then Spanish, signage.

"LA is the most culturally diverse city in the world." Bella was sure that was true.

"Now wait for it, for when you see it, you will gasp," is something Bella said every time the silvery Walt Disney Concert Hall loomed, like some giant, half-opened pile of sardine cans.

She walked her guests around the perimeter of the concert hall. That was the best part - the outside - where, from various points, spectacular views of the city could be seen. They moved on to the garden named for Lillian Disney, featuring a water sculpture made from broken pieces of blue delft.

The Cathedral was far more to Bella's taste. She loved the lighting, the ambience, the tapestries, and even the garish crypt below, with panes of too-brightly stained glass. "Like a cartoon." Bella then led her guests to Gregory Peck's prime resting place.

The church in which Chloe's Christmas pageant took place was old by Los Angeles standards. The Gothic structure was a cozy, dark place, with a long nave, ending in the chancel. Bella knew such terms as nave, apse, chancel, and flying buttresses from her Fine Art studies. She once wrote an essay on Gothic cathedrals to impress a handsome young professor who had recently returned from France, where he studied Chartres Cathedral for his doctorial dissertation.

From Bella's perch on the aisle at the back of the church, she was well positioned to see the children as they walked to their places at the front, where they enacted the nativity play, and sang psalms in a variety of languages: French, Spanish, and Korean. Chloe seemed like an angel herself in an ivory dress with tiny gold embroideries and matching coat. Jessica spent a fortune on Chloe's wardrobe, which Chloe appreciated, being quite the Diva even at eight.

"That's the most glamorous outfit," Bella complimented Chloe. So her granddaughter would not think her appearance was everything, she added, "And you are so smart, too."

Bella believed how her own confidence came from experience, from living close to seventy years, having loved and lost - friends, lovers, husbands, jobs, situations - over and over, until she didn't mind losing anything ever again, excluding her health.

She was of the age when losing her health was a probability, if not sooner, then certainly later. She often counted how many good years she had left. Not so long ago it was thirty, and that seemed long enough. Now it was twenty, which was not that long. Soon, if all went well, she'd have ten and then five, and then two and then one, and then maybe she would wonder if she'd reach the next birthday, like her mother, who died just after she turned ninety-two.

This shrinking time line was scary - no, it was terrifying. Bella could not fathom how humans lived with the certain knowledge they would die. What amazed her more was that knowing whatever they did or didn't do - fought the fights, loved and hated, strived, failed or succeeded - their life inevitably came to an end, no matter how difficult the struggles, how powerful the love, how intense the work, or how much the suffering or the ease of their journey.

The church was dimly lit. Women's hair shone brightly under the light from the hanging lanterns. Bella fixated on two redheads, and on some of the Korean mothers with glossy hair wearing beautiful designer clothes.

Jessica whispered, "The Koreans send their children for extra lessons, even when they're doing well."

Bella wondered, "Does my hair shine too under this light?"

The light: In the beginning, there was darkness. Then God made light. Bella surrendered to feeling spiritual. She gazed up at the circular stained-glass window. Maybe the halo around the face of Christ would break into light?

"Yea, though I walk through the shadow of the valley of death, I shall fear no evil." Bella was comforted by those words, and thought of her mother, who had died so recently.

Was the halo becoming brighter? Bella wondered what she would do if she saw Jesus' ghostly manifestation.

The Priest intoned, "For those who have departed and whom we miss."

The congregation responded. "Lord, hear our prayers." Bella tried to stop the tears.

"For all who are lonely and suffering and sick."

"Lord, hear our prayers." The lights dimmed with each response.

Bella focused on the lonely and suffering, those out there in the cold of Los Angeles, which was nothing like the cold of most of America, or China, or Russia. She thought of suffering animals, and more tears came.

Bella rummaged in her purse for a handkerchief; she always

had one with her. She collected soft, cotton, printed handkerchiefs from the forties, which since the advent of eBay, she could easily purchase. Greta was the only other woman Bella knew who used handkerchiefs, though Greta's were all white or cream with her initials.

On to The Lord's Prayer and, finally, "Silent Night," which sent further tears cascading down Bella's cheeks.

Finally, with a few words from the Priest, the pageant was over. The lights brightened, the children walked down the aisle out of the church, and after came a rush of parents to find their spawn.

"That's my formal religion for the year," Bella said, shaking off her melancholy.

"I cried, too," Jessica said. "I miss Granny so much."

Jessica was Joyce's first grandchild. She had six others that came after, but Jess was her first.

"I miss her, too," Bella said.

There were many years Bella was not close to her mother, and times Joyce was so angry with Bella they were almost enemies. Those ugly times had to do with Archie, who entered the scene when Bella turned sixteen. Only after he died, twelve years ago, could the once-close bond with Joyce be repaired.

Archie was a small, stingy man, and Bella could not understand why her mother married him, other than he was totally opposite to her father. Speedy Mellman was a womanizer and a drunk, and Bella did not blame her mother when she finally kicked him out.

What Bella could not fathom at the time was the speed with which her mother remarried. With hindsight, Bella now understood: in those days, especially in South Africa, a woman without a man was considered pitiful. Bella married at twenty-one, and she was not considered too young. Guy was twenty-four. When Janine Fine, a school friend of Bella's, remained unmarried at twenty-seven, everyone - particularly Janine's mother - was concerned. When Janine went to Canada and found a man to marry, everyone was relieved.

When Bella was first divorced from Guy, she learned it was not easy to be unmarried. She needed courage to go to a restaurant with a girlfriend. If Bella was invited to a party, she was expected to bring a date. Many were the times she braved going on her own. "I am not inviting anyone, just because he's a man, to make me a whole person." This didn't endear Bella to hostesses who now felt they had to find a single man, so that the table placing would be even at sit-down dinners.

Fortunately, by the time the twenty-first century rolled in, this taboo had changed: women had no problem dining without a man and restaurants were filled with groups of women dining together. Bella no longer attended formal dinners, so the problem of even numbers went away and, in any event, she didn't think society circles cared so much anymore. She was grateful to the strong women who had gone before, who had bothered fighting so hard for simple things like equality.

Young women like Nicole had absolutely no idea how it felt to be devalued because you had no partner, date, or husband.

"There were times women did not even have the vote!" Bella pointed out.

"But that was so long ago," Nicole shrugged.

"Not so long ago. When I was your age, the sexual revolution had only started. No woman would just get up and dance unless she had a partner."

"Awesome."

"No, awesome is not the right word, awful would be more appropriate." Bella didn't like common overuse of the word "appropriate," but there were times the word truly was... appropriate.

Once a month Bella and Shelly went to dinner. They had a standing arrangement. One time Bella chose the restaurant, the next time Shelly had her pick. The two women found an abundance of interesting eateries all over Los Angeles.

"I look forward to our dinners more than a dinner with any man," Shelly said with a sense of surprise.

"Well, I am more interesting than most men," Bella laughed.

"My dates are so boring, I can't wait to get home," Shelly complained. "I feel so relieved when I can shut the door, get into bed, and turn on the TV."

"Seeing as I don't have dates like you, I would not know."

"You could have," Shelly said.

"Why would I want to? Now, a love affair, that's different, but a date? No. I'm fine with my own company."

Fifty-something Shelly thought Bella amazingly adventurous. "I could not go to a movie by myself. I just couldn't."

"Why not?"

"I don't know," she replied. "I would feel uncomfortable. I think people will feel sorry for me, like I have no friends. I couldn't go to a restaurant alone, either."

"That's different. I don't like eating in restaurants on my own. But I would feel no shame in doing so. No shame at all. The shame comes from feeling you are incomplete without a man at your side. That's a stupid shame. I find it a shame that many women - especially older women - are incapacitated by it."

Bella didn't realize how influential her words were, for two weeks later Shelly told her, "I went to a movie, all on my own. A matinee."

"A big gold star for you." Bella knew something had shifted if Shelly ventured into such unknown territory.

"And you know what? I didn't like the movie. So I walked out and went to the next theater and loved that one!"

"The movie, or the experience of being on your own?"

"I loved them both."

Bella noticed that after this, Shelly was a little bit less anxious about securing a mate. She stopped whining about finding "someone," at least for a few months.

Bella decided this was something of a victory, for both her and Shelly. And she was wise enough not to mention the achievement.

Bella got the idea of how George Agadees made his fortune from Marina Painter.

Marina's well-known and very-rich uncle, Harvey Painter, had for many years obtained the concession to harvest all the abalone on the Eastern Cape coast. The exclusive franchise was like a license to print money, and profits from abalone - which was sustainably harvested at the time - gave him the wherewithal to live incredibly well. Harvey was rumored to be gay and his exploits - fabulous weekend parties at his house in Hermanus, which was near the abalone beds - were the subject of gossip. In those days, being gay was very hush-hush. Bella was incredulous that in her lifetime, same-sex couples could marry. Greta had actually been invited, she said, "To my first same-sex marriage." She was thrilled, and reported the event as the sweetest wedding she had ever attended.

In Harvey's day, most of the harvested abalone was sold to China. When he sold his company - long before the fall of apartheid - he made millions.

He suffered a debilitating stroke soon after - gossip attributed this to excess. He was not able to observe the unraveling of the industry he basically began, as China expanded into Africa, and illegal harvesting decimated the naturally abundant mollusks.

Abalone were now factory-farmed far away from the turbulent Atlantic Ocean where they had clung to the rocks for eons, impervious against the currents. When Bella was on vacation in Hermanus, a holiday hamlet much favored by Capetonians, she asked the hotel maid what her son did.

"He's a poacher," the woman replied in that inimitable

Cape-Coloured Accent. She saw nothing wrong, and was proud that her son's work brought in money: abalone poaching was probably one of the few ways for Coloured People to make a living in the area.

Bella often noted, "China is the New Imperialist." Though nobody she told disagreed, nobody seemed to care much either.

She could rant on, given a bit of encouragement. "At least the English built schools, and taught the indigenous people to read and write. The Colonials were prejudiced and unjust - we know all about the failings of an Empire - but at the same time, they installed modern infrastructure and they tried to impart what they genuinely believed were their superior values.

"But not China! They only build roads to carry what they mine to ports. They keep to themselves without imparting any cultural wisdom, and import most workers from China, so they can continue paying slave wages. The only local people who seem to benefit are corrupt politicians whose well-lined pockets turn them into millionaires."

The appetites of the Chinese market decimated abalone. Bella despised the foolish and uneducated Chinese belief in the aphrodisiacal power of rhino horn, which further endangered another creature close to extinction. On her trip to the Mala Mala Game Reserve, a ranger told Bella that seven rhinos were poached in one sorry day.

A lot of what happened in the world made Bella both angry and outspoken: the constant humiliation of women in Arab countries, the way animals were abused in factory farms, the denial of basic health care to boost outrageous corporate profits, and the meager salaries of teachers and nurses.

When Bella ranted on about yet another horrible issue, Shelly warned her, "A heart filled with anger can't find love."

"Oh shut up!" Bella said with good humor. Shelly managed to turn any conversation into a reminder that Bella should find a man.

Chapter 19 -
Position
"Experience is expensive."

When Bella turned sixty, she didn't find life that different from fifty-nine, but when she was sixty-two, she felt that eighty was five minutes away. After Bella turned sixty-nine, she imagined saying, "I am seventy." Regardless that some people claimed age didn't matter, seventy was old. Seventy differed from sixty-nine in a way she considered far more significant than twelve months.

"Next January I will be old," Bella told Greta as they set out for Greta's birthday lunch. Greta said nothing. She knew better than to tell Bella she didn't appear to be old. Or that she "looked good for her age."

Bella and Greta always went to the fancy Neiman Marcus restaurant, Mariposa, to celebrate each other's birthdays. They both agreed that this tradition would ensure them two divine lunches every year.

There was a clear pattern to the celebration. They met up around the jewelry department - a perfect place to spend a few minutes - in case either of them was late. They chose what their nonexistent boyfriends should buy them. Greta usually picked rings or necklaces, while Bella liked earrings. Bella never went without earrings, from the moment her ears were pierced at the age of eighteen. Joyce would not allow her to wear earrings until then. And she listened. The world was different then, and Bella now knew she'd been a little scared of her mother. She could not imagine what Joyce would have thought of nipple piercing, or worse - tattoos

- which seemed to be ubiquitous now, even for women.

After selecting out pieces of jewelry, Bella and Greta took the escalator to the basement, where they perused dinner services in the housewares department, adjacent to the restaurant. They took their time and embraced the fantasy.

Bella picked a blue-and-white Ralph Lauren pattern. "For my yacht."

"For my private plane." Greta chose a gold-and-white Herend pattern.

Greta, who always booked the table when they dined together, had reserved a choice table where both she and Bella could see the other patrons, who were almost exclusively female.

"Well done!" Bella exclaimed as they sat down at a table where neither of them had to face a wall. She never understood why - if she had to face a wall while dining - there wasn't a mirror so she could see the room, even if only in reflection.

The two women made their choices from the small, perfectly proportioned menu, which stated the calorie count of every dish - information that never stopped Bella from ordering a side of fries which came wrapped in a paper folder like an ice-cream flute. Both Bella and Greta anticipated what they thought was the very best part of the meal: a tiny cup of chicken broth, which was offered gratis, and a huge puff of Yorkshire pudding served with jam and butter.

"Bella, you aren't seventy yet, and in case you don't know, sixty-nine is a fun number. It's the French favorite," Greta joked.

"I never understood that. What's so wonderful about having an erect penis in your mouth? Nothing could be more uncomfortable, unless you have a very large mouth. Your jaw begins to ache, and then, if you can bear the discomfort until the end, you get some glutinous stuff that's more like snot than anything else spritzed into your mouth, making you gag. How in the world have young boys managed to convince girls that giving head is the thing? I find it astonishing!"

"You're brutal!"

Bella finished her tiny soup and tore into the Yorkshire pudding. "Not brutal, Greta, brutally honest. As for the men, unless you've just washed, those jokes about fish are not far off. Then there's your hairs in his mouth."

"God, Bella, don't you know that women wax or shave their pubes these days?"

"Yes, I do know, and I do. I don't like hair."

Greta sighed, "Giving a man head shows you're affectionate."

"Blow jobs show you have power," Bella explained. "And not just the power to bite the thing off."

Greta bellowed. "Men love them. I think they prefer it to regular sex."

Bella lowered her voice. "God didn't do well when he designed our sex organs. They should have been totally separate from the waste-disposal areas of the body. What was God thinking?"

The neighboring table was within hearing distance, and Bella noticed that the two young women had stopped talking.

"I like giving head." Greta squared her shoulders. She was not going to let her older friend dissuade her, particularly as she had embarked on a hot new romance with a married man a few years younger than she, who was - of course - leaving the wife he "loved," but wasn't "in love" with.

"Oh, please." Bella threw her head back. "What is there to like about a blow job, other than you feel powerful that you can give him pleasure?"

"That's the whole point."

"We couldn't help overhearing what you're talking about," one of the young women at the adjacent table offered.

Very sheepishly, Bella and Greta glanced at each other, but said nothing.

"No, don't worry, you are amazing!"

"Amazing!" The blonde young woman did something funny with her bee-stung lips. Her darker companion swept her incredibly straight, long hair over to the side and fiddled uncomfortably with her large-faced Cartier watch, which if - Bella thought - wasn't the real thing, then was a good replica.

"And so, what's your opinion?" Bella's affable attitude let the two youngsters know she was happy to include them in the conversation.

The dark-haired woman swept her hair over her other shoulder, then back again, as though her swishing hair might help with the answer. "It's what men expect."

Bella wished her hair would swish. "Perhaps, but my generation fought for you to have a choice. Young men have so bamboozled you young girls, that you feel you have to do it, or you won't be desired." Bella was certain that both women had breast implants.

The blonde joined in. "They demand it. And from a young age, too."

"And you oblige?" Bella rolled her eyes. "You don't like it, but you do it. Don't you think that's incredibly idiotic?"

"You're awesome," the brunette gasped. "Amazing!"

The blonde concurred, "You are awesome!"

"The pill changed everything." Bella wasn't sure exactly why she bothered with this women's history lesson, but a compliment was a compliment, and she liked being called "awesome" and "amazing" over and over again, even if the adulation was from two juvenile fools with silicone boobs.

"You know, when I was your age, if women had sex, we risked falling pregnant. We all had abortions, which was no fun. Horrible, really. Seriously horrible."

It was an experience Bella had pushed down in her mind: the sordid doctor, and the dark little room in a sparsely furnished flat. When Joyce saw her later that day, she commented, "You look so pale." Joyce usually didn't notice much about Bella. She was too busy trying to find a replacement for Speedy, who had fallen in love with his secretary and was about to leave Joyce.

Bella was on a roll. These young women needed educating.

"The pill came along and we were free to have sex as often and with as many men as we liked. But our brains and our biology were wired to want a partner who will fend for us while we are pregnant, and help to support our offspring. Girls, cultural anthropology is nothing new. Endless books have been written about the subject. But I doubt if anyone has written a decent book about blow jobs."

"You should write one," the blonde suggested.

"Maybe I will," Bella threatened. "Even the name, 'blow job' - yes, it's a job! That means we should get paid for our labor."

The brunette declared, "I'd make a fortune."

"Me, too," the blonde giggled.

"But what about if you really love each other?" the brunette mused. "That's different, don't you think?"

"This conversation is getting too philosophical for me," Bella said. "I need to get going. Let's get the bill."

Bella had an appointment after lunch to have her annual mammogram. She had put the dreaded procedure off for months since she got the reminder notice.

She was calmer than usual this time. She knew she wouldn't get the results immediately. They'd inform her of a problem later, with a phone call. No phone call after five-to-seven working days, and she was in the clear. There was no point in worrying, at least for today.

Bella remembered with apprehension that her colonoscopy must be around the corner. Five years had passed since she last endured the dreaded procedure, which she'd already endured twice before. Each time was horrendous. Not the actual procedure, but drinking that awful drink until her stomach and intestines threatened to burst, and then getting rid of all that shit before going to the hospital at some ungodly hour, only to wait forever until they took her in to see the doctor.

Trying to remain healthy wasn't fun, nor was testing to find out how unhealthy she'd become. Bella's favorite part of trying to remain healthy was training with Sven. He was part torturer, and part therapist. He knew when to push Bella, and when she needed a less strenuous session. Since Bella had trained with Sven for many years, she knew about Sven's life, and he about hers. "We are like family," Sven said, and how true this was. An hour three times a week with just each other made them close. Sven lived through Bella's problems with friends and family, her fear of flying (Sven told her, "You are not flying, the pilot is"), and her feelings about getting older and fatter, as well as unloved and useless. Somehow he always had something helpful to say, and if that didn't work, he made Bella do push-ups or leg lifts or whatever would take Bella's mind off herself. In truth - as Sven always pointed out - her life, and his, too, were just fine.

Bella lived through Sven's countless unsatisfactory love affairs with women Bella knew would not please his mother, or any mother for that matter. She'd listened to Sven's heartbreak when he fell madly in love with a drug-addicted, sociopathic stripper who really was a hooker and who did nothing but lie to him. "Make sure you wear a condom," Bella nagged Sven again and again.

"I always do," Sven claimed.

Fortunately, the stripper was out of the picture when Sven - who "always wore a condom" - impregnated a relatively normal young woman, and the resulting little boy totally changed Sven from a sex-mad Viking to a doting father and a (more-or-less) satisfied partner.

After a particularly strenuous set of stomach crunches with Sven - Bella hoped the exercise might displace some of the previous day's lunch from Neiman's and a midnight snack of her favorite Lindt chocolate - Bella flopped down on the mat with utter relief. "It's so good when you go down."

Inwardly, Bella winced at her choice of words, and when Sven said, "That sounded kinda funny," Bella knew exactly what he meant. And so, thinking about the conversation at Neiman's, Bella decided to ask Sven, as a representative of the male sex, "What do you think of oral sex?"

Sven replied, "If the woman knows what she is doing, I like it. But so many don't."

"What about you? Do you like it?" Which was what Bella actually meant when she asked Sven the question.

Sven was specific, "Yes. With a new partner, it's very exciting, but not later. I don't think people in long-term relationships do it." In other words, Sven no longer went down on the mother of his son.

Bella thought of doing a survey on the subject. Who else could she ask? For a day or so she considered all the men with whom she came into contact. The valets at The Portland? Norman at the gym? The young man who walked his two terriers? He was gay and would have a different take on the matter. However, although Bella believed such a survey would be enlightening, she realized there was nobody other than Sven she could comfortably question about the subject of blow jobs. Thus, at least for the moment, Bella decided her cultural anthropology would be put on hold.

Bella reached the point in the story where Rosy Hemmings, Winston's future wife, was to be introduced.

Rosy lives with her widowed mother, Peggy Hemmings, at Fairlands, a gracious old house in the Johannesburg suburb of Westcliff, where the mining magnates whose fortunes came from gold and diamonds built mansions.

Rosy is an artist or maybe a potter.

When Rosy meets Winston, it's love at first sight. They are a match. Both beautiful, both from wealthy families.

Their stylish luncheon wedding on the grounds of Fairlands is the talk of the town.

Bella knew people like the Hemmings. Many of them were her friends, and she could easily picture the wedding scene. She imagined Grant Butler as the wedding coordinator and considered calling him in New York for some input on the latest in weddings. Instead she bought every single bridal magazine, only to discover nothing much had changed since she married Guy. Her choice of wearing a pink wedding dress was rather radical, but Bella had to be different, even if in little ways. In retrospect, her dress would have been prettier in white, or at least cream.

Fairlands was easy to bring to life. Huge banks of hydrangeas, old oaks giving shade to terraced lawns, and a rose garden with upright standard roses. The house would be of local stone, and designed by Sir Herbert Baker, who in the early nineteen hundreds was the architect of the magnificent Union Buildings, the seat of government in Pretoria. Mandela's inauguration ceremony was held there in 1994, and having been to the buildings herself, Bella imagined how magnificent the presidential celebration must have been.

Shelly became overly involved helping Bella pick Rosy's wedding dress. She wanted a strapless ball gown with a skirt as big as an ocean. Bella wanted a Grecian column: definitely not strapless.

"I can tell you, because I go to lots of weddings, that modern brides go strapless." Shelly often wondered about Bella's clothes. She didn't dress badly, but Shelly thought Bella dressed oddly. Shelly remembered how happy Bella was when the madras top with a mandarin collar she found on eBay was delivered.

Shelly said, "It looks like an artist's smock. Or even one of those big shirts men used to wear with droopy-cuffed sleeves. Your figure is totally hidden."

Shelly simply could not fathom why Bella liked baggy clothes. Her figure wasn't bad "for her age."

Greta arrived in the middle of the bridal dress discussion. "If you think you're going to pick the clothes for the movie - if it's ever made - you're mistaken. That's left to the costume designer."

"I know that!" Bella said. Greta could be annoying.

Though the scenes at Fairlands were easy to visualize, Bella found herself challenged when describing A'marula. She hadn't been to the Eastern Transvaal in a long time.

The necessity of more research made Bella happy. What did people do before the Web, that wonder of technology?

A sign, "A'marula," would be affixed to a huge Marula tree at the property's entrance gate. There could be a scene of blacks - the Tsonga - eating Mopane worms. The Mopane moth lays eggs on the Marula trees and the fat caterpillars are an important source of protein. In the cities, they are a delicacy, and Bella could always tell they were being fried from the distinct smell wafting from the kitchen. Anna, her maid, laughed when Bella wrinkled her nose in disgust at the fat white grubs. "They are not as bad as your prawns."

Bella recalled a Sausage tree with its enormous red flowers, which were horrible smelling. Bats were the main pollinator, and when the tree's huge pods - like giant sausages - were mashed to a pulp, they were used to treat skin ailments and even skin cancers. The tree's nectar was delicious to impala. She loved watching impala - the way dominant males protected females and their young, and the bachelor herds comprised of young males and old males past their prime, though Bella thought them still handsome and strong. She always found watching animals enlightening, and compared their behavior to that of humans. Bachelor herds were like young men in gangs, and dominant males were like... well, like Guy.

A Baobab could be a focal point in one scene. Maybe even a tree that had fallen, so its huge innards were visible. As children,

Jessica and Ivan called the Baobab "the upside down tree," as its branches look like roots. Unlike other trees, when these die they rot from the inside and suddenly collapse, leaving a seriously enormous heap of fibers. Bella had photographs of her and the children clambering around the massive mound of a fallen Baobab from one of the trips they took to Mala Mala.

After learning more about South Africa trees, Bella proceeded to grasses and flowers, none of which were truly interesting, but the thatching grass used to roof most of the buildings in wildlife areas intrigued her. Even the airport terminal at Kruger National Park was thatched. When Bella saw pictures of thatch-roofed structures in ads on the Internet, she had a moment of nostalgia: a memory ache that reminded her of her roots which, like the Baobab, were upended.

Guy called when she was mesmerized by the unique proclivities of flap-necked chameleons. Guy called her quite often, sometimes for no reason at all. She was always happy when he did because it was evidence of their connection.

"In my next life I would like to be a biologist," Bella told him.

He replied, "What's wrong with this life? Go study."

Everything was so simple for Guy. Except for being a kind and faithful husband.

Chapter 20 -
Dropping off the Perch
"Everything is made from stardust,
but is regular dust still stardust?"

Bella hadn't seen Serena in at least four years. Usually Serena and her fourth husband, John Hickey, came to the United States every year to visit John's daughter in San Diego; but for the past couple of years, John had been ill. He survived two hip replacements, and some plumbing additions to his aging blood vessels; thus Bella was surprised when she picked up the phone and heard Serena's voice.

"Hello, *daaahling.* We are here." There was no mistaking Serena, who affected the most upper-class English accent imaginable, even though she was born in Rhodesia - now Zimbabwe - and didn't set foot in England until she was well into her thirties.

Bella believed if Serena had been born in Los Angeles, she would surely have become a movie star, for she possessed that starlight quality, as well as the ability - and desire - to entrance every man she met. However, Serena was born in Africa and in Africa she remained, marrying and divorcing to end up with the Scottish-born and thoroughly upper-class John. Bella was led, with a tiny bit of envy, to believe he was rich enough to indulge Serena's profligate ways, and charming enough to have a wide selection of fancy friends for Serena to entertain.

Bella arranged to meet Serena for lunch at The Ivy. The day was cold for Los Angeles, and thus Bella booked a table indoors. She was, as always, early. Serena, she knew, would be late and make an entrance - which she did, showing up in a navy-blue Armani blazer,

160

a cream silk shirt, and cream pants falling off her almost anorexic body.

"You haven't aged a bit," Serena said, as Bella rose to greet her.

"Neither have you," Bella lied.

The two old friends sized each other up. Bella knew Serena noticed how much weight she'd put on. Serena was certain, though mistaken, that Bella didn't notice her recent face-lift or the addition to her breasts. After the initial impact of observing what damage the inexorable passage of time had wrecked on each other, they got down to gossiping about mutual friends. They had known each other for many years and had history, which was one something Bella's friendships in LA sadly lacked.

"John and I had dinner with Belan and Suki Dugraigh one Saturday, and Belan was dead the following Wednesday. It was such a shock. So many people I know have dropped off their perches. I had to redo my address book." Serena had always been droll.   .

She continued, "These days, nobody is screwing or suing. All people talk about is their most recent operation and damned backaches." She paused. "Do you have backaches? I don't."

Serena didn't wait for Bella to reply, and Bella was not going to tell Serena that if she picked up anything heavy, a month-long backache ensued. She was also not going to tell Serena that her fingers hurt, and she'd developed Tennis Elbow - very misnamed in Bella's case, for she never played tennis - or that one knee would simply not get better after a fall she'd taken months previously. Bella was not going to complain about a thing to Serena.

Serena carried on, "I feel great, but I still take pills for my thyroid. Anyway, they keep me thin. But let's stop talking about our health. You will never guess who I saw at a dinner at the Frankenheimers. Tinka deFreis. You know Leslie left her for an actress. A young actress."

Bella grinned. She never liked Tinka, who became more pretentious than ever after she married Leslie deFreis of deFreis Winery. Moreover, like so many of Bella and Guy's friends, Tinka dumped

Bella when she and Guy divorced.

Serena was a mine of information regarding people Bella hadn't thought about in years. "Molly Dubbs divorced Bobby when she found out he was having an affair with his secretary. So what's new? And Paddy Becker died and left most of his money to his first wife, which just about killed poor Claire. She spent a fortune trying to get the will overturned and wouldn't listen to anyone."

After Serena's third glass of wine, she divulged how miserable she was. "I really can't stand this 'getting old.' We were beautiful. Our good looks got us everywhere and gave us everything."

"Speak for yourself. I was never as attractive as you, Serena."

Bella noted Serena didn't disagree.

"Thirteen to sixty. It's a long time to have that weapon. Now I can't even charm an eighty-year-old butcher."

"A butcher?"

"My butcher used to throw in extras - special cuts and so on."

Bella giggled.

"It's nothing to laugh about. What happened? It's awful. I don't want to go out anymore. Me, who never liked staying home one single night! I can't be bothered to get dressed. Some days I don't. I mooch around the house all bloody day. John couldn't care less. He's losing it. And since I can't drink, people bore me."

Despite the three glasses of wine she'd drank like water, Serena had been warned by her doctor to lay off her daily champagne, which - she told Bella - was "not that difficult."

"You are obviously not an alcoholic," Bella replied.

"No." Serena shrugged. "And then we have the merry optimists like Jane Fonda, who maintains that eighty is the new sixty. Or those annoying people who insist we must enjoy each and every day. As if I set out to not do so. And there's that worst of all statements, 'You are only as old as you feel.' Well I don't feel thirty, or even forty. And how can I feel youthful when I hear about this friend or that one getting sick and dropping off their perch? And I can't stop thinking that my mother died at seventy-two. It was the biggest change in my life when my mother died. I still can't accept it. I never stop missing her. She died fifteen years ago and I still think, 'I must tell Mummy.'"

Bella agreed. "I wish my mother was alive, even though she irritated me so much. I feel guilty about that."

"Don't feel guilty," Serena instructed. "It's a mother's job to irritate her daughter. Thank God I couldn't have kids. They would have hated me."

Serena had dogs instead. Poodles of all sizes, and at least four or five at a time.

On occasion, Bella wondered how Jess would handle her not being around. Their relationship was extremely close. Bella imagined her fall from the perch would be hard on her daughter.

How would she fall off? Bella considered this often, and found the possibilities most unpleasant. No, more than that - she was downright terrified. Would cancer get her? Her heart? Or merely an accumulation of old-age ailments like her mother? Would she have an accidental death, or die during "The Big One" - the earthquake that those in the know assured all Californians was overdue?

Someone from City Hall once came to explain to the residents of The Portland what they should do in the advent of The Big One: don't stand in a doorway. Get under a table if possible. If you're in bed, roll off and stick as close to the bedside as you can. Be prepared with three days of water, food, pet food, flashlights, matches, candles, batteries, and cash on hand. But most importantly, medication.

After that, Bella bought a couple of decent flashlights, and she put a blanket in her car along with some heavy old boots which were recommended in case she had to walk through torn-up streets. She also stowed some dog food for Charlie, a large bottle of water, and six cans of sardines. Bella once heard that if a single food could keep you going the longest, that food was sardines: oil, protein and calcium - from the fish bones - in each tiny tin. She also included her antidepressants in the survival kit.

What if she succumbed to some noxious disease like the one that befell Karmen, the manicurist? She contracted bacterial meningitis and was dead in a few days. Bella and everyone else who'd come into contact with Karmen that week were contacted by the city's health authorities, who insisted they take an antibiotic - such was the risk of infection.

After lunch, Bella took Serena shopping. Serena was a world-class shopper. Whilst Serena tried on shoes and clothes, Bella's thoughts meandered down dark and dire alleys.

She peered at her newly manicured nails. Did dead flesh feel, or not feel, like nail cuttings? No feeling at all? She wondered if she should be cremated. Which was worse, being buried or burned? Bella pondered offering her body for science. Would her corpse be too worn-out for useful experiments?

"What do you think? Tell me honestly." Serena kept popping out of the change room.

"Honestly, I'm jealous you can fit into all those tight-fitting styles."

"Bella, pick something out for yourself. I want to buy you something."

"I don't want anything, and anyway, there's nothing here that would fit me. They don't have clothes my size anywhere down this street."

Finally, having spent what Bella deemed a fortune, Serena declared, "I'm pooped."

"Are you scared of dying?" Bella asked as she drove Serena back to The Beverly Hills Hotel.

"Oh Bella, don't be so morbid. We all die. If I lived here I'd be scared of going broke. Are you scared of dying?"

"Yes, I am. Not really of the dying part, but the fact of not being here anymore. I want to see my grandchildren marry and have children, and watch their children grow. I want to see how the world progresses."

"I'm glad I don't have children," Serena replied, "seeing the world is such a mess and getting worse by the second. And I'd have been a dreadful mother. I have no patience."

Serena turned her infertility into something positive and Bella admired that in her old friend. Despite acting as if she didn't care a hoot about anyone but herself, Serena was always a good friend to Bella.

"Bella *daaahling*," Serena drawled. "You know what we have to do? We have to remember the good times. Remember our trip to Swaziland when I was still married to Ron? That was fun!"

"It was fun until I found Guy with the Israeli singer. He was supposed to be playing tennis and, I have to say, that revelation spoiled my trip. He was awful in that way, as you well know."

"That's husbands, or should I say men. They're all the same. I can tell you because I've had quite a few of them. You know what? I think you're lucky to be single. You don't have to put up with the bullshit, which gets worse as they get older. My John had an affair with his second wife. Imagine that! I wished he would go blind. You know, men can go blind from those pills that keep their willies up. Quite frankly, I didn't think he had it in him. But I won't get anything much from John if we divorced. So I stayed. Better the devil you know. I'm not like you, I've never been alone."

Serena looked at her Ebel watch, one of her many elegant timepieces. This one had small diamonds around the bezel. "I'm so late. John will be furious."

"Ah," Bella thought, "the marital order of things."

Bella hugged Serena as they said their good-byes. An age or forever may pass before they saw each other again.

"Now, don't you go dropping off your perch just yet," were Serena's last words to Bella.

"I won't, not just yet."

Driving home, Bella felt oddly happy. She gazed at the way the palm trees silhouetted against the darkening sky, and was grateful she had amusing friends like Serena who were still defiantly holding on to their perches.

In one of her How-To books, Bella read that characters begin to have minds of their own. How true that was!

Beatrice Agadees, Winston's unmarried aunt who lived in the town of Nelspruit near A'marula, was turning out merely eccentric instead of the strong woman Bella wanted. Bella thus changed the kind of clothes Beatrice wore from bohemian to classic khakis. So much of what a person was perceived to be was on the outside. People were like packages: a great many wrapped in newsprint, others in fine tissue, a rare few in Tiffany-blue or Hermès-orange boxes. Beatrice had to get out of flowery prints and into a brown paper bag.

Rosy, who Bella wanted smart enough to recognize the signs of Winston's devious nature, was turning out fragile and unable to cope with anything except being a gracious hostess to the endless guests who came to A'marula.

Rosy had to give up on her art/pottery, though Bella still could not decide which one.

She reached for some dark chocolate with salt. Bella promised herself only four pieces, but she ate the entire bar before going to bed where, after hours of watching TED Talks, she struggled to fall asleep. When she finally succeeded, Bella dreamt about being unable to remember where she'd parked her car. It was a recurrent dream. Not quite a nightmare, but disquieting, nevertheless.

Chapter 21 - Breaking Out

"Keep going in any direction."

Perhaps the unseasonably warm December weather was the reason, or the new moon? Or maybe Bella so desperately wanted to break out of her routine that she accepted an invite from her French-born friend Claudette to join her, her husband, Marc, and her son, Vidal, in a game of *Pétanque*.

Bella almost cancelled the arrangement - she didn't enjoy playing sports, and was hopeless at ball games of any kind - but she was pleased she ended up going. Whilst she spoke only a few words of bad French - despite lessons at The Alliance Française for a couple of years - she enjoyed practicing her meager language skills. She almost felt as if she was in another country at the *Pétanque* court, which was oddly located at the all-American Rancho Park. Los Angeles' famed diversity never ceased to astonish Bella.

The players were mostly French. No surprise, as the game - throwing hollow metal balls to hit a target ball - was played in villages all over Provence. Marc and Vidal, most patiently, taught her how to play.

Bella had a good time and resolved to join the group the following week. She'd been seeking something different to do, and decided the universe had presented this particular opportunity.

"It's much better for you than sitting in front of the TV," Marc said.

"What makes you think I sit in front of the TV?" Bella inquired. Ironically, by the time the following weekend came around,

Bella's enthusiasm for the game had waned. Moreover, she was delighted that the cold-and-cloudy winter weather she adored had finally showed up. The day was perfect for lying in bed and binge watching *The Newsroom,* a TV drama that justifiably castigated the networks for their abysmal reporting of the news. Anyway, with the rain, there'd surely be no *Pétanque.*

Bella was also happy that Sven was away. He always took off during the holidays to visit his family, who lived in Florida. She could relax and sleep in, and though she promised Sven she'd work out without him, she knew she wouldn't be that disciplined.

There was a time when she actually exercised even when Sven was out of town, but she'd long given that up. Now, she treated Sven's absences as a holiday for her body, and she lay in bed, luxuriating and taking more time than usual to read the *Los Angeles Times* and crack the Sudoku puzzle.

After Sven returned, and when Bella got down to the gym, Norman was - thankfully - finished walking on the treadmill, so she didn't even have to make a pretense of conversation.

She wasn't in the mood to talk to anyone, nor watch the TV Norman had left on Fox. She switched it off with a flourish, as if to point out what a right-wing fool he was. Bella put in her earphones, turned up Herb Alpert, and allowed herself to drift...

She was thirty-five and dancing with Tommy Stanton to Herb Alpert's music on the tiny dance floor at Annabel's in London. Bella loved Tommy that night, which had more to do with the music than with Tommy. She didn't want him to leave his wife, not that he'd ever mentioned doing that. Bella believed she had the best of him: lunch at least twice a week at one of Tommy's favorite restaurants, where the waiters knew him, and the occasional dinner. Bella was thus left to fly, or rather flutter, and live a life that she found, at the time, to be fun.

She recalled those chaotic days in London. Newly divorced, with two young children, she was - in retrospect - lost. In order to fit in with the fast crowd she'd been introduced to by her best friend at the time, Suzie Crawford, Bella began to drink more and more.

Bella increased the incline on the treadmill.

Thankfully alone, Bella allowed her tears to flow freely before Sven arrived. By the time her session with Sven was over, her tears were long dried. Any pain she felt was from squats.

Then Sven's new client arrived.

Bella had seen Harriet Gebhart, but she did not know her. Sven met her as he passed through the lobby of The Portland. She wanted to be in good shape for her pending vacation.

Harriet turned out to be overbearing and always arrived before Bella's time was over to do her cardio. There was nothing Harriet had not done better, bought cheaper, or seen more of. She wanted to be Bella's friend. Bella did not want that. Even Sven, who by nature was easygoing and tolerant - he had to be, considering his self-absorbed and entitled clientele - told Bella, "You will not like being her friend." Bella needed no such warning.

"I am going to Antarctica on a cruise." Harriet danced into the gym wearing knee-length purple shorts and a white T-shirt emblazoned with a large, sequined red heart. This was, perhaps, a fun outfit for someone, but on enormous-breasted Harriet - who was probably around Bella's age - it looked silly.

"I'm sharing a cabin; it's the first time I've ever shared."

Bella felt sorry for whoever had to share a cabin with that boastful woman. Harriet kept telling Bella how she loved young men and was able to have so many of them. "You should try it," Harriet suggested, with a lascivious grin.

Bella could think of little worse than screwing a slew of younger men, except sharing a cabin on a cruise ship all the way to Antarctica with Harriet.

169

When Harriet returned from her trip, she was glowing.

"Oh, I had the best time. It's the way to find a man. You have to go!"

Bella had never once complained to Harriet about not being able to find a man. Nor had she asked Harriet how she managed to have a choice of young men. Bella tried to avoid any conversation with Harriet.

"She's not your type," Sven again warned Bella after she was invited to a party at Harriet's condo.

"I know that."

Bella couldn't fathom why some women presumed that all single women were desperate not to be so. This outrage was akin to men, when they found a woman disagreeable, declaring, "She needs a good fuck."

The next time Bella saw Harriet in the gym, her youthful catch was with her. He was patently a fish out of water, but he was affable. Sven told Bella, "The boy drinks like a fish." He also told Bella that he thought Harriet might be taking drugs. She was up one day, and down the next. She was agreeable, and then argumentative. "I think she's bipolar," Bella assessed.

Harriet put her arm around her man's neck, and staring at Bella announced, "Just go on a trip. Go on, take the plunge and go."

Being both polite and kind, Bella said, "I'm so glad you've found happiness." God had done at least one thing well when he designed thoughts to be invisible.

Bella bade Sven and Harriet and her man farewell. "Watch out for melting glaciers," she said, and pranced up to her condo with relief.

Bella took a shower in her gorgeous new shower cubicle. She dressed and applied her makeup, as she always did. Bella was never sloppy. She knew that when she caught sight of herself in a mirror and she looked bad, she felt bad.

Then, wearing new dark-blue jeans she'd bought at Nordstrom - labeled "Not Your Daughter's Jeans" or NYDJ because the waistband was at the waist and not below the navel - a soft cotton shirt, a small kerchief around her neck for a bit of colour (Bella adored scarves), and earrings, Bella went to the movies on her own, the way she preferred it.

Thankfully, Harriet soon changed her time with Sven so that Bella no longer had to see her. A couple of months later, Sven informed Bella that Harriet had sent her boyfriend off to a rehab in Arizona, sure that it would help him stop drinking. After that didn't work, she kicked him out.

When Bella next saw Harriet in the foyer, Harriet said, "I'm going on a cruise. You should come with me."

"Where are you going?"

"This time I'm off to Russia. I might find a better class of men on this trip. It's more expensive."

"Well, I hope you do," Bella said. "I wish you the best of luck."

Bella was sincere. She felt sad for Harriet, who seemed to pin her worth not only on the quality but the quantity of the men she could collect.

When Bella next bumped into Harriet, the adventuress said with great gusto, "I've given up on men. They're not the be-all and end-all."

Bella quipped, "You can live quite happily without one. I do."

"Oh no, I'm not alone! I'm in love with the most wonderful woman. I don't know what took me so long to discover that I'm gay. Maybe you're gay, too. That makes sense, since you haven't been with a man for ages."

"What makes you think that?"

At that very moment Sven arrived and Bella, again wishing Harriet the best of luck, left to go into the gym.

Bella told Sven the news. "I hope they live happily ever after."

But Bella never found out whether that happened, for soon after, Harriet moved from The Portland. She was a renter and did not own the condo.

When Bella spied Harriet at the supermarket some months

later, both women pretended they did not see each other.

Bella fleshed out some supporting characters.

Jacob Muller owns the land adjacent to A'marula. He is one of those ruddy men of the earth with leathery skin, wiry, and gruff. He is a confirmed bachelor and lives with his sick mother.

Dora is the Tsonga woman who takes care of Jacob's sick mother, but at the same time is also Jacob's secret lover, and has been for many years.

For decades, The Immorality Act banned sex between whites and nonwhites, including Indians and what were called "Coloureds." Bella found it hard to imagine that policemen actually went around snooping and arresting sexually nonconforming suspects: checking semen on sheets was South African detective work!

When Bella was at university, her mother had a maid named Patty, who was arrested with an Australian in a hotel room. Bella, being an incensed liberal-arts student, went to visit Patty in jail at "The Fort," colloquially named for its stone, fortlike appearance, and is now the seat of the new South Africa's Constitutional Court. The second time Bella went, Patty had been discharged. The apartheid government did not want to upset Australia. Patty never returned to work. Bella didn't know what happened to Patty until about four years later, whilst having a drink at the bar of the Carlton Hotel, she was greeted by a shriek. "Miss Bella!" And there was Patty, draped on the arm of a Japanese businessman.

"I can see you're doing well," Bella laughed. "Be careful."

"I will, Miss Bella. Don't worry about me."

Chapter 22 -
A Big Pain
"Water can both sustain and sink a ship."

"Better the devil you know." Bella remembered her mother's words when Guy and Wife Number Two were contemplating divorce. Bella had become accustomed to Wife Number Two, and seeing as many people found her snotty and condescending, Bella felt, if not younger or more beautiful, a more genuine person.

There were times Bella handled Guy's second marriage well. She could almost completely anaesthetize the lacerations that splintered in her heart every time she attended Jewish holiday feasts or Thanksgiving dinners or certain other family events like birthdays at Guy and Wife Number Two's sprawling house in Brentwood.

Bella found herself truly fond of Haley - Guy's daughter with Wife Number Two - who was but six years older than Bella's granddaughter, Chloe. Haley treated Chloe sweetly, and Chloe adored her.

Greta could not fathom how Bella managed the relationship. "I don't know how you do it."

"I don't, either."

Bella's therapist explained: "Guy is still the man in your life. Though I have to admit, your connection with him is one of the most unusual I've ever encountered."

That idea contributed towards Bella's contentment. "I have a man, but I don't have to be with him." The arrangement made sense to her, if not to anyone else.

But now Guy was with Irina: the mongrel, a European mélange, a child. And, even worse, she was the same age as Jessica.

When Bella complained to Sven about how young Irina was, Sven asked, "How old is Guy?"

"Seventy-three."

"Halve his age," Sven instructed.

"Thirty-six."

"Now add ten. How old is the girl?"

"Forty-six, same age as Jess."

"So she's the perfect age for him."

Using the same formula, Sven, who was forty-two, worked out the appropriate age for his woman: "A woman of thirty-one is perfect for me."

"I hate you!" Bella cried. "I hate all you men."

"No, you don't," Sven laughed.

"I do," Bella declared as she continued with stomach crunches. "I hate the way men my age discard women our age."

"Not all men. You told me about a man who wanted to take you to dinner. You discarded him."

"Not because of his age. He was not attractive to me. And you know what Sven? I can understand why men prefer younger women."

Sven, usually with something uplifting to say, kept quiet.

"Young women look up to older men. They treat them with adoration, with the same unconditional acceptance puppies treat their new owners. Usually the older man has money, which makes him even more appealing."

Sven didn't like talking about women and money. He'd been told once that the earnings of a trainer were not sufficient to attract a mate, and so he changed the subject. "Were you so happy when you were younger?"

"No."

Bella surprised herself at how quickly she answered, and she pondered this paradox for a long time afterwards.

When Guy called Bella two weeks later to invite her and Jess to see one of his newly acquired paintings by an artist he liked, Chen, Bella suspected that Irina would be there, too. She knew Guy so well. He wanted her approval of his new lady, even though he surely knew Bella wouldn't be giving it.

"Come inside and meet Irina."

Guy, as usual, appeared like the quintessential rich older man dressed for a wintery Sunday afternoon: taupe cords, a hand-tailored pale mauve shirt, taupe suede loafers, deep-mauve cashmere socks, an interesting brown leather belt, and a tan. He also seemed nauseatingly pleased with himself. Bella grimaced. She also gave herself a pat on the back for being correct about the Irina ambush, and for being smart enough to have washed her hair and for attempting to shine in new dark-blue denim jeans, a pale lilac silk shirt - lilac was Bella's best colour - and a matching pashmina. Bella and Guy presented as colour coordinated. Their mutual colour choice happened frequently, and friends and family commented on how uncanny this was.

Bella's eagle eyes assessed Irina. Thin. Fine, stringy blonde hair. Shapely legs. A nose, obviously done but not that well, which nevertheless made her appear prettier than she would have been without the uplift. No children. She could devote all her attention to Guy.

Bella wondered, "What can this young woman ever truly know about him? I understand this man, with all his personal assets and faults. I have been witness to most of his life, long before he climbed his way out of the impoverished neighborhood where he grew up. I have cheered him every step of the way, even when another woman was sharing his bed."

Despite her constant smile and odd, tinny laugh, Irina was obviously - and understandably - nervous. At a most inopportune moment in the conversation she asked Bella, "Can you please tell me, what are your interests?"

For a moment, Bella was stumped.

"I'd have to look them up on my Facebook," she joked, but her wit didn't register with Irina.

All in all, Bella was proud how well she handled the meeting. She chatted to Guy about people they both knew, with Irina glancing from her to Guy as if she was trying to take in a tennis rally. She giggled, swished her fine hair, and changed position - crossing her legs, uncrossing them, and moving her arms this way and that.

Bella was simultaneously pained to note how Guy and Irina, sitting at each end of a long sofa, were nonetheless joined by a wave of palpable adoration.

The thrill of a new love. A frisson of glee flitted into Bella's brain when she remembered how loudly Guy snored. Much older now, this had to be worse. Bella knew that in order to get a decent night's sleep, Wife Number Two sometimes slept in what she called "my little studio." The studio was where she pretended to be a high-end children's-clothing designer, which was - like jewelry design - amongst the much-favored professions of rich wives desirous of a so-called career.

When Bella got home, she took Charlie for a walk. Nicole came out to join them.

"You look beautiful, but so sad."

Bella began to cry, just a bit. She told Nicole about the meeting.

"You should have, like, ignored her. Or asked what she was doing with an old man. Like, for his money, of course."

Nicole adored Bella and couldn't bear to see her in pain, but she was not mature enough to understand restraint. When Charlie's walk was over, Bella called her friend Fiona in Dallas.

Fiona was helpful with certain matters of the heart. She had experienced much tragedy in her life. She lost her husband, Duncan, to drugs a couple of years previously. He was found dead at Caesar's Palace in Las Vegas, where he'd taken one of his hooker drug dealers for the weekend. Fiona had grown used to Duncan disappearing and then returning, promising love, before running off with other women. The last few years of their marriage had been awful, and Bella spent endless hours helping Fiona search for

Duncan everywhere from downtown alleyways to fancy hotel bars when Fiona lived in Los Angeles.

"Life's easier for me since Duncan died," Fiona admitted. "It's so utterly final. I would have hated to know about all the other women he would have been with if we only split up. I totally understand how you feel. You had to deal with that awful Wife Number Two, and now this child. I think it bothers you to be ashamed of feeling as jealous as you do. But you shouldn't. You're human, and once you love someone, you always will."

Fiona always knew how to say the most comforting thing. Shelly would never have understood; once she left a man, she was over him. Shelly lacked deep feelings. Greta had never been married. She understood pain, but she never understood why Bella continued to be part of Guy's family once they were divorced. "You're punishing yourself," Greta said again and again, and though she was partly correct, Bella could not quite make her recognize that having children with a man meant being forever tied to him. Greta, having long broken all ties to her family - whom she told Bella were not worth knowing - could not comprehend Guy's importance.

Family. That was the key reason for Bella's tangled relationship with Guy. But there was also another reason: Guy wanted her in his life, too.

Talking to Fiona was just the right medicine. Bella felt vindicated and supported. She thought how lucky she was to have friends like Fiona, Greta, and Shelly - and Nicole, too. And she thought of Guy, and how lucky she was to be able to love him in her way and not have to deal with the things she didn't like about him, which was why she'd divorced him in the first place.

Bella wrote, and rewrote, and rewrote as her story progressed.

Winston and Rosy settle down, spending most of their time at A'marula. Rosy loves the place, and wants to have a baby.

Winston spends more and more time away from A'marula in Johannesburg and Cape Town, where he still has a home. He lives the fast life and is not faithful.

Rosy is becoming disenchanted with Winston's absences. She begins to suspect that when he is at A'marula, something is going on between him and Lena.

Lena, silly girl, is in love with Winston.

Brown knows this, and warns his daughter that no good will come of it.

Beatrice, always observant, notices everything.

The story was clear in Bella's head, but getting the words written down using the constraints of Final Draft was proving to be exceedingly difficult. The screenwriting books said, "Show the action, don't explain." How in the hell was she going to show all the explosive emotions that everyone was feeling?

At dinner Greta inquired, "How's the script going?"

Bella truthfully replied, "I am learning a lot about South Africa."

Greta replied, "Well, I'm learning a lot about Bernie."

Bernie was Greta's latest. He wasn't married, which was a plus. He had no money and was in the music business, which was a minus. He'd also been married three times. He had a son who didn't talk to him. His daughter was a successful movie producer.

"You haven't told me one admirable thing about him," Bella pointed out. "He must be good in bed."

Greta smiled. "He's very sophisticated." She knew Bella appreciated sophistication.

"So what's he doing now? You said he was in the music business?"

"He's writing a screenplay. Like you."

❧·❧

Chapter 23 - Thin

"Eat only what you can fit on a saucer."

Bella had not seen her friend Tina Kohn for more than two years. This was not because Bella didn't want to see her, but because Tina, after her accident, became a recluse and didn't want to see anyone. Not even Bella, whom Tina adored.

Bella missed Tina. There were particular things she could only talk about with her. Tina understood Bella's relationship with Guy, and why she stayed emotionally connected after the legal connections were severed. Tina also once had a drinking problem and was now sober. She had an appreciation of the absurd, which Bella found refreshing. You couldn't faze Tina Kohn.

Bella was a good friend, and totally accepted Tina's need to exclude herself from frequent contact. Bella occasionally sent Tina e-mails, and was not hurt when they were ignored. When Bella bumped into Tina's husband, she merely told him to send Tina her love.

Tina's life had been hard for a long time. Her adult daughter was sick with a rare blood disorder, and her husband was having one of his serial affairs. Then a drunken woman ran onto Wilshire Boulevard directly into Tina's car. The woman was instantly killed, Tina's arm was broken, and her neck was damaged sufficiently enough to require surgery. She was so traumatized she decided to retreat from the world, at least for a time. Who could blame her?

"I still see the woman's face smashed against my windshield, with blood smeared. I can't get that picture out of my mind," she'd told Bella just after the accident.

So it was out of the blue when Bella finally received a call from Tina. "I'd love to see you."

When Bella agreed to visit the following day, Tina warned, "Don't be frightened, I look like a skeleton." She added, "I'll make lunch for you."

Bella fully expected Tina to cancel, as she'd done before, but she didn't. Thus Bella made her way to Tina's Spanish-style cottage in Cheviot Hills as promised. When Bella rang the bell and there was no reply, she wondered whether Tina decided not to answer. But eventually she did, and there Tina was - as she said - thin.

"Oh my God, I didn't think you'd come," Tina said. "Don't look at me, I just got up. I haven't showered or even brushed my teeth. Come in, sit down. I'll be with you in a minute."

Though Tina didn't give Bella much time, Bella's eagle eyes took in a gaunt person in a long black T-shirt, with pin-stick legs and arms, and a solid sweep of straight, almost-black hair, with bangs over cloudy blue eyes.

Tina's "minute" took about half an hour. Bella leafed through a pile of classics, illustrated in comic-book form, set out on the coffee table. She paged through *Romeo and Juliet* and after that *Les Misérables*. The comic books, as well as a collection of vintage teddy bears piled on the sofa, made Bella smile in acknowledgment of just why she adored her old friend.

Bella checked her watch. Perhaps Tina had a change of heart and would not come out of her bedroom? Bella decided to give her five more minutes before she'd quietly leave. But then Tina showed up, bathed and dressed. She looked fabulously emaciated.

Tina said her weight loss was the result of some unknown physiological problem that prevented food from staying in her system. "When I eat, it just passes through me."

"I'd like that to happen to me," Bella said, admiring Tina's lank legs encased in tight, turquoise jeans. "Your legs are amazing!"

"The best thing about being this weight," Tina said, "is that I can buy cheap clothes and they still look good."

A skinny, three-quarter-sleeved white T-shirt - Bella couldn't decide whether it was cheap or expensive - hugged Tina's narrow frame, and the scooped neckline showed off her bony shoulders.

"Damn it, Tina, your clavicles show," Bella said.

"But what about my hands and neck? They don't look pretty being so thin."

Bella peered at her own hands. They were fat. She had a manicure the day before and her nails were perfect, but her fingers were now too thick for most of her rings - she hadn't bothered to stretch them except the two she wore every day. One on the middle finger of each hand: a diamond ring from her maternal grandmother and an opal her mother gave her for her twenty-first birthday.

Though Tina invited Bella for lunch, there was nothing prepared. When Bella admitted she'd had nothing to eat - she never ate breakfast - Tina insisted on making Bella a sandwich. Though Tina's weight might indicate an empty refrigerator, the fridge was well stocked. At least Tina's husband wasn't starving, Bella observed, as Tina fixed a cheese, tomato, and avocado sandwich whilst giving Bella the choice of ham, chicken, turkey, or even a bowl of homemade vegetable soup.

"What about you?"

"I'm not hungry. I'll have something a bit later. I can eat anything I like. It all goes through me," Tina mentioned again. "It's not so nice, you know."

Bella didn't quite believe Tina, for she remembered the satisfaction of being skinny. Bella had shrunk down a few times in her adult life. Once after she divorced her brief mistake of a second husband, Phillip - the one who turned out to be gay.

More recently, Bella lost weight when she developed the horrible affliction, Tinnitus, which plummeted her into a severe depression. The ringing of Tinnitus began one awful February morning. Bella then endured nine months of hell: doctors, audiologists, psychiatrists, behavioral therapists, meditation, and helpful noise machines to distract her from the sounds that never left her brain. But slowly, very slowly, the purely internal sounds finally left her. And when they did, the pounds appeared again. As slowly and as surely as the departing Tinnitus, Bella's weight rebounded, until she was even heavier than she was before the Tinnitus began. She was really not that fat, but by LA standards, where sizes began at zero, Bella was obese. So, as a chastened warrior - defeated in her battle against becoming larger than size twelve - Bella went back to purchasing clothes from the bleak battlefield at the back of department stores, where sizes Large, Extra Large, and upwards were assembled in segregated defeat.

After Bella left Tina, she felt fatter than ever. Her brand-new jeans, which did as they were advertised to do - make her appear one size smaller - felt so constricting she couldn't wait to take them off. Her bra began to chafe a refrain: "You are fat." Her shoulders, under her long-sleeved, V-neck sweater, felt so heavy that they joined the bra's chorus: "Fat, fat, fat." She frowned at the way her middle finger puffed on either side of her rings: "Fat, fat, fat!"

As if the ether knew how she felt, the very next day Bella received a whole bunch of e-mails about weight-reducing methods like Raspberry Ketones and Green Coffee Beans. She realized that these were targeted to her since a couple of weeks prior she bought a particular vitamin B complex with some "perfectly safe" ingredient added to take away her appetite. After only one dose, she began to shake. She took one more dose, which had the same effect, and then threw the bottle away.

Bella found herself wandering around the Internet, seeking up ever-more infallible, thin-inducing products: Sensa crystals, Garcinia Cambogia (from a pumpkin-shaped fruit that grows Indonesia), plus a variety of weird products lauded by bona fide doctors who must have a stake in their sales.

She knew full well that the healthiest way to lose weight was to eat less, and she resolved to do just that for the hundredth time, whilst bemoaning how unfair life was that fat and years became added simultaneously. Why did older people need the fat? There had to be an evolutionary reason. To be noticeably thinner, she'd need to lose so much weight that she'd have to get sick, like Tina; or be almost suicidal, like she was with the Tinnitus.

As Bella undressed and prepared for bed, she sang, "You have left me, my years have gone, you have added to me, my fat has come."

She thought of silly diet names: Bella's Belly-Up Diet, Bella's Breathe-and-Get-Over-It Diet, and Meditate and Diet: How To Do It. She giggled. The antidote to being upset at just about anything that disturbed her was to be able to laugh at herself, and Bella suddenly found herself remembering her all-time giggle maker: doing the twist, naked, in front of the bathroom mirror. So, in her beautifully renovated bathroom, stark naked, she did the twist and burst out laughing.

When she got into bed, instead of eating a full bar of those divine squares of Lindt chocolate whilst watching Stephen Colbert, which she did most nights, Bella decided to only have half. When she woke up the next morning, she felt both happier and thinner.

Another side character, and more research.

Hannes de Villiers is the local taxidermist to whom Winston brought the huge male lion, 'Big Baas,' that he shot before he murdered his father and mother. Winston wanted a suitable trophy of his life-changing kill. Hannes takes pride in his work. He has impressive examples all over his large thatched-roof studio in Nelspruit.

Beatrice does not approve of anything to do with hunting, and takes every opportunity to let Hannes know how she feels. Seeing as they live in the same small town, this happens quite often.

Bella researched hunting animals and animal trophies. One Internet site offered a leopard hunt. To bag one, a dead impala was hung on a conspicuous branch to lure a leopard to come out and feed.

Bella simply could not conceive why people shot animals for sport. Sport! How could they call big-game hunting a sport, when the animal has no chance against an automatic rifle? She could not relate to the psyche of people who'd shoot a leopard, especially seeing that the rare animal is facing extinction.

On various sites, hunters - young and old, male and female - posed proudly with their dead animals. One particularly odious photograph showed a leather-skinned woman of around forty, rifle at her side, grinning over the carcass of a magnificent, dark-maned male lion. She had bowling-ball boobs and a tan that showed off her capped teeth. Bella got so mad, she posted the picture on her Facebook page and the appalling picture went viral.

As if innocently selling washing machines, hunting-expedition companies advertised enticing deals: Father-Son Special; Five-Animals-Guaranteed Special, and Honeymoon Hunts.

Prices varied. One hunting company offered $28,500 for a maned lion, trophy included. A lioness was much cheaper at $7,000. For a white rhino, which Bella knew to be almost extinct, Bella found an offer of $65,000. For a Cape buffalo: $14,500. Warthogs went for a mere $300.

Wanting to express her outrage, Bella wrote an e-mail to Frik Fleisher's Hunting Safaris, one of the larger operations.

Their polite reply claimed:

While we understand your concerns, hunters do more than any other group to make sure endangered animals such as the leopard do not go extinct. It is precisely due to hunting that African wildlife will survive. We also employ many local people, who could not otherwise find jobs.

She replied to this by asking what percentage of a dead leopard went to the locals and how much to Fleisher's. She didn't expect or receive a reply, but they'd made her at least consider their perspective. She read differing opinions, pro and against hunting, and eventually concluded that those pro were delusional. There was no rational view that killing a species would save it. Like going to war to make peace.

Bella researched taxidermy, too, because she wanted to include scenes in which Winston had Big Baas's head stuffed and mounted.

Every company claimed they were "the best" and made "the most lifelike" trophies. Hunters could choose from full, shoulder, or pedestal mounts. One taxidermist offered to make a dead zebra into an ottoman. A shoulder-mounted elephant would set a hunter back $7,500; a full elephant, $68,000. Bella wondered who on earth would want an elephant mount, full or shoulder.

All this research directed Bella to the pressing issue of animal cruelty. She signed online petitions, which she passed on to Shelly, Nicole, and Greta, as well as any other friends who might pay attention.

In Bella's World, orcas would never be cruelly captured and kept in restricted tanks - tantamount to torture - for the amusement of humans. Elephants would be banned from circuses. For those monsters that killed elephants for their tusks - along with anyone who bought the ivory - she'd have all their teeth pulled out. For the so-called blood sports - dog-, bull-, and cockfighting - the punishment would be slow and painful death. And Bella didn't even support the death penalty.

However, the very worst was the way animals were treated in factory farms. After Bella saw an image of the living conditions of cows on corporate dairy farms, she stopped eating meat and chicken, and started drinking only almond milk. She also announced to everyone she knew, after watching the brutality involved in the skinning of animals, that she would no longer buy leather shoes or bags.

To Bella, Greta said, "Fake leather is cheap and nasty looking, but I understand that you want to be more humane." To herself Greta said, "There she goes again, holier-than-thou Bella."

Nicole said, "Awesome."

Shelly said, "Guess I won't be buying you a Gucci bag for your birthday."

❧·❧

Chapter 24 -
Musing

*"How odd it is that we are so similar
and so unique."*

Bella adored her primary physician, Dr. Fehrer.

Ernest Fehrer was not a typical doctor. He seemed to care little about money; he cared about his patients. When Bella needed to see him, which was when she came down with The Fear - her dread of cancer - Dr. Fehrer's equally wonderful secretary, Anne, always managed to fit Bella in for an appointment, usually the very same day.

Dr. Fehrer didn't make Bella feel like a hypochondriac when she believed her heart was beating abnormally. He gave her a contraption to monitor her heartbeat, and they discovered together that her palpitations were caused by a day of intensive coffee drinking.

Dr. Fehrer made jam and brought his patients tiny jars of his homemade concoctions, which were so delicious that Bella told him, "You could make a fortune on these jams if you ever stopped doctoring; though I hope you never do, as I never want to have to find another doctor."

Recently, Dr. Fehrer resolved to memorize every one of Shakespeare's soliloquies. When Bella saw him for her annual checkup, Dr. Fehrer boasted, "I have already committed twelve of the most well-known to memory. Which one would you like me to recite?"

Bella thought for a moment, and made her choice. "*Richard III.*"

Bella relished demonstrating that her knowledge of Shakespeare went beyond "*Friends, Romans, countrymen*" and "*Romeo, Romeo!*

Wherefore art thou Romeo?'

Without further ado, Dr. Fehrer stepped to the back of the examination room as if the small, sterile space was center stage at The Old Vic. Eyes glittering behind his frameless spectacles, he launched into the monologue. *"Now is the winter of our discontent, made glorious summer by this son of York..."*

Done with that, Dr. Fehrer asked Bella to pick another. This time she left the choice up to him. He launched into *Hamlet* with such bravura that she saw him as a man of passion, instead of the sympathetic, calm, and scholarly Dr. Fehrer she'd known for years.

"He didn't just recite; he orated. I almost fell in love with him," Bella told Shelly.

"I'm seeing him for a checkup next week. I'll ask him to recite something for me."

In Shelly's case, Dr. Fehrer performed *The Merchant of Venice*, and gave her two jars of preserves. "I think he's got a crush on me," she remarked.

Shelly liked to believe many unsuitable men had a crush on her. She deduced that Marco, one of the part-time valets at The Portland, was smitten after he offered compliments on her haircut, which he said made her look much younger. When model-handsome hairdresser Cusco invited Shelly to accompany him to an art-show opening - because his boyfriend was out of town - she was convinced Marco was bisexual. Shelly knew her neighbor Mr. Fay was infatuated with her, as was her accountant.

Shelly held no reservations about her physical allure. She wore high-heeled shoes, her hair teased and tousled, and her breasts pushed out with a confidence that Bella found admirable, and even charming. Thus it was with trepidation that Bella decided to tell Shelly to stop wearing the black leggings she often wore because they showed off her crotch.

Bella started with a little beating about the bush, but eventually came right out and said the words: "Those tights are too tight, down there, if you know what I mean."

"Why didn't you tell me before? You know, Bella, I'm a big girl. I can take criticism. If you see I've got a boogie in my nose, I want you to tell me. I'd tell you, too. Friends do that."

Bella felt fortunate that she possessed the ability to make good friends. She was not one of those women who maintained, "I get on better with men," as if women were lesser company, and their conversations and concerns were not worthy of discussion. "We can be aware of the world and all its troubles, and still care about the colour of a lipstick," she said.

For years Bella frequented Bettina's, an upmarket nail salon that catered to mostly well-off, older women. Many had been clients for so long they arrived with caregivers.

The ladies were of a type - married or richly divorced; faces lifted and peeled into baby-pink wax; casually dressed with a fine gold bracelet or necklace, a decent handbag, and low-heeled shoes; and hair coloured to hide the grey. They were women who Bella believed to be comfortable with themselves and their position in life.

As Maria - from Vienna - attended to Bella's nails, she liked to close her eyes and eavesdrop on drifts of conversation: trips, events, who was sick or died, vitamins, husbands' illnesses or deaths, restaurants, and - always - opinions on movies and movie stars. Some of these women had known each other forever. They had history.

From time to time, Bella tried to join their conversation. She gave her assessment of a movie they were discussing, or added some snippet about a health product, after which they pointedly ignored her. Bella decided she wouldn't bother to be sociable and rather be a fly on the wall, which required no effort.

When she elected to try out Matrix - an artfully designed modern nail salon, newly opened and within walking distance from The Portland - the experience was totally different. At Matrix, Bella was at least twenty years older than the next client. Nobody talked, or even glanced, at anyone else. iPads and iPhones replaced chitchat.

Occasionally someone remarked on Charlie's good behavior. He was lying by the chair, beside Bella, as if in a coma. "My dog would never stay still like that," was the usual comment.

It was while at Matrix that Bella received a call from Lonni Blumberg.

Bella had known Lonni for decades. She and her husband Donny moved to Los Angeles around the same time she did. Bella never had much to do with Lonni when they lived in South Africa. Their friendship was solely based on them both relocating. They saw each other once a year, if that.

"Guess who I saw riding a bike when Don and I were in Carmel?" Lonni could not keep the delight from her high-pitched voice.

Bella didn't need to guess.

Lonni added, "He wasn't alone. She looked young enough to be his daughter."

Lonni was fishing. Bella refused to bite. She shrugged her shoulders as if she couldn't care less.

Lonni baited her line with a choice morsel. "He looks amazing."

Bella avoided the lure and agreed, "He's in good shape, for his age."

Bella made a mental note to unfriend Lonni Blumberg on Facebook when she got home. She switched off her phone, closed her eyes, and did three sets of Kegel exercises. The muscles of her pelvic floor were getting stronger, but Bella wondered whether this strength would truly help avoid incontinence? Joyce was afflicted when she was eighty. That will be in ten years! An icy pang pierced Bella's attempts at relaxation. "If I die in ten years, people will not say, 'Oh dear, how young she was.'" How mysterious it was, this process that gradually turned young flesh to old. How did the skin suddenly manufacture dark spots? That very day, Bella found a new one, on the bridge of her nose. She first thought the vague, brown smudge was makeup, or a tiny bruise, but upon closer inspection, yet another damned age spot revealed itself.

The Vietnamese pedicurist, Lu, began to massage her feet. Bella paid extra for this luxury. Ten minutes, ten dollars.

Her mind drifted to the painter Lucien Freud. She watched a program on his life the night before. He painted the naked body - old and young, male and female - in all sizes, even hugely fat. He painted his daughter, his lovers, and himself, as if the human body was a glorious landscape filled with mountains, ravines, crannies, fields, and pools. His vision was brutal and exquisite and completely original. Like Picasso, da Vinci, and Michelangelo, he was a creative genius; and death took him, as it did Einstein, Newton, and everyone who ever changed the world for the better. Bella found it oddly comforting that even people whose contributions were so enormous died like everyone else.

When Bella was around ten, she planned to be a famous painter, like Picasso. At twelve, she wanted to be a dress designer, like Dior. Then, for some reason, her dreams stopped. She fell in love with Guy, she had children, and she divorced. Her dreams changed form. They became wisps. Wisps became disappointments - some big, some small. Acceptance replaced the wisps. The way things were was good enough, most of the time.

With her nails newly gelled - she was persuaded to try the gel - Bella walked back to The Portland with Charlie. She saw Nicole as she arrived from work. Nicole complained - as she usually did - about how Manilla, a coworker who was having an affair with the Vice President of the company, was determined to show her up.

"I remember those office politics so well," Bella said. "Only I was the one having an affair with the boss." She added, "Mind you, only at one agency. We're still friends, or at least we would be if we ever bumped into each other."

Bella thought she was being subtle by pointing out how fortunate

Nicole was. Her job paid well. The office was nearby. She rarely worked overtime. But Bella's subtlety passed over Nicole, like a sudden gust of wind that failed to blow off the remaining leaves from the trees before winter set in.

"I didn't grow up wanting to be an assistant, booking models at an agency."

"What did you want to be?" Bella asked.

"I wanted to be a model. But I didn't get taller than five-four."

Shelly waved to Bella and Nicole from her black BMW.

"I'm off to meditation," Shelly shrieked.

Shelly was forever nagging Bella to come with her and learn to meditate.

"I meditate whilst I walk Charlie. I've told you a hundred times!"

This was true, for when Bella waited for Charlie to pee - which he wanted to do every few feet - she was there, in the present, not thinking of anything but fully aware of whatever was right in front of her: impossibly tall palms against a cerulean sky, or old-style scented roses when they were in season. She always stopped to smell a rose, testament to the saying.

Perhaps because she came from Africa, Bella noticed how little nature remained in urban Los Angeles: the noisy crows, which were as smart as six-year-old children; hummingbirds that made a tick-tick noise as they foraged amongst the hibiscus; spiderwebs that stretched across the tops of hedges; and the odd nervous squirrel.

At night, when she took Charlie for a last walk, she scanned the navy heavens in awe at the Mystery of Creation. The light-years that marked the distance of far-away stars, the wandering planets, the brightness of Venus, and the moon as it slid from hiding to full each month.

The only thing that disturbed Bella when she walked Charlie

were dog owners who pulled their leashes tight and declared, "My dog doesn't like other dogs."

"It's you who doesn't like other people," Bella informed one particularly obnoxious woman.

Bella finally agreed to accompany Shelly to a meditation session.

There were six other meditators plus the leader, Jograg, a young Indian with a beatific smile, who said, "You can call me Jo."

The room felt like a tomb. There were no windows and the walls were painted dark blue. The subdued chatter stopped as Jo put on meditation music and everyone, including Shelly, settled into the Lotus position. Bella could always touch her toes, which amazed people, but the Lotus was out of the question. She'd never been able to cross her legs like that, even as a child.

Jo offered an oddly shaped cushion. "This will help," he smiled.

"Now breathe in… and then breathe out," Jo intoned.

Bella could not get comfortable.

"You'll get used to it," Shelly whispered.

"Can't I lie down?"

Jo said, "You'll likely fall asleep if you lie down."

Bella thought it would be lovely to fall asleep to the soporific sounds of the gongs.

She got through the hour and even felt as if she had a few moments in that spiritual place, where Jo said she could go, once she was adept. Bella concentrated on the blue light Jo said she'd find with her eyes closed. When the hour was over, she assured Jo that she'd return, but she didn't.

Shelly said if Bella didn't like the class, she should meditate on her own. Hoping she might discover the well-being everyone said they got from the practice, Bella tried. She downloaded meditation music, and for one week sat on an upright chair, with her feet on the floor, and waited for the ten minutes to end. She was amazed by how tedious ten minutes felt when she was doing nothing other than focusing on breathing in and out, which Bella concluded she did all the time, whether she paid attention or not.

"Maybe my chakras are not where they should be," she told Shelly. "Maybe I don't even have chakras," she teased, ruffling Shelly's feathers.

"Everyone has them."

"How do you know? You can't see them like you can see a stomach."

Bella glanced at her stomach. Damn, it was getting larger! That made her remember the colonoscopy she was booked to have the following week, for no reason other than she'd reached the age when Dr. Fehrer thought such procedures were necessary.

Her whole body was cut-and-paste from now on. An old crown had to be replaced. A painful right elbow necessitated a shot of cortisone, plus twelve sessions of physiotherapy. A sore right knee, which Sven said would get better but it hadn't. Dr. Francine - Bella's chiropractor - went over the areas with one of her stainless-steel instruments, which hurt a lot and only helped a tiny bit. Her fingers were misshaped and arthritic, like those of Bella's grandmother-on-her-mother's-side. She ignored the pain and took Krill Oil, which Marina Painter - her great friend in South Africa who was almost a doctor she knew so much about health - said was helpful. She hoped the oil, extracted from tiny, shrimp-like crustaceans would work and not join the bottles of half-finished, highly promising cure-alls that languished at the back of her kitchen cupboard.

Bella's writing felt reinvigorated. She was moving along, slowly but surely, and already outlining the third act, which she thought would begin as Rosy prepared for houseguests: Winston's English friend, Charles Somerville, and Charles's American girlfriend, Kathy.

Charles found his niche running an art gallery specializing in African art and artifacts. He told only Rosy that he's planning to propose to Kathy whilst at A'marula. Winston hasn't been told, as he can't keep a secret. Rosy also had a secret: she's pregnant.

Rosy makes sure everything is perfect: the thatch-roofed guesthouse - with its locally fashioned, tree-branch bed - is dressed with white linen. There are toiletries for the outdoor shower and vases with flowers. There wasn't better to be found at a five-star safari camp.

Rosy has also made sure that the hide - a tree house–like enclosure overlooking the waterhole where the animals come down to drink - is cleaned up and filled with pillows and quilts. This is where Charles plans to propose.

Charles and Kathy arrive, and after a lazy lunch, Rosy drives them to the hide. The plan, which Winston is not aware of, is that Rosy will find an excuse and leave them alone, so Charles can propose. Winston thus thinks he has the late afternoon to himself.

From the hide, a procession of animals can be seen coming down to the water to drink: impala, zebra, giraffe, and finally two young male lions.

Bella imagined it would be cinematically dramatic to show the two young male lions expel an older male and take over the pride.

Many years ago, when she and the children went to Mala Mala with her mother, they'd witnessed this generational power struggle.

The Ranger explained, "Two young lions have already killed three of five cubs. Once all the cubs are dead, they'll attack the old male, who will be forced out. The lionesses will come into estrus almost immediately. The old male may be permitted to hang around for a while, but he'll have to fight the hyenas for the dregs of the kill. He won't last long."

They didn't actually see the last two cubs being killed, but they did see one young male walk into the reeds with a small body dangling in his jaws. This primal image of seemingly harsh ferocity was one Bella would never forget.

Bella didn't know which lions she pitied more: the tiny dead cubs, the old lion doomed to starvation, the young males who'd have to constantly defend their pride from other usurpers, or the females who - after failing to defend their young - had to submit to the new males. And then there was the lions' prey. She thought a world in which animals ate other animals was a big design flaw of God's, one that Bella could not get her head around. Not only animals, but insects, too. The savagery of insects was even worse.

One day, when Sven complained about how he thought one of his unfortunate paramours might have stolen his iPad, Bella replied, "If she was a black-widow spider, she would have eaten you whilst you were mating."

Sven didn't quite get the joke, but he told Bella that the mother of his adored, now three-year-old child and he were getting along much better since they parted.

Chapter 25 -
How Bella Got Famous
"Life is a series of accomplishments and
failures that begin with learning how to walk.."

At one of her first monthly Homeowners Meetings at The Portland, the Board demanded Bella remove the yellow umbrella on her patio and replace the sunshade with one either white or beige. She was defiant. "What do you have against colour? What's wrong with yellow, or blue or red for that matter? The world is full colour. The trees are green, the sky is blue, the sun is golden. I am not getting rid of it."

The Board passed a new rule, which to their chagrin they couldn't enforce retroactively: white or beige umbrellas only.

"We'll give you the money for a new umbrella," the Board President offered. Bella refused. She kept that yellow umbrella flying long after it wore out, just to show them.

The Board soon introduced another rule: dogs can't walk through the lobby. Dog owners could pick up their dogs, or else enter through the garage, which necessitated opening and closing the automatic garage door. Just for Charlie, this was a thrice-daily mechanical happening - that was six times opening and closing, whatever the weather - which amounted to an awful lot of wear and tear and a reckless overuse of electricity. The garage doors forever had to be fixed, and the mechanism frequently overhauled. Bella knew that the Stupid Dog Rule was probably to blame.

There were times Bella ignored the rule and walked Charlie through the lobby. He was always an angel; he never barked at other dogs and remained impervious to attacks from the Fellses' pair of Maltese terriers.

Charlie never peed anywhere inside, and if he was desperate, he went through the doggy door onto Bella's patio. Nobody Bella ever met showed any fear of Charlie. Not that Bella met many people in the lobby other than the valets. The building was not a hive of activity, being home to mostly retired people who had downsized from large homes. Some entitled residents could hardly believe the indignities they had to endure living in a condo, where they had to accommodate the desires of other homeowners.

When Mr. Fells moved in, he and his wife commanded that the Board unearth all the trees and ivy in the wide beds surrounding the building. "They brings rats," he declared. "They must be removed."

At the first Homeowners Meeting Mr. Fells attended he made an impassioned speech about the disgusting dangers of rats, and ivy's rodent-habitat appeal. By the next month's meeting, he discovered that the trees and ivy were staying. Fells began to shout and rage, which segued into a coughing attack so bad, Bella thought he might die mid-rant.

One afternoon, when Bella decided to walk Charlie into the lobby - seeing as the front door was open and she didn't need to ring to be buzzed in - she found Judi Gabor, one of the Board Members, holding her diminutive white more-or-less-poodle talking to the ever-patient Keisha.

In her high-pitched foreign accent - Bella knew Judi Gabor was from some South American country, but could never remember which one it was - she sniffed, "I thought we aren't allowed to walk dogs through the lobby."

"Dog?" Bella replied, "What dog?"

Judi Gabor glared at Bella, momentarily at a loss for words. Normally Judi Gabor - Bella never referred to her other than with her full name - could not stop talking. Bella strode to the elevator pulling Charlie, who clearly wanted to greet Judi Gabor's dog.

Bella recalled a scene like this from a very old movie, in which a wife walked in on her husband in bed with another woman. In shock, the wife slammed the door, and stomped out. By the time she re-entered her bedroom, the lady in question had been bundled out the window. "Where is that woman you were with?" the wife demanded.

"Woman? What woman?" Bella appreciated the unknown depths of her brain from whence she'd resuscitated that scene.

This episode compelled Bella to write a letter to the Board, which she'd planned to do for years. She pointed out the time had come for the No-Dog-In-The-Lobby rule to be scrapped. She exposed the ridiculous ritual of the garage doors opening and closing, citing the wear and tear as well as the waste of energy. She stated that if any dog became a nuisance, that particular dog could be Lobby-Banned.

Her words were plain and clear, her point was sharp, and so it came to pass at the next meeting, the Board saw sense and changed the rule. Strangely, Bella thought, they sent a copy of her persuasive letter to each and every resident of The Portland with their own letter explaining the decision to change the rules pertaining to dogs in the lobby.

Thus, Bella Mellman, long-time resident, became famous at The Portland.

For some weeks after her letter was distributed, Bella received fulsome congratulations from Portland residents about the wonderful thing she'd done, some even from homeowners who did not have dogs.

Little victories like this helped Bella quell those familiar feelings of worthlessness, which frequently flitted across her mind, like clouds on a mostly sunny day.

The screenwriting How-To books were very specific.

Well-written scripts usually incorporated an established structure. There were five Plot Points, eight Sequences, and specifically timed Beats, Acts, Midpoints, a Climax, and a Denouement. Bella wondered why scripts had to be so formulaic. Maybe that's why so many movies were predictable? This made Bella contemplate insects and their three-part bodies - head, thorax, and abdomen - which in turn made her think of biology classes, and then High School, where she also didn't go for rules. In her senior year, she was affectionately voted Class Captain by her peers, who knew how much she didn't like the regulations required for the position.

She wasn't actively rebellious but merely preferred doing things her way, in a way that made sense to her. She never understood why her mother wouldn't allow her to shave her legs until she was older, so one day she did. Joyce didn't even notice. Nor was Joyce aware Bella always turned back the grandfather clock - which chimed the hours - when she went out at night, so she had extra time. Bella found Joyce's idea of a curfew to be unfair. Joyce never noticed that, either.

But dammit, after reading more and more about writing a script, even Bella could see that her favorites all conformed to Classical Structure. And so she worked hard to construct *The Lions of A'marula.*

"I'm plodding along," she told Greta who was, most irritatingly, forever inquiring about her progress. And there was progress. The story, Plot Points and all, was taking shape.

With Charles, Kathy, and Rosy out of the house, guess who goes to see Winston? Lena, of course. And Winston has been expecting her, which is the reason he did not go to the hide.

Poor Brown. He knows what is going on, but is powerless to stop it.

Meanwhile, at the hide, Rosy's plan to leave Charles and Kathy alone is forced upon her earlier than anticipated, when she discovers a thin train of blood trickling down her thigh. Horrified, she knows this is an early miscarriage. She races the Land Rover back to the house.

Brown sees Rosy arrive, but there is nothing he can do to stop her going to her bedroom, where Winston and Lena are having hot sex. Rosy pauses at the bedroom door and listens, her disappointment about the lost pregnancy forgotten. She quietly opens the door. At first Winston and Lena don't notice her, but when they do...

Bella did not like sex in movies. She never felt comfortable sitting next to a stranger whilst people on the screen were busy humping away. And sex had become so graphic. And still so fake.

No, she would not show Winston and Lena actually screwing. Rosy would listen to grunts and moans as she waited by the closed door, which would say everything necessary.

When Rosy opens the door, the camera will focus on faces, not naked bodies. Showing the whole body was also popular. Nothing is hidden anymore. Bella did not like the trend one bit, even though she knew a human body was natural and shouldn't have to be shamefully hidden.

Bella's much older, distant English cousin Biddy Lovejoy once told Bella that she and her odious husband Roy were "naturalists." She explained that they go on naked vacations "at least three times a year."

"It's not about sex," Biddy claimed. "In fact, the experience is quite asexual. It's about freedom."

After learning that information, Bella, never saw them again when they came to South Africa on vacation; she always found some excuse to avoid them. Fortunately, when they came to America, Bella told them she would be out of town, and they gave Los Angeles a miss. So there would be no nudity in *The Lions of A'marula*, at least not in the screenplay.

Winston could grab a towel? Maybe Lena could be seen running, in deep shadow, down the corridor? There would be no breasts, no bottoms, no penises, and no glimpses of pubic hair. Bella couldn't believe that penises were now being shown in regular movies.

"Why not?" Jessica said. "Mom, it's a body. We all have them."

Hysterical, Rosy runs to the pool house and locks herself in. Winston rushes to her, attempting to persuade her that what she saw was not what it seemed. This denial further enrages Rosy. She screams, through the locked door, that Winston will pay dearly for his betrayal.

Out of the blue, Bella remembered Arlene Abbot, whose husband once called to inform Bella, "Your husband is having an affair with my wife." Guy and Bella had not been married for long.

Bella went crying to her friend Marina.

Mrs. Painter, Marina's mother, sat Bella down and said, "A leopard will not change his spots." The aphorism was a common one, and Bella never forgot it as Guy cheated again and again.

Guy was also unfaithful to Wife Number Two. He made hardly any effort to hide his indiscretions, but unlike Bella - who turned into a detective, going through Guy's pockets searching for hairs and so on - Wife Number Two made no effort to find him out. She went a more mercenary route and shopped. Bella heard that she spent tens of thousands on designer clothes.

Unsurprisingly, Guy's infidelity wasn't the reason for their divorce; it was more of an age thing. She wanted to fly, and Guy wanted to settle. They didn't like doing the same things. A divorce settlement would give Wife Number Two the wherewithal for a first-class takeoff.

As for Guy, the only reason he'd remain faithful to Irina would be because of diminishing testosterone levels, not any changing spots.

In the rapidly fading light, Winston sits silently on a pool lounger where he is able to see if, or when, Rosy opens the pool-house door.

Sunsets in the African bush are both magical and amazingly fast: day falls into night with a magnificent blaze of red orange that can take your breath away. Bella found it easy to visualize gorgeous shots of animals as the light quickly faded: impala gathering quietly, lions waking from their lazy day-sleep in the shade of a clump of Bushwillow, and the lace silhouettes of the Acacia Thornbush.

Meanwhile, back at the hide, Charles gets on his knees and proposes to Kathy.

Back in the staff compound, Brown berates a sobbing Lena. She packs some clothes in a carry bag and plans to leave A'marula when day breaks. Brown leaves her to her sad work.

It's almost dark when Rosy opens the pool-house door.

She does not see Winston, and with furious determination she marches towards the storeroom.

Winston follows her and watches, not alerting Rosy to his presence.

Inside the storeroom, Rosy props up a ladder to bring down a suitcase from a large shelf above an open window. The noise of a couple of cases tumbling to the floor is shocking. But what is more shocking is that she has disturbed the sleep of a Black Mamba, coiled behind one of the suitcases. The snake bites. It is one of a mated pair. The other is seen slithering down the trunk of a Marula tree outside the storeroom window. Brown notices the lone Mamba. He knows if one is around, another is nearby.

Bella knew this snake had to be deadly, and none was more feared than the highly aggressive Black Mamba. Its readiness to attack might be exaggerated, but when disturbed, a Mamba always attacks. During the mating season, Mambas are even more aggressive than usual. The Black Mamba's venom acts fast and is powerfully neurotoxic: death has been known to occur in twenty minutes. Two drops are fatal to humans and a bite can express more than twenty drops per fang. Most chilling, a Mamba doesn't hang post-strike, but withdraws and waits for the victim to die. Which is what happened to Rosy, though not in the obvious way.

Rosy knows the bite, if untreated immediately, will be fatal. As she watches the blood running down her arm, matching the sad trail down her thigh, she notices Winston, standing at the open door.

Winston inspects the bite, instructs Rosy not to move, and rushes off to - he says - fetch the antivenom kept in the main house's well-stocked box of emergency medical supplies.

Instead, he calmly takes the Range Rover and drives to the hide to pick up Charles and Kathy.

When they return, Rosy will be dead.

Winston will claim he doesn't know where Rosy was when he departed to bring Charles and Kathy back from the hide because night had fallen.

Whilst Brown did not witness what happened inside the storeroom, he did see Rosy go inside. He also saw Winston enter, and then leave to go pick up his friends. He remembers the female snake, which alerted him to a nearby male.

Brown can't be sure, but he suspects something is seriously amiss.

Chapter 26 -
Dark and Brooding

"If you can't be content with what you have received, be thankful for what you have escaped."

Unlike a lot of people who went on about how much they didn't like Christmas, Bella enjoyed all the Festive Times of the year. She loved sparkling lights and street decorations. Aside from buying Chloe ornaments, Bella always took her granddaughter to see the pretty displays along Wilshire, where they'd compare the merits of the exhibits at Saks, Neiman's, and Barneys.

Bella's holiday array along her hall table was worthy of a fine store. She plonked fake ivy, berries, and grapes around her collection of blue-and-white Japanese pottery, and hung wired angels from the lamps on either side. She decided to dispense with a tree since she didn't have space in front of any of the windows. Bella adored the way some people placed their trees that way, so those who passed by enjoyed them, too. Instead, she hung her accumulated ornaments from the two chandeliers in the dining area of her living room.

Jessica, as usual, hosted a lovely Christmas lunch. Bella was delighted that for once Ivan could come, as he didn't have to babysit Farrel Bootch in Hawaii, where the Bootch family owned a mansion on the Big Island. Farrel had come down with a bad flu and his Hawaii trip was postponed.

Guy and Irina were out of town, which made the luncheon more enjoyable for Bella, Jessica, and Ivan, who each - for their own reasons - found the matching of Guy and Irina stressful.

As for New Year's Eve, Bella hadn't bothered celebrating the night since arriving in the United States. She'd never enjoyed New Year's Eve parties. They brought up the memory of Guy kissing other women as the clock struck in the New Year, and reminded Bella of drinking too much and being exhausted and hung over the next day. It was also the night Bella's sociopathic lover JP moved in with her, and moved out soon after with unfathomable excuses for doing both.

Bella was early to meet Greta for lunch, and so she stopped at a nearby coffee house to let the time pass. Bella sat on the outdoor patio and imagined having coffee at such a place on a daily basis, as many people did, when Greta called. "I'm going to be late. Please forgive me." Greta knew that Bella was unimpressed by unpunctuality.

A man at the table next to her said, having overheard the conversation, "Change of plans? Dare I say I am pleased? I have been looking at you and wanting to start up a conversation."

His name was Peregrine Filleroy. Though seated, Bella could see he was very tall, taller than Bella's sociopath, JP. He was very thin. She found out later this was from his addiction to smoking heroin, which wasted his muscles. He had the kind of intelligent, emaciated masculinity that Bella found attractive. His hair was fair, but he was all darkness, which surrounded him like smoke. He was English, with one of those regal English accents that made words sound like caresses to Bella.

"The name comes from France. Somewhere down the line, one of my ancestors was the bastard son of a French king. *Fils royale.* Get it? But there is nothing aristocratic about me."

Bella glanced at the small tattoo - a Celtic symbol - on Peregrine's wrist.

"I had it done when I was boozed up. Now everyone has them, not just artists."

"Are you an artist?"

"You could say so."

"I come from Lithuanian royalty," Bella said straight-facedly.

People could tell anyone anything about their roots in Los Angeles, the city where everyone is permitted to regularly reinvent their ancestries, embellish their accomplishments, and discount their letdowns.

Peregrine seemed to believe her, and Bella, a frighteningly honest woman, put him straight. "My grandparents were Jews from Lithuania. They emigrated to escape the pogroms in the early twentieth century."

Before Bella left to meet Greta, Peregrine Filleroy asked for her phone number. She was hesitant, but gave him her card - cream stock with the type embossed in brown - not expecting to hear or see him again. With the assurance of a mature woman who knew what was what. she flung out as she departed, "You will like me."

Two days later, he called and they met at the same place for coffee.

Bella washed her hair. She wore jeans and a white shirt that she thought was flattering. She put on mascara, which she normally never did during the day.

"And for what!" she exclaimed later that day when she told Greta about her second encounter with Peregrine Filleroy.

"He's a longtime drug addict. He's had periods of sobriety. Four years, five, six, but interspersed by addiction. He has no job, no money, and has been sober for three months now and is having a hard time. He's lost all he ever had, from what I can ascertain. And he alludes to having once had a whole lot."

Bella met Peregrine again. "You tell me your story, and then I will tell you mine," he said.

Bella told him that she had her own demons, and that many years prior she'd also stopped drinking. He wasn't very interested and quickly moved on to his story, though he was maddeningly vague, insinuating more than explaining.

She didn't know whether she could, or should, press him for more details.

"Did you inject it?" Bella asked.

"No, I'm too fastidious for that. Believe it or not, I am a fastidious person. I like fine things." Peregrine peered down at himself, as if viewing a person he didn't recognize. Bella decided that sliding beneath the surface of Peregrine's rumpled white shirt, worn jeans, and shabby black-leather sneakers lived a man who was, as he said, "Particular."

"I am depressed," Peregrine stated when they met yet again. "Who wouldn't be depressed?" He shrugged. "I have no money. I have no friends and no lover. I have made a mess of my life."

Normally, this sad litany would make Bella run. A man with no job, no prospects, and no home. Bella didn't even know if he owned a car. He always arrived before her, and she always left first.

She asked, "Have you ever been married?"

"No, I've never been married. But don't think I'm a fly-by-night. I've had long-term relationships."

Bella could easily imagine the intensity of Peregrine's love. She could also imagine the angst he caused when his love either wore out or was broken by the splintering of addiction.

Usually it was Greta who needed Bella's ear when talk turned to the complications of romance. Now Bella took her turn.

"I can't concentrate. I'm fixated on the next time I'll see him. I think he's as scared as I am. We're awkward with one another. I don't quite know what to say. He keeps saying things, and then adding, 'you know,' and I say, 'yes,' as if I do know, but I don't. And he's too young for me. Probably mid-fifties. Maybe even younger."

"I think it's wonderful."

"I felt it the second I saw him, before he said one word to me as he sat in that chair having coffee. What the hell is it? Now that I know him a bit better, he's not as intelligent as I thought he was. He's got a swagger of confidence, but he's without direction. He's too old to be so lost. Men like Peregrine are normally completely unappealing to me. Even his art is awful, from what he showed me on his cell phone."

"At least he has a cell phone," Greta commented.

"He can't draw. He said so, with pride."

Greta added, "For some young artists, the inability to draw is a badge of honor. There isn't any need to draw since the camera was invented. Artists make art differently these days. But he's a bit too old for that kind of attitude."

"Well I'm too old for him."

"No, you are not," Greta insisted. "He's middle-aged and so are you. It's not as if he's twenty and you're forty, that would be creepy."

Nicole said, "You're like, in love. It's kind of cute."

Bella did not like being called cute. When older folk did something young people believed was a sole prerogative of youth, the kids proclaimed the action to be cute: "How cute, they still have sex," or "How cute, look at the couple still holding hands." Nauseating.

Bella began to take more notice of young women, how thin they were, how fresh their skin was, how high their heels were as they tottered down Robertson Boulevard, in and out of boutiques with clothes that only went up to size eight. She became more keenly aware of her advancing age, and that there was nothing she could do to stop it.

The unforgiving bathroom mirror spoke up: "Lose some weight!"

Nicole asked, "Have you got any condoms?"

"Of course not."

"Well get some."

Bella had not insisted a man wear a condom since she was eighteen, when condoms were used to avoid unwanted pregnancy, not an unwanted killer disease.

Bella imagined what it would feel like to kiss Peregrine. What would his lips feel like? Would even just kissing a former heroin addict be safe? She often had small lesions in her mouth, from biting her cheek or grinding her jaw when she slept. No, she could not kiss him. Death was coming soon enough as it was.

When she met Peregrine again for coffee, he appeared healthier. He was dressed in a black-leather jacket, indigo jeans, and fresh-looking black sneakers. He was clean-shaven and seemed more relaxed.

He had moved in with an old love. "Nothing romantic," he insisted. But still, he had to leave to go to a movie with her and a friend. "I feel I have to be polite. You understand, of course?"

Bella nodded. She was so damned understanding it made her sick.

The next time they met, he was seriously searching for a job to keep him funded until he'd completed enough artwork to hang a show that he'd been promised with the "best new gallery in Berlin."

She asked him to dinner at her condo. She'd been wondering for a while whether this was a good idea.

"Why not? He's not a killer," Greta said.

"You want me to get into an unhealthy romance to keep you company. So I can be as miserable as you. I already feel miserable. I feel like a hollow vessel that is not going to get filled, and it hurts. I want to cry. Suddenly, my happiness depends on Peregrine Filleroy, and I know he is useless for anything other than a hot affair."

"What's wrong with that?" Greta asked.

"Look at the pain you're in with your married man. He isn't good for you. Not just because he's married. He won't fit into your life. He is crude, not educated like you are. He likes watching sports, going to car races. You would hate that. Peregrine would not fit into my life, either. My children would despise him, and me, for falling for a heroin addict. They'd compare him to JP, and there are toxic similarities. I'd probably have to pay for him and I don't want to do that. He'll mess me around. He already has."

"How?"

"He's had stomach flu, twice, when we've had arrangements to meet." Bella added, "What BS!"

Greta didn't look sympathetic.

"Maybe he did?"

"And maybe he couldn't get away from the woman he's living with, the one with whom there is 'nothing physical.'"

"A little romance might be fun for you."

"It is a little romance, a very, very little one. It's so little, it barely exists other than in my own mind."

Nicole was more helpful. She told Bella, "You are having an attack of Limerence."

"What's that?"

"It's a sort of mental disease, kind of like love making you crazy. I can't explain it properly, you have to look it up."

So Bella went to her computer and researched the meaning of Limerence. It was a term coined by psychologist Dorothy Tennov in her book *Love and Limerence: The Experience of Being in Love,* which was published in 1979 after she interviewed more than 500 people about love. Since then, the condition has been defined as a syndrome related to Obsessive-Compulsive Disorder, mostly in the stages of early romance.

From what Bella deduced, Limerence seemed to be an involuntary state of over-attachment involving intrusive thoughts and feelings. The feelings ranged from euphoria to despair, contingent on the perceived emotional reciprocation.

One Sunday, whilst waiting in vain for Peregrine to call, Bella chose to distract herself from her Limerence attack and finally see *The Levitated Mass,* which was nothing but a large boulder that a sculptor installed over a walkway at the Los Angeles County Museum of Art.

Just about everyone had seen the rock by now, but she had avoided doing so as a form of protest regarding the stupidity of this so-called tour de force.

The boulder weighed 340 tons, and its travels atop a massive transporter with 176 wheels made it a Star. Crowds cheered the rock on its way, as if the Inanimate Object was a Living Thing.

Bella thought it ridiculous that dragging a large rock from a quarry, and suspending it above a walkway in LA was defined as art. But once she got close to the thing, and walked up and down the walkway under the boulder, she was forced to admit that *The Levitated Mass* possessed some kind of mysterious presence.

What would happen if there was an earthquake? Was the rock moored fast enough? Imagine being killed by a work of art...

Bella's feelings for Peregrine suddenly seemed as stupid as the big rock. The waves of Limerence were as ludicrous as Peregrine's name which, when it appeared on Bella's phone, made her heart literally jump. "Literally," another *L* word, like "Love." Bella went through words that began with *L*: libelous, licentiousness, lucidity, lesbians, and laughter.

Charlie was not happy walking back and forth under *The Mass*. There was nothing against which he could mark. If Charlie could talk, he might say, "What the hell is this? No grass. No bushes, not even a pole! Just a featureless walkway with a giant rock hovering over the middle." Then he made a poop.

"So that's what you think?" Bella said.

And then Peregrine simply vanished. He didn't call. He wasn't at the coffee shop. A few months later, having not seen Peregrine, Bella was more or less her old self again, and she was able to reflect on the absolute mystery of the way one look allowed Peregrine to ignite that primal part of her, or whatever one chose to call the overwhelming emotion: Passion, Libido, Yearning, or that silly-sounding Limerence.

Meanwhile, Greta was recovering from her married man after he dumped her when his wife found out about the affair through his carelessness with his iPhone. The two friends spent hours discussing the ins and outs of attraction and what an enigma the chemistry of attraction was. They agreed that this type of magnetism was many times more mysterious than anything else in the whole wide world. Scientists could explain things from quasars to quarks, but nobody could even half explain the insanity of Limerence.

Bella outlined how her movie ended at her next appointment with Dr. Francine. Dr. Francine asked insightful questions that made it clear some important points needed reworking.

She added, "I have a client who took four years to write a book."

That was not what Bella wanted to hear, and for the first time since she'd been going to Dr. Francine, she left without feeling better.

When Bella asked Nicole what she thought, Nicole asked the dumbest questions.

Nicole's understanding of Africa was abysmal. She imagined wild animals roaming the streets no matter how many times Bella explained that Johannesburg was a big modern city with high-rises and shopping malls, and it suffered from the same bleakness that modern architects and developers had inflicted - with callous disdain - on American cities.

Modern architects were not amongst Bella's favorites.

"Look at that!" she grimaced, as she and Greta drove past Getty Center. "It looks like a beige institutional lump thrown on top of a hill."

Bella said the same thing every time they passed by. Greta always replied, "I like it." Greta liked clean simple lines and subtle colours. Her taste was diametrically opposite to Bella's, but Greta was the one who mostly visited Bella's colourful condo, and not the other way around.

Bella commented, as she always did, giving the architect some kudos, "The view is spectacular when you stand inside and look out at LA stretched below, but surely a landmark building should be just as attractive on the outside, as the glorious views from within.

"Tell me again what happens," Nicole asked when Bella described how Rosy dies.

"She is bitten by a snake."

"I get that," Nicole claimed.

Bella further explained, "Brown spots the Mamba's mate on a branch outside the storeroom. Knowing the ways of the creatures that inhabit the area, he puts two and two together, and works out that Winston did nothing to save Rosy. You see, Brown is a man of the bush. He knows that Mambas live in pairs."

"That's awesome," Nicole said, even though she didn't have a clue exactly what the mate had to do with the events, or why Brown's understanding was important, but she wasn't going to admit that to Bella.

Bella continued, "Rosy's funeral is held at A'marula in the small cemetery where the local Tsonga and Winston's parents are buried."

The funeral scene almost wrote itself. All the characters would be present. Brown, Beatrice, Delbert, Hannes the taxidermist, Jacob, Dora, Charles, Kathy, and Rosy's mother are all present. Some local Tsonga sing.

"I love African music," Nicole said, though Bella knew that the music she loved was nothing like what the Tsonga would actually sing at a funeral.

"What about Winston? Nicole asked

"He plays the part of the Grieving Spouse to perfection."

"It's an awesome story. But where's Lena?"

Bella wanted to throttle Nicole but instead she clarified that Lena had run off.

"Maybe you should read some murder stories?" Greta suggested when Bella asked her if Rosy's death was too far-fetched.

"I don't like murder stories," Bella replied.
"Then why are you writing one?"

Chapter 27 -
The Moving Picture
"In movies you brush your teeth to a tune."

Bella often went to the movies in the afternoon, on her own, which she preferred as she could sit precisely where she wanted - midway on the left, against the side wall - and eat her large bag of popcorn without worrying whether she was making noise. It was a ritual. If she found herself too close or far from the screen, she could move without upsetting anyone.

Bella was particular about movies. She did not like animation unless it was Japanese, and even then not so much. She was not a lover of science fiction. Action movies were boring and formulaic, and every ubiquitous car chase was utterly tedious, whether the actors dashed insanely around the streets of Los Angeles or the highways of outer space. Bella's preference was thrillers, dramas, documentaries and foreign movies. She liked movies and books that made her think, or taught her something she did not know.

She was upset that Sunday when she decided to go to the movies. Ivan and Jessica were going up to their father's house for a barbecue. Guy had also invited Bella, but she'd declined the invitation seeing as Irina would be there.

Bella's reluctance to go to lunch had nothing to do with Irina or her age. Had Guy been with an age-appropriate saint, Bella still would have declined the invitation. When Guy was married to Wife Number Two, Bella gritted her teeth when she went to Guy's house for certain family occasions: Jewish holidays, Thanksgiving, and significant birthdays, like Guy's seventieth. She put her mixed emotions - jealousy, admiration, disdain, and on occasion genuine fondness - about Wife Number Two aside, so that Jessica, Chloe, and Ivan would gain a sense of family, which Bella thought was important, particularly since their children had not been born in America. But that time was over. Bella was determined not to deny her pain.

Neither Jessica nor Ivan called Bella after the barbecue, but curiosity got the better of her and she called Jess, who was not informative.

"Mom, you'll have to accept her. You must get over it."

"Don't talk to me in platitudes," Bella huffed.

"I have to rush Mom." Bella was relieved. Words with her daughter, which always upset her, were avoided.

Bella called Ivan.

"You should have come to lunch."

"Why?"

"You're getting older, you should spend time with your family."

Bella was momentarily speechless. "I will call you later," she said and put down the telephone.

Ivan sometimes had the bite of an asp.

Bella recalled all the times she had made Joyce cry. Now was payback time.

Bella called Greta and her repressed tears burst forth.

Greta, by nature a peacemaker, said, "Jess doesn't want to get involved, and you can't expect her to. Guy is her father and she adores him, too. As for Ivan, well, you know your son; he didn't think about what he was saying. He didn't put it elegantly."

"No, he did not!"

For a woman with no children - or maybe because she didn't have them - Greta was wise. "They let out all their hurts on you, because they know you'll still love them."

Greta changed the subject. "Tell me about the movie you saw. I heard it's good?"

"A veneer of pretty cinematography coated the most insipid story."

"Was there a story?" Greta inquired.

"Basically the story was boy meets girl, boy lets girl go, girl returns, love leaves, girl leaves. The end."

"So, it was depressing?"

"Not in the way you mean," Bella explained. "It was depressing because it showed the ordinariness of true love, and how that's impossible to sustain for any real length of time."

"Not always. Look at you and Guy. It's love all right. Not everyone's idea of love, but it's love."

"What's the use of loving someone you can't live with?"

"You're lucky. You don't have to live with him. But it's love. And it's going to last because you aren't together."

Greta had just returned from San Diego where she'd gone to visit one of her old married friends who wanted to introduce her to a man. It didn't work out, but that did nothing to destroy her natural optimism.

"They have another friend coming to visit from New York next month. I might like him." Greta's sense of hope was unyielding.

That night, Bella tossed and turned, as she did when she couldn't sleep, which was rare. She switched on her reading light and finished *Collapse*, a book by Jared Diamond that explained why societies fail.

Wide-awake - societal collapse was hardly a relaxing subject - Bella went to her computer and wandered around the Internet: yes, Swaziland was a monarchy, the Marx brothers were brothers, and

Gap had great offers all the time.

Bella loved technology. Technology didn't scare her, though she could not see why Twitter was so popular, and nobody could adequately explain to her what a hashtag was.

She went back to bed, found something that seemed soporific on Netflix, and managed to finally fall asleep to a TED Talk on food production. When she woke, her tears unexpectedly returned. She sat up and folded her hands over her eyes, thinking how odd the action was, this cupping of the hands over the eyes, as if to hide emotion. Nobody was watching.

"Are you over it?" Jessica asked Bella when she called, as she usually did, after dropping Chloe off at school.

"Yes," Bella was firm.

When Ivan called a week later, he was his usual self, which meant he had no idea how deeply he had hurt her. "How are you mom?" he inquired.

"I'm fine, just fine." Bella meant that. She couldn't stay mad at Ivan. He was her son, and she'd heard enough complaints from other mothers about their thoughtless sons to realize that sons could be very cruel to mothers. Of course, there were the exceptions that proved the rule. Grant Butler adored his mother, but he was gay; the same could probably be said about Olivia Blauss's son. Suzie Crawford's three sons adored her, she said, but none lived on the same continent as she did. Becky Blumenthal believed that her daughter-in-law ruined her relationship with her son. Maggie Lowenthal didn't even speak to her son. Bella's aunt Frieda, her mother's sister, cried about her son who she said, "Wouldn't care if I died," which was more or less true, though he was rather upset when he found out he'd been cut out of her will. Not that Frieda had much money, but as her son said, "It was the thought." Joyce told him, "It's true. The thought counts, and you never thought about your mother."

Eventually, Bella decided that Guy and Irina, as a couple, had to become just another brushstroke in the multi-layered painting of her life.

Shelly was less sanguine. "I'd like to rip her out. What does a young woman want with an old man?" Then Shelly answered her own question, "He gets the nurse, she gets the purse."

That was funny, and Bella had never heard the joke before, but she didn't appreciate Guy being thus reduced. "Maybe she loves him?"

"Oh, Bella! Love? What's that got to do with it?"

"So now you're the cynic?"

Shelly sat up straight and tall. "Some of your cynicism has rubbed off on me, and I'm happy it has."

"Oh, really?"

"Yes, I've become more like you. I don't want a man in my life just to have a man. I don't even want to get married. I'm giving up the search. It's far too much bother. I like my life just as it is. If someone comes along, well, I'll be here. But if he doesn't, I'll be fine, just like you."

Shelly repeated, with a huge smile, "Just like you, and I mean that as a compliment."

Bella did not know what to say. Then she let out a yell. "Hallelujah!"

Shelly jumped up and gave Bella a high five. "To us."

Bella concurred. "To us!"

Bella believed she tied up the story for a happy resolution. She believed she mastered the dreaded arc. As always, before putting things into Final Draft, she outlined what would happen.

Winston leaves A'marula playing the role of the grieving widower and charming young women who see him as a catch wherever he goes: Johannesburg, Cape Town, London, and Paris.

Winston hasn't a trouble in the world, especially since his aunt, Beatrice, agrees to keep an eye on A'marula for him.

Bella was delighted she found a way to place scenes of Rome, London, and Paris into her script. She loved old cities; narrow cobbled streets, charming outdoor cafes, and stately buildings would entice rather than offend. This cinematically appealing change from the African bush would have Winston cavorting around Europe. She imagined him in a montage.

Winston exits a London taxi with two winsome models; Winston walks into a five-star hotel in Paris; Winston and a blonde bombshell wander around the Coliseum in Rome, with hints of the horrors that took place there when gladiators were forced to battle, not only each other, but also wild animals, like lions.

Though Bella loved the visual palate of the Old World, there was much she adored about America, or rather California. In particular was the ability for everyone to reinvent themselves, to craft an identity that's been waiting to be tried. Just about all the people she knew were learning or developing something new about themselves.

Greta, who never boiled an egg, was taking Japanese cooking classes. Shelly was studying real estate, and planned to become a property developer. Nicole was keeping up with her writing group and taking sailing lessons. In Nicole's case, this nautical interest was awakened by Brandon, a young man she'd met at her new gym.

George Agadees's trusted old accountant, Benjamin Tobin, warns Winston that he's spending too much, and if he isn't careful there won't be enough money to maintain A'marula. George's will stipulated that maintaining A'marula was his highest priority.

Lena returns. Beatrice notices that she is pregnant, and though Lena tries to keep out of her way, Beatrice gets the truth out of Lena: the child is Winston's.

Brown now tells Beatrice that he suspects Winston intentionally didn't help Rosy after the Mamba bite. Beatrice does not believe him. Nobody can be that bad!

After the warning from the accountant, Winston hatches a dastardly plan. He'll set fire to A'marula, and there'll be nothing for him to keep up.

With that in mind Winston arrives at A'marula. It's his first visit since Rosy's death, and the first person he sees is Lena, with her six-month-old baby daughter sleeping in a sling on her back.

Jessica and Ivan were both carried like that on their nanny's back. She was a Zulu and her name was Nomalanga. She preferred to be known as "Nanni," which is what she was: a loving woman whose own children lived far away, cared for by her mother and the old aunts of her clan in a village in what is now known as KwaZulu-Natal.

Bella couldn't help wondering why she, and everyone else she knew, accepted this injustice. The women themselves made no complaint. The men? As far as Bella could remember, no fathers were involved. They gave their sperm and left the women to themselves.

Lena has expectations that when Winston sees her, he will declare his love for her and the child. Instead, he pointedly ignores them both.

Beatrice is anxious to see Winston to disprove Brown's theory.

Winston, Beatrice, and Brown take a drive around the property in the open Land Rover.

Whilst on the drive, Winston spots a Kudu male with a magnificent set of horns.

He stops the Land Rover, picks up his rifle and, despite horrified shouts from Beatrice, shoots the animal. Thrilled with himself, he jumps out of the Land Rover and gloats over the bleeding carcass. Brown turns to Beatrice and in his eyes, she sees the truth. Winston is a monster.

Beatrice impulsively picks this moment to accuse Winston of Rosy's death.

Winston levels his gun. Beatrice is aghast as he takes aim. She smartly ducks as he shoots. She screams to Brown to start the Land Rover. We've seen previously that Brown often asked Winston if he can learn to drive, but Winston wouldn't permit it. However we've also seen Brown taking practice drives after Winston left for Europe.

For a few heart-pumping moments, the Land Rover refuses to start, but eventually Brown kicks it into gear and off he and Beatrice drive, leaving Winston screaming insults and firing reckless shots that miss the Land Rover's tires.

Meanwhile, a pride of lions on the prowl has picked up the scent of the downed and bloody Kudu bull, and the huge cats pad quietly through the bush expertly tracking the source of the blood scent.

Winston is oblivious to the danger about to explode from the tall grass as he runs after the Land Rover.

A running animal is all the lions need to set them off, and two lionesses easily bring Winston down as prey.

Police find the remains of Winston's body. No foul play is suspected. They assume he went walking about and was taken by the lions. Such accidental deaths are not unknown for those sufficiently reckless to venture into the bush alone.

Bella could not believe she got so far. All the strands of her story were coming together. Her plot might be a bit unbelievable, she thought, but with a smart director and some talented actors it might work. She and Shelly spent hours playing at casting *The Lions of A'marula.*

Shelly liked Leonardo DiCaprio. "He can do a great South African accent," Shelly pointed out about his brilliant performance in *Blood Diamond.*

Bella explained, "Winston doesn't have to have that thick South African accent. He is not Afrikaans. Remember, he goes to a school where they talk like the English upper class. Rosy does, too. Lots of my South African friends sound almost English."

"I think you do, too," Shelly said.

Americans loved Bella's accent, and most thought she was from England. Some even asked if she was French, but any English-born person could tell she was from the colonies.

Bella liked Orlando Bloom. He was dark and brooding. He had an evil look to him, too. Jessica saw him at her gym once. She said he was gorgeous and friendly.

"Rosy could be a newcomer," they agreed, and left it at that.

They had fun casting Beatrice.

"Meryl Streep can do any accent," both Bella and Shelly noted, but Bella thought such a star wouldn't bother with a small role. Bella liked Angelica Huston. "She's a grand presence, and she could be of Greek decent."

Together they searched the Internet, and came up with quite a few possibilities for Talented Actresses Over Fifty: Diane Keaton, Jeanne Tripplehorn, Melissa Leo, Jamie Lee Curtis, Annette Bening, Sharon Stone, Patricia Heaton, Melanie Griffith, Kathleen Turner, Sigourney Weaver, Glenn Close, Susan Sarandon, and Helen Mirren.

Shelly said, "I would cast Sharon Stone. Definitely."

"I'd be in heaven if any of them played the part. I'd be in heaven if anyone made the movie. Or even optioned it. Actually, I'll be in heaven when I finish writing it."

Chapter 28 -
Decades

"If you are over the hill, why not enjoy the view?"

When Bella's oldest friend, Pearl, turned seventy, she and her husband took their whole family on an African Safari. "There were twenty of us, with the grandkids."

When Heather Glass, another old-time friend from South Africa who also lived in Los Angeles, turned seventy, she and her husband took their family - twelve altogether - on a luxurious eastern-Mediterranean cruise. In addition, Heather hosted a luncheon for her seventeen best lady friends in a private room at a fancy restaurant. Bella remembered being amazed that anyone had seventeen best friends all living in one city. But from what Heather said of her friends - including Bella - as she honored them in a sentimental speech, she actually did.

When Greta's cousin Jocelyn married for the third time to Felix Faberwell, of the Florida property developer Faberwells, she celebrated her seventieth just a week before Bella's with a luncheon for sixty at her beachfront holiday home in Palm Beach.

At the luncheon, a Japanese chef made a lobster and caviar cake in the shape of the numerals seven and zero, and a famous Fado singer performed, as Jocelyn was into Portuguese music that year.

"I think as we get older the simple things in life become more important," Jocelyn said in her speech to her sixty friends.

Greta spent, for her, a fortune on a new outfit: taupe linen pants, a top, and a coordinating scarf by Eskandar, a designer she always admired. "I needn't have bothered," she told Bella. "They dress quite peculiarly in Palm Beach."

Bella's school friend Emmie, who lived in Perth, came to visit Bella two days before she turned seventy, which she planned to celebrate at her eldest daughter's home in Portland, Oregon. Emmie's twin sons had flown in from New York and Berlin, respectively, and her younger daughter also came from New York.

"I should have spent it with you," Emmie told Bella afterwards. "My kids all acted like disagreeable two-year-olds. Lunch, supper, dinner, and every meal led to an argument. All I wanted was to go shopping and sleep."

Guy was still married to Wife Number Two when he turned seventy. She organized two parties. One luncheon for family and "old friends" - meaning her idea of unsophisticated people - plus a fancy dinner for everyone she wanted to impress.

Bella was invited to the luncheon, but she was prescient enough to know that she'd come down with a migraine on the day.

Shelly always said of her seventieth, which was still some time off, "I'm giving myself a total lift. Everything!"

Greta nagged Bella as her seventieth birthday approached, "You must celebrate. Have a party. I'll help."

Bella mulled this over, but she didn't feel like having a party. As always, her birthday was too soon after the holidays. Everyone was tired of celebrations, and either complaining about or avoiding them. January was a time to hunker down, not party.

Ivan asked, "Mom, will you be terribly upset if I'm not here for your birthday?"

"No, I won't be upset. Where are you going?"

"Digby bought a new yacht. He wants Farrel and me to be there when he takes delivery. You know what he's like."

Bella said she had no idea what Digby Bootch was like, but she wouldn't be at all upset if Ivan couldn't make her seventieth birthday, and she meant it. Ivan felt guilty anyway and gave Bella a more-than-generous gift certificate from Neiman Marcus.

"Buy something special," he told her. "Something you want."

As if Bella would buy something she didn't want.

Wondering how much yachts cost, Bella did an Internet search and got lost cyber-wandering around shipyards and luxury yacht brokers. This was a world she knew nothing about, and she spent a whole evening combing through yacht inventory deciding which one she'd choose to buy. Eventually she decided that if she was ever in the market, she'd have one made custom, seeing as she didn't like the way any of the interiors were fashioned. Obviously yacht customers had no taste - at least not her kind of taste - even though from the outside, mostly gleaming white and resting proudly on the ocean, the ships were magnificent.

Jessica suggested a brunch seeing as Bella's birthday fell on a Sunday. "We can have it at my place," she offered. Bella appreciated the proposal and mulled over that, too. But somehow the brunch didn't get off the ground either, and the week before her birthday, Bella caught a really bad cold, so she was relieved she hadn't scheduled a party.

It wasn't flu, just a cold, and everyone had "the" cure for the common cold that "really worked," but only if she would do precisely as prescribed: saunas and ginger, ginger and lemon, lemon and cayenne pepper, zinc, vitamin C, and colloidal silver. Bella resolved never to tell anyone the best cure for anything, for that was terribly annoying. Nor would she ever inquire, "Did you have a flu shot?" with the air of superiority those who already had one evinced. A cold lasted for an allotted time, no matter what anyone did.

Eventually Bella chose a small celebration: lunch at The Ivy with Jess, Chloe, Greta, Shelly, and Nicole. Bella asked Jessica to invite Guy on his own, but he coldly declined.

Bella was not as upset about Guy's refusal as Jess. "It's not as if he's married to her, or that they've had a long-term relationship. Who is more important: you, the mother of his children, or Irina?" Jessica complained. Bella simply smiled.

Three days before Bella's birthday, her sister-in-law, Josie, called from South Africa to inform her that her beloved brother, Derek, had suffered a heart attack. He was fine, and there wasn't much damage to his heart, but the doctor said, when Josie asked if the attack was serious, "All heart attacks are serious."

Bella was happy that she hadn't organized a Big To-Do. She didn't feel like a celebration at all now.

On the eve of her birthday, Pearl rang from London. They met when they were thirteen and had remained close, despite living on different continents and having totally different life trajectories.

"There is nothing nice about turning seventy," Bella said. "All those people who say it's fabulous are liars."

Pearl wholeheartedly agreed.

Emmie called from Perth, "I love you and always will." They spent some time reminiscing about the good old days when they were university students and faced their futures with charmed ignorance. Emmie said, "We were so immature."

Bella agreed, "We thought we knew everything."

Matthew English, Bella's best male friend, called from Tanzania where he owned a trucking company. After Bella's divorce from Guy, Matthew had almost become a lover. "Thank goodness we didn't do it," they both agreed.

Jack, an old lover now married, called. He phoned Bella every birthday, forgetting only once in all the many years since their brief and intense romance, which they both remembered with tender nostalgia.

Derek called on Skype. The moment Bella heard her brother's loving voice, she began to cry. Josie said, "Derek can't drink yet, but I'm having a glass of champagne in your honor."

Serena Hickey called from Plettenberg Bay, where she was spending a few days at her holiday home. "Bella my old friend, this really is the big one. It's like being eighty, but it's seventy." Bella understood exactly what Serena meant.

Ivan called. "Digby and Farrel send their love," he added. It was a very bad connection and Bella couldn't make out whether they were in Malta or the Maldives.

Bella's Facebook was filled with birthday wishes.

Guy called around eleven in the morning. "Happy birthday to you…" Bella let him sing till the end of the song, but not wanting him to hear her voice crack she put the phone down. "I can't talk to you now." She sobbed, she wailed. She picked up Charlie and hugged him. "It's a big day."

When Jess called, Bella said, "Cancel lunch at The Ivy. I don't feel like pretending to be celebratory."

"What do you want to do?" Jessica asked kindly.

"Let's have a regular lunch, like we usually do on Sunday. Nothing fancy. Just us."

So that is what they did.

When Bella called Greta to cancel, she understood.

"We'll still have our lunch at Neiman's, as planned, next Thursday. You'll feel better by then."

Shelly was sweet. "Who wants to celebrate getting old anyway? But I'm taking you to dinner and a movie next week. No discussion. I'm booking."

And so, treating the significant day like any other, which in truth it was, Bella, Jess, and Chloe had lunch at the French restaurant at American Rag.

After lunch, they browsed the housewares, and then the shoe department and clothes. In the vintage section of the store, Chloe found a shirt she thought might fit her. It didn't, but Bella bought it for her anyway. After lunch they went to a movie. The day was lovely, in the end.

When Bella woke up the next morning, she looked at herself in her antique mirror and said out loud, "Good morning seventy!" She got out of bed, stretched her arms up and counted to seventy. She resolved to stretch every morning, to keep her body lithe. She bent to touch her toes and counted to seventy. Blood rushed to her head and she felt the tendons at the back of her thighs painfully stretching. "I am seventy and I can touch my toes."

The next day, Bella saw Norman in the gym. He asked, "So what's it like to be seventy?"

"It's like childbirth, or falling in love, or having a headache. You have to experience it yourself to know." Bella set the speed on the treadmill to "3" and the incline to "8," noting with no small satisfaction that Norman was huffing away at "2.8" with no incline at all.

Bella was writing the end of *The Lions of A'marula*.

Endings were difficult: marriages, relationships of all kinds, and even jobs. Beginnings were much easier.

Bella had once plunged into romances, moving from country to country without much thought. She came to America on a vacation and stayed, she said, to purge JP from her life. This became necessary as she could not stop herself from seeing the man, despite clearly understanding that having anything to do with him was an invitation to more heartache.

She was stuck on her script's ending. Bella knew, from her own experience, that when a movie's ending is unsatisfactory - and that doesn't mean a sad ending - even a fine movie is spoiled. Conversely, a satisfying ending can make a fair movie seem excellent.

Lions had eaten Winston. He got his just deserts. But what about those left behind? Bella had an idea, but her idea was so schmaltzy and cloyingly sentimental, she balked.

The How-To books were clear: the questions set up in the first act had to be answered in the third. Bella read act one through for the first time. She became utterly despondent and almost cried. "It is so damned amateurish."

Greta said, "What do you expect? You are an amateur." That was one of the things Bella liked about Greta. She said it as she saw it. "But for God's sake, finish it."

"What's the difference to you?"

"You've been a nightmare since you began."

So Bella wrote the last bit, schmaltzy as she thought the ending was.

As Winston's only living relative, Beatrice inherits A'marula. She doesn't want the land and all the responsibility of running the operation. She tells the lawyers handling the trust to give it all to Brown and his Tsonga clan. "It was once theirs."

Bella was aware that real people were not so generous. In fact, arguments about money were a huge cause of permanent family feuds.

Her own father and his sister never spoke after their father died. Shelly didn't speak to her brother. The fights could be over thousands, or hundreds of thousands, or millions. They were all the same. Money. And here was Beatrice being so unbelievably magnanimous. However -

According to the trust made by George Agadees, A'marula must go to the next of kin. If there is no next of kin, it would be sold to the highest bidder.

Continuing her magnanimity, and with Lena's blessing, Beatrice adopts Lena's little girl, whom Lena named Elizabeth after Winston's late twin, mistakenly thinking he would have appreciated the sentiment.

Thus, Lena's child with Winston will eventually inherit A'marula. The Tsonga clan from whom the land was stolen so many years ago, when white people came from afar, would get their land back.

It was a politically correct conclusion. Bella was sick of political correctness, which made people afraid to say what they felt, saw, and thought, especially about differences.

Men and women are different. Our brains are different. Our bodies are different. Our chromosomes are not the same. And anyone can see that people have different-coloured skins, which makes a person who says, "I didn't notice his colour," sound like she has her eyes closed. Noticing is not the same as disrespectful action.

Cultures are not merely different. Some are different and horrible. Some religions are crueler than others, though in Bella's opinion none of them have improved the human condition when their history - or even their present - is carefully considered.

Joined with political correctness, in Bella's opinion, is the abuse of the world "appropriate."

Jess was forever saying, "That's not appropriate, Mom," making Bella want to scream. But she said nothing. She'd learned that screaming was an inappropriate response.

As for Beatrice, she finally accepts her long-term beau Delbert's standing proposal of marriage.

However, Delbert decides they will be happier keeping things as they are, and Beatrice is relieved.

Chapter 29 -
And the Winner is...
"Stars disappear during the day."

Bella adored watching Hollywood award shows: The Golden
Globes, The Oscars, even The Emmys, though she wasn't a fan
of popular TV. What she loved most was the fashion. The award
shows were the brightest thing about February, a month that made
winter seem endless, even in sunny California.

She wished that instead of only the contenders, every single
woman who walked down the red carpet would be shown. How
many dresses had been bought by women - who weren't award
contenders sporting designer gowns on loan - for the event? What
a waste, like the money spent on wedding dresses, which could be
better utilized for any number of things that newlyweds actually
need. Yet when Jessica got married, Bella became like every other
mother of the bride helping her daughter find "the" dress. They
searched every bridal store and every bridal department. Jess tried
on endless gowns, but finally decided to have one custom made.
Like Bella's wedding dress, it now hung, furtively in a dust bag at
the back of a spare-room closet.

Bella's wedding dress was rose pink. The bodice and elbow-
length sleeves were a confection of tiny lace flowers. The rest
of the dress was Thai silk, and a cummerbund band showed off
Bella's tiny waist. "I can't believe how small your waist was," Nicole
said when Bella showed her the dress.

Bella gestured at her much thickened middle and exclaimed,
"What happened?"

"The dress was made by Madam Delores. She was a divinely elegant Hungarian, and the only couturier in Johannesburg. She also made me a suit and one cocktail outfit. That, with a glamorous nighty and robe, was the extent of my trousseau."

Nicole had no idea what a trousseau was.

"I don't know if I'll ever get married," Nicole sighed. "It's not like the old days."

"It isn't. Then, nobody shacked up together. I told Guy I wanted to live with him and not get married, as I'd never had much faith in the institution. Guy was shocked. Even insulted. But then, I was always more modern than he was."

"You are still so cool," Nicole complimented. "A pink dress! Awesome."

"Did you know Indian brides wear red?"

"Actually, I do. My friend went to an Indian wedding."

"And they don't drink if they're Muslim. Guy and I went to a Muslim wedding, and one of our friends brought those little airline bottles of vodka for us to pour into our fruit punch. Horrible sweet red stuff on every table."

Nicole sighed. "I want to get married. I want a house and children and a husband who loves me. I want the whole shebang."

"Well then, don't walk around with that bra strap showing. I've told you before. And not such a short skirt. And stop smoking. Why are you still smoking? I thought you'd given it up."

"I wish you were my mother."

Nicole's mother lived in Florida, with her fourth husband. They had little contact. Nicole's father was not in the picture.

Bella hugged her young neighbor. "I will always be here to give you motherly advice. But you have to listen."

"Don't I always?" Nicole pulled at her bra strap and tucked it away.

Bella watched The Oscars with Greta and Shelly.

She laid out a splendid spread: smoked salmon, kettle-fried potato crisps, grapes, a cheese board, and Lindt chocolate balls in three different flavors. Bella did not like big Oscar parties. What was the point of a party when everyone wanted to watch the television rather than socialize?

Bella never before wished she had anything to do with the movies, and she could not fathom why this year she felt she should have done something in that sphere: editing, directing, or costuming. "Those jobs weren't an option when I was growing up," she explained. "We didn't even have television in South Africa until 1976."

"You're kidding!" Shelly exclaimed.

"No, I'm not. The apartheid government did not want South Africans to see what was going on in the big, wide world. And The Dutch Reformed Church - you'll never find a more misnamed Church - thought their narrow little fundamentalist world would collapse if we had TV. Actually, they were right. But it took bit of time

"You could have been a comedienne," Greta offered. "You are really funny. Brutal, but funny."

"No, I don't like being on stage. Maybe I could have been an Art Director?"

"Or a Cinematographer?" Shelly suggested.

Greta laughed. "Have you ever seen Bella's photographs?"

Bella could not defend her lack of talent in that direction. "I take the worst photos. Everyone says so. It's like my driving. But I love pattern. Flat things. That's why I paint."

"You could have made movies," Shelly insisted. "I love your art."

Bella ignored the compliment. "The truth is I am not a

235

collaborator and moviemaking is a collaborative venture."

"It must be nice to be a star," Shelly sighed.

Through her volunteer work with various women's charities, Greta had met quite a few movie stars. "They are nothing like the roles they play. Nothing. And in the flesh, they're very ordinary. Usually shy, with little to say. We think they're all interesting and clever because they mouth smart words, that is, if the script is any good. But those are neither their words nor their thoughts."

"Still, they are like royalty."

Bella said, "The Queen poos."

Greta added, "The Queen farts in bed."

Bella carried on, "The Queen's bra straps hurt... The Queen masturbates... The Queen has bunions."

Shelly joined the fun. "The Queen has hot flashes." They laughed like teenagers, going on and with ever more silly human things that the poor Queen did or didn't do.

The stars began to arrive in their borrowed designer gowns and jewels, their perfect makeup and hair. Critiquing them was the best part of the evening.

"With all those stylists, she chose that!"

An older actress gave out an Oscar. The ravages of age were shocking on her once startlingly beautiful face.

Shelly said, "When I see that, I get scared of getting old."

"It is scary," Bella agreed. "But you're not quite there yet."

"She looks good, for her age," Greta said and then, glancing at Bella said, "Oops, I shouldn't have said that."

Bella made no comment. Instead, she cut herself some cheese and spread on fig preserve. "I am craving cheese. I must need calcium for my bones."

Shelly stated, "I am not having another birthday."

"That's going to stop the march of time?"

Shelly sometimes said the most foolish things. Bella told her how sick Guy once got after a long flight and Shelly said, "But doesn't he travel first-class?"

"Yes, he does," Bella replied. "But the germs didn't know."

"Oh yeah, I guess that was a stupid thing to say," Shelly was willing to admit.

The three friends ate too much, criticized avidly, and had the best time. They marveled at the inanities required when TV personalities asked all the stars the same questions: "Who are you wearing?" - as if the designers of Armani or Dior or Marchesa were draped around their bodies - or "Who do you want to win?"

Greta wondered why no stars had tummies, and every butt was uplifted and firm. "Spanx," Shelly announced with an insider's grin.

Bella shook her head in wonder, "I know lots and lots of women wear them - the woman who invented them made zillions - but I tried Spanx once, and I was so uncomfortable being smoothed out, I couldn't wait to get home and take them off. They're right up there in the same category as high heels: instruments of torture we endure to make us feel sexy" - Bella shrugged - "and for whom?"

"For men of course," Shelly answered.

"For women, too. Look how we notice every little defect in ourselves," Greta correctly pointed out. Then she noted, "I've never been to The Oscars and I've lived here most of my life."

Bella said, "I knew someone whose mother went every year. She was a seat filler."

"What's that?"

"They sit in a chair when someone goes to the bathroom. So the theater always looks full on TV. Seat fillers have to dress up as if they're invited guests."

Shelly sighed. "I'd like to be invited to one of those after-parties."

Greta had once been. "It was too noisy for conversation. Nobody flirted. Wives hung onto their husbands like picture hooks."

"With you around, I'm not surprised," Shelly quipped.

Bella added, "When I was younger, everyone flirted. Married people flirted. I suppose that's why we all got divorced."

Greta had more to say about parties.

"Years ago, when I worked for a PR firm, part of my job was

attending endless functions to celebrate store openings, product launches, and of course movie events - premieres and so on. The point was not to have fun, but to pay back or pay forward. You have no idea how much money is spent on food and flowers and swag bags, trying to get name guests to show up. Hardly anyone had anything in common, and the only thing to do was to get drunk on all the free wine. That became part of my job, too. And getting people to leave when the show was over."

"On that note, I really must take Charlie for a walk."

"That's the problem having a dog, you have to walk it," Shelly declared victoriously.

Bella had been trying - and failing - to get Shelly to adopt a dog from the pound. "It beats a man," Bella explained. "And you will be doing a truly needy creature a great service."

"I'll walk with you," Greta offered.

Shelly, with a flounce that said, "I am not getting a dog," left to go back to her condo.

The winter night was pleasantly bracing, and Charlie, as always, was ecstatic to be taken for his walk, though he hardly walked at all. He stopped constantly to sniff, and when the scent was right, he peed. He did this over and over again, which sometimes drove Bella crazy. "Come on, how many pees does a dog need?"

"Look how gorgeous the moon is," Bella observed.

The moon was full with a bright halo. Bella always searched for the moon when she and Charlie walked.

Greta squinted upwards. She was not the kind of person who noticed the moon.

A while later, Bella pointed out the way that drops of water, from the nightly sprinklers, sparkled in the neatly clipped grass sidewalk. "They look like diamonds! Better than all those diamonds at the Oscars."

"It's all wet." Greta didn't like wet.

"My grandmother used to say that there are so many grains of sand and so few diamonds."

"She thought you were a diamond, of course," Greta laughed. "Of course she did."

The diamonds in the grass made Bella think of more eternal questions than what designer a celebrity was wearing, or whether she could have worked in the movies if she was born in Los Angeles. She felt a rush of bliss that she could find joy in the grander scheme of things, like the immense sweep of the Mysterious Universe, and that she - Bella Mellman - held a unique place amidst the wonder.

Even Greta must have sensed something, for she finally commented, in a tone approaching awe, "That moon is something else."

Charlie, as was his habit, peed and then did his business. He chose a spot under the street lamp, so Bella could easily see to scoop up his poo in a degradable blue plastic bag. She decided his selection of location was a small, godly kind of gift, like finding a parking spot right outside her destination, or getting back to her car just before an officer was about to write a ticket, or managing to contain her bladder before she wet her pants.

And for an ecstatic few seconds, as such heavenly rushes are, Bella felt herself a winner.

Bella made six copies of the first draft of *The Lions of A'marula*. She gave one to Greta, one to Shelly, and one to Nicole. She also gave one to Jessica and one to Ivan, not expecting her children to bother.

Bella gave them a week and then asked, "Have you read it?"

She gave them another month before inquiring again.

Greta was in love again and couldn't think straight. Shelly was having grown-up children troubles and Nicole - well, Nicole hardly ever read anything.

Bella expected Nicole to finish last, and was pleasantly surprised when Nicole informed her, "I finished it."

"And?"

"Don't get me wrong, it's awesome; but I thought you'd be writing about your own life, I mean, like, your life in Africa."

Shelly finished the script next. "I thought it was interesting."

Bella knew that meant she didn't think much of her effort.

Greta was last. She was more precise. "I found a lot of grammatical errors, which I know will be fixed. But you know what I didn't find."

"Tell me."

"I didn't find you"

"What do you mean?" Bella felt the tears welling.

"There was nothing of you in the script. That story could have been told by anyone. I can't quite explain, but when you tell a story, when you tell me about your life, you tell it in such a way that I'm spellbound. You know what I think?"

"What?" Bella pinched her wrist, stopping the tears. This was something she'd once been taught to do, but she did not recall by whom.

"I think you should write about your life."

After some weeks of feeling worthless, eating too many chocolates and far too much soy-based frozen yogurt smothered in chopped almonds and chocolate sauce, that is exactly what Bella did. Which is how *The Fabliss Life of Bella Mellman* came into existence. She hopes you have enjoyed her efforts.

Postscript

"The intelligent person is not only open to new ideas - she seeks them."

Something peculiar happened to Bella shortly after she turned seventy, but not all at once. With hindsight Bella thought what occurred could have begun when Guy took up with Irina. "If Guy could, well why not me?"

Meeting Peregrine might have played a part. Or she had a last-gasp surge of hormones? Maybe it had to do with global warming? Or perhaps charged particles from the collapse of the nuclear facility after the tsunami in Japan? Bella saw a map of that radiation on an Internet site, and the toxic mix was heading for California but was *not* reported on the nightly news. Could be the basic fear that all was to end? Or rather, she herself was to end? After all, seventy might be called the new fifty, but if you died at seventy nobody commented on how young you were. The obituaries were filled with people who died in their seventies.

Whatever the cause, Bella woke up one morning, and said to the great, unknown spirit with whom she talked, "I want someone to love me."

This wasn't a plea, but a declaration.

Nothing had changed about her opinion of men, love, or age. Nothing at all. In fact, if anything, she had become even more cynical since an old married lover had made contact and wanted to meet up with her in Paris - despite having just celebrated his forty-fifth wedding anniversary and posing as The World's Best Husband on his Facebook page.

Bella wondered whether her desire to be loved was a passing thing. Most likely in a week or so, faced by the dearth of suitable prospects, the feeling would vanish. There was no possibility that someone with the charm of Peregrine, the confidence and manliness of Guy, the sensitivity of Matthew, the sense of humor of Roland, and the wild passion of JP would magically materialize.

Greta said, "People win the lottery every week - in fact, twice a week." She added, "In lots of different states."

Bella invested in lottery tickets since she first arrived in Los Angeles. "If you don't take a ticket, you can't win the prize," was something she always told her children, even though there wasn't a lottery in South Africa at the time.

When she mentioned how she felt, Nicole said, "You are gorgeous. I don't see why an awesome man won't sweep you off your feet."

With an I-told-you-so smile, Shelly announced, "The yearning never leaves us; so come on, be brave. Come with me to the next Date & Mate. It's fun. You might meet someone."

This elicited a groan from Bella, who had no intention of ever going with intrepidly optimistic Shelly to any such event.

A week or so later, there was a new man on the treadmill.

From the length of the nail on the little finger of his right hand, which revealed he was not a manual laborer, Bella judged him as Middle Eastern. He was over six feet tall, head shaved bald, and dressed in proper workout black. Was he attractive? Maybe. Bella wasn't sure. Was he married? Who knew? Men pretended not to be. What did he do?

"I have many interests," he avoided specificity when Bella inquired, with due subtlety. "All over the world," he added a tad boastfully.

Evidently he was visiting. "My favorite older sister has bought a condo in this building. She moved in last month. I am paying her a visit."

Before Bella could learn more, Sven arrived, and Bella, with a mildly apologetic smile, ended the conversation.

"Perhaps we can have some tea a little bit later in the week?" he asked.

This could be interesting, Bella said to herself as Sven started off her session with leg lifts. And then the man blew his nose, right into his towel. That ended whatever could have been, instantly.

On Jessica's entrance table, Bella saw her script... exactly where she'd left it three months prior.

Bella knew Ivan would say, "I'll get to it when I have time," so she said nothing when she noticed *The Lions of A'marula* on his coffee table.

Bella long knew that neither of her children were interested in her creative efforts, and she decided not to take offence. Children, at whatever age, wanted their parents to be nothing but parents. Bella had read numerous books by the offspring of the talented and famous, so she was assured that was always the case.

But something wonderful - really wonderful - was about to happen.

Farrel Bootch saw her script lying on the kitchen counter at Ivan's bachelor pad in Hollywood. He began to read it whilst waiting for Ivan to shower and dress. Without saying a word to Ivan - for once acting totally on his own accord - Farrel took the script home with him and, after completing the script, informed his father that he'd discovered a gem.

In turn, Digby also loved the story. He offered to provide financing and encouraged Farrel to proceed. Digby was thrilled that his son was finally enthusiastic about something. He'd hoped this kind of thing would happen when he employed Ivan, and in a circuitous way, Ivan was responsible, even if Farrel's passion was inadvertently ignited.

And so, after all the legalities were signed, *The Lions of A'marula* went into pre-production, with both Ivan and Farrel producing together.

Greta was thrilled for Bella and rightfully claimed an accolade. "It all started when I gave you that Florentine notebook, remember?"

Greta's life was plodding along. She'd tried to forget about Glen, who was still married, but "planning" his divorce. "He treats me like a Queen," she maintained, excusing him for his tardiness in getting the divorce, which in all likelihood he'd never actually obtain.

Shelly could not have been more pleased to know a real Hollywood screenwriter. She'd finally obtained her real estate license and had just sold her first condo at The Portland. Her boss said Shelly had a talent for sales and she was thrilled with her newfound position. She stopped whining about how she wished she'd find someone special, and began a lighthearted affair with Ari Rabinowitz, a young Israeli contractor who was employed to get a house in shape before Shelly's agency put it on the market.

Nicole was in love. Her paramour, Tarquin Goodred, was a partner in a start-up IT venture that had something to do with booking models. Both the romance and the IT venture seemed promising.

Many of the residents of The Portland somehow heard about Bella's potential success, and people who never spoke to her before were now effusive. Bella was flattered, even though she knew the sudden neighborliness was not genuine. Or was she wrong? Greta always said that Bella's personality was naturally intimidating.

The script was making the rounds of Actors' Agents, and Farrel and Ivan were interviewing Directors. They were also planning a trip to Africa to scout locations.

Bella wondered, when the film was made, if she would appear in one of those articles she so hated about success in latter years. She hoped she would.

The End

ॐ·९०

Acknowledgements

Jill Schary Robinson, our fearless leader, and the writers of
The Wimpole Street Writers Group.

Shari Goodhartz, my well-named editor.

Jackie Woods, book designer supreme.

Valerie Woods, publisher at BooksEndependent,
a person I so admire.

To friends, family, Microsoft Word, iMac and the Internet.

About the Author

Shirley Sacks was born in South Africa in 1943. She left South Africa in 1976 and lived in London for several years. She has lived in Los Angeles since 1987. She has a degree in Fine Arts and has shown her work in galleries all over the world. She has also worked in advertising as a copywriter, and wrote a column for *The Sun*, a South African magazine. This is her first published novel.